HOSTILE

Luke Scull

ABOUT THE AUTHOR

LUKE SCULL is a British author and videogame designer. Luke's first novel, *The Grim Company*, was shortlisted for the Gemmell Morningstar Award and earned a starred review from *Kirkus* as well as praise from *the Guardian*, *the Sun*, and *the Daily Mail*. Luke's game design credits include several acclaimed titles for Ossian Studios. He has worked on *The Witcher*, *Neverwinter Nights*, and *Baldur's Gate* franchises and is currently design and writing lead for *Pathfinder: The Dragon's Demand*, as well as unannounced titles for the *Dungeons & Dragons* brand.

You can keep up to date with Luke's various projects on his website at www.lukescull.com.

REVIEWS FOR THE GRIM COMPANY

Extraordinary, bold and brilliant. A stellar exemplar of what the genre has to offer today. — *TOR.com*

The best fantasy you will read this year — *SF Book*

Highly memorable with a great cast and an even greater story all wrapped up in a mature world, told by a true story-teller — *SFBookcom*

A fantastic story that is ripe with action, strong characterization and a tight plot... This is one debut not to be missed and marks Luke Scull as one of epic fantasy's talented debutants' — *Fantasy Book Critic*

A rollicking dark fantasy adventure novel. It moves with verve and pace... and is threaded through with a great sense of humour' — *The Wertzone*

Luke Scull is more than good. He's the sort of author you buy on publishing date and read on the way home — *The Bookbag*

Luke Scull will hit the fiction world like few before. Honestly, it comes in my TOP 10 books of all time — *Booktoreview*

Brilliant — *Tor.com*

If you like your glizzards glistening and your mages mean, this rollicking debut will suit. Hugely enjoyable. — *Daily Mail*

This is a work of a fiction. All characters, organizations, and events portrayed in this novel are either products of the author's imagination or are used fictitiously.

ISBN-13: 9781036922955

Cover design by: Phil Williams

For fathers everywhere

HOSTILE

1

A crimson sun bled across the sky above Longleat Safari and Adventure Park, its savage dawn light threatened by encroaching thunderclouds. Savannah Grace eyed the ominous, slate-grey clouds clawing at the horizon, grateful she'd brought her waterproof parka.

She'd been an animal keeper at the park for six months now and absolutely loved her job. With a name like *Savannah*, it seemed destined that she would end up working with wildlife after finishing university. The move from London to rustic Wiltshire had taken a while to get used to, and the pay wasn't great—in fact, she earned less now than she had as an intern at her uncle's insurance firm—but she got to work with the most marvellous creatures on Earth. Her family had always obsessed too much about money. Savannah's interests were more aligned with living in harmony with the planet than worrying about her bank balance.

She pulled her coat tighter in the spring dawn chill. This early in the day, only a handful of employees disturbed the sprawling Longleat estate. She waved to several while making her way towards the park entrance. The majesty of Longleat House rose in the distance, a stunning example of Elizabethan architecture that contained 128 rooms and had housed the Marquess of Bath for generations.

Savannah didn't like the ostentatiousness of Longleat House, though she was grateful for the role the Thynne family had played in establishing a wildlife sanctuary in such unlikely surroundings. The park supported several important scientific research programmes, as well as providing a home for rescued and endangered animals that could no longer survive in the wilds. Savannah dreamed of one day working in Kenya or South Africa, protecting the animals there from the capitalist predations of humanity. For now, Longleat was a solid first step in realising her ambitions.

She hurried by the various restaurants and shops designed to tempt guests to part with their hard-earned cash in return for greasy fries or soggy pizza, or perhaps an overpriced T-shirt to commemorate their visit. Half Mile Pond was just ahead, a man-made reservoir that acted as a buffer to the much larger safari park beyond. She thought she glimpsed the immense bulk of a hippo rippling through the dark water. A pair of sea lions lounged on the rocks nearby.

In the middle of the artificial lake, the climbing sun suffused Gorilla Island in crimson gold. There was no sign of Nico, the park's oldest inhabitant. The great silverback spent less and less time outside the house that occupied much of the island. He was likely the only gorilla in the world with access to central heating and satellite television, enjoying his favourite cartoons.

A boat was moored at the edge of the water. Savannah recognised Bob, one of the Jungle Cruise guides. He was a heavy, grizzled Welshman pushing sixty. Despite his no-nonsense appearance, he was friendly and a good storyteller, with a voice that carried. He seemed to be consoling Maria, who looked like she'd been crying again.

‘Morning,’ said Bob, as Savannah approached. ‘Don’t mind us. I’m just giving Maria here a pep talk.’

Maria gave Savannah an embarrassed smile. Her brown eyes were wet with tears. ‘Just me being silly,’ she said.

‘No, don’t be daft,’ Savannah replied, hopping on to the deck of the boat and giving the woman a hug. Maria was some ten years her senior, but there was an almost childlike fragility about her. ‘I can’t imagine how it feels to be married so long and then… Any luck finding your own place yet?’

‘I’m still at my friend’s, in Warminster,’ Maria replied. ‘I’ve been looking for a flat to rent, but it’s just so expensive. I wanted to visit my family this year.’

Savannah nodded sympathetically, though her father had paid a year’s rent up front for her roomy, two-bedroom apartment in Bath. The local town of Warminster was only a few minutes down the road and was a much cheaper place in which to live. ‘Perhaps your family could visit you?’

Maria shook her head. ‘They don’t have the money for flights, and my dad works every hour God sends. The Spanish economy is still recovering from the crash.’

‘Oh,’ said Savannah. She hadn’t thought of that. ‘How are my boys? How’s Charlie?’ she asked, embarrassed and keen to change the subject.

‘They were acting a bit strange.’ Maria fiddled with the heart pendant hanging around her neck. ‘Charlie wouldn’t come with the others when I called.’

'Well, you know Charlie.' Savannah smiled. He was the eldest of the four brothers that lived in the Chimpanzee Enclosure on the opposite bank of the Pond.

Maria sometimes worked night shifts, and her responsibilities included checking in on the enclosure. The apes liked Maria, which occasionally gave Savannah pangs of jealousy. Still, she knew that she, not Maria, was their favourite person. Maria was an infrequent visitor in the night, while Savannah fed them and played with them and groomed them, almost as though she was their big sister.

'Bad Charlie,' Maria agreed, smiling back. She yawned, and Savannah noticed the bags under the woman's eyes, the lack of care that had gone into applying her makeup. 'I should get some rest,' said Maria. 'Lovely to see you.' She turned to Bob. 'Thanks for your advice,' she said earnestly.

'You're welcome, lovely,' he replied. He watched Maria clamber off the boat before turning back to Savannah. 'And you, lass,' the Welshman said, 'care for a ride across the water?'

'Yes, please,' Savannah replied eagerly. The boat trip across the Pond to the enclosure would take only a few minutes and save her feet the longer, roundabout trip. Her phone vibrated in her coat pocket. She checked it and sighed. It was Brandon again. Her ex still hadn't gotten the message. He was a nice enough guy, but the distance between Longleat and London was too far to be convenient, and besides, the animals had always been her first love.

Bob turned the boat, and they set off towards the opposite shore. The grey clouds looked closer now. For a moment, the sun was swallowed by a passing bank and a great shadow seemed to descend over the lake. Silence immediately followed, broken only by the trickle of water against the hull and the low thrum of the boat engine. Savannah raised her head towards the clouds and revelled in the utter calm. It was moments like this where she felt the most free and powerful. She was the goddess of the lake, and this was *her* domain.

A bestial roar shattered the calm. Startled, she almost toppled off the boat. 'The lions are awake early,' she called out to Bob, hoping he hadn't witnessed her embarrassment. Even several miles distant, the angry roar of a male lion could freeze the blood.

'Big cats have been restless lately,' the Welshman called back. If he noticed her near mishap, he didn't mention it. 'All a bit queer if you ask me.'

As the boat neared Gorilla Island, Savannah's eyes were drawn to a hulking figure standing in the doorway of the solitary house. Nico, the famous silverback for which the island was named, was twice Bob's size and likely just as old.

At first, Savannah thought he had been drawn out by the untimely roar of the lion in the safari park. As she watched, Nico turned his great head to regard her. His amber eyes flicked to the chimpanzee enclosure, and then back. He shook his head, his gaze boring into her. Was Nico warning her not to go there?

It was Savannah's turn to shake her head. She was being silly. Nico might be ancient among his kind, but he was just a gorilla. Still, she couldn't shake the feeling of unease that settled over her as the sentinel of Gorilla Island watched their passing in silence.

The boat reached the opposite side of the lake a minute later. Savannah bid farewell to Bob and watched as he turned the boat around and began the short trip back across the water. It was a simple life, she reflected, sailing up and down the lake all day. Pleasant though he was, Bob was a simple man. She wanted so much more for herself. She wanted to see the world. To experience everything there was to see while she was young and carefree.

The enclosure was unusually quiet as she approached. Normally, the brothers would hear her coming and hoot in excitement. She'd only been working at the park for six months, and already they had grown to adore her. But this morning there was barely a sound to be heard. She could see three of the four apes lurking in the upper reaches of the structure that ran almost the entire length of the enclosure. There was no sign of Charlie.

Her phone vibrated again. She *tsked* when she saw it was Brandon trying to call once again. Why did he keep trying to call while she was busy at work? She made a mental note to block his number later.

She shoved her phone back into her pocket as she made her way to the storage shed beside the enclosure. The boys would definitely be hungry. Savannah filled her bucket with the proper ratio of roots, nuts, leaves, and assorted vegetables and made her way to the enclosure's main entrance.

She anticipated that the apes would immediately come knuckling towards her, eager to inspect their breakfast as they'd done every morning for the past six months. But they didn't move. Instead, they huddled together on the wooden apparatus. They hardly so much as glanced in her direction. The chimps seemed subdued, *spooked*, even. She remembered Nico's odd behaviour and felt a tightness in her chest.

Stop it, Savannah, she told herself. She was being ridiculous.

'Charlie?' she called out, worrying something had happened to her favourite boy. 'Bad Charlie,' she had nicknamed him affectionately, for he was wilful and liked to play silly pranks. She smiled, remembering the time he had stolen the feed bucket and forced her to chase him around the enclosure.

There was no response. She opened her mouth to call him again but stopped when, finally, she heard it: an eerie panting noise, like the struggling breaths of a dying man. She saw Charlie sitting under the apparatus between two iron cables. His back was to her. Charlie was the largest of the brothers, easily the weight of a man and appallingly muscular beneath his dark brown fur.

As she approached, concern warred with dread in her chest. What if he was sick? The panting sound he was making was not normal. He twitched suddenly. Behind her, Savannah heard the other apes whimper and skitter away.

'Charlie?' she called again. Still no reaction. It was as though he was focused on something in front of him. Something only he could see.

When she was less than six feet away, the big chimpanzee finally turned his head.

Savannah froze as her gaze met his. Something was wrong with Charlie's eyes. They looked as though they were filled with blood. He opened his mouth, not to smile but rather to announce savage intent, a gesture that in the wilds was more feared than a great cat's growl. Charlie's canines were twice the length of any human tooth, his fangs capable of rending flesh and bone and committing violence beyond the comprehension of most sane minds.

Sudden terror gripped Savannah. 'Please, Charlie, it's me,' she said, her voice choked with fear as she backed away. She managed to steel herself and forced her voice to become calm. 'You know me.'

His prodigious muscles tensed, but something in her tone must have penetrated Charlie's crazed brain. He hesitated. Recognition flickered in the bloodshot fury of his simian gaze.

'Yes…that's right, it's me, Charlie. It's me. You're sick. Let me call for help—'

The phone vibrated again.

Charlie noticed it and barked in fury. Savannah hurriedly tore the phone from her coat pocket and tried to cancel the call. Instead, she fumbled the device. It hit the ground with a soft *thud*. And then:

'Hello? Savannah? I can't believe it, you answered my call! God, I missed you.'

Brandon's babbling broadcast to the entire enclosure, his Estuary English whine like fingernails down a chalkboard.

Charlie howled in fury, his body shaking. He met her gaze, and all trace of familiarity was gone. Now, there was only a sick rage, a bestial desire to tear and maim and render beauty into unspeakable ugliness. Savannah screamed and turned to flee.

She had barely taken half a dozen steps before Charlie reached her.

2

John Sharrock was having a bad morning.

First, Alfie had woken him at four in the morning, pawing at the duvet cover and making pitiful whining noises. The smell hit John moments later, and he fumbled for the bedside lamp, dreading what he'd find. A lumpy puddle of yellow vomit met his horrified gaze. It was hard to believe so much could come out of such a small dog.

John had shoved the dog off the bed and jumped up, rolling the soiled blanket into a ball so he wouldn't have to look at the partially digested mess. Alfie hovered nearby looking shamefaced. The shih tzu's distress had made John feel incredibly guilty.

By the time John had replaced the bedding and settled back down to sleep, night was already giving way to the grey light of dawn and the first delicate notes of birdsong. John was a night owl and rarely went to bed before the early hours. Sleeping in till midday made him feel like some sort of ghoul, only grudgingly part of the world of the living. It was a bad habit he had fallen into since his wife had left.

The garage had called just as John was leaving his house on the way to the post office. The mechanic grimly informed John that his car would cost more to repair than it had cost to buy in the first place. John had owned it less than a year. The red convertible had been his reward for himself after securing his big book-deal. Now, it sat broken on the driveway, the front panel on the passenger side a mangled wreck and one wheel fallen off. A forlorn end for what had been his pride and joy.

That was what happened when you went driving around town after too much to drink. Never mind that he hadn't done anything like that in his thirty-four years before that fateful night. Never mind that his marriage was already falling apart. John had made the dumbest mistake of his life. Now, he was facing a lengthy driving ban and a future without Maria. At least no one had been hurt. It was a miracle he'd made it home after smashing into the parked vehicle that seemed to his alcohol-addled mind to appear from nowhere.

Halfway to the post office, the heavens had opened, and John realised he had forgotten his coat. The spring rain came hard and fast, and he was drenched before he'd taken another twenty steps.

He was definitely having a bad morning.

Unfortunately, the middle-aged jobsworth staring at him from behind the counter seemed determined to make it even worse.

'It's too large to post as a large letter,' she said again. She dropped the parcel, and it bounced off the slot in the plastic measuring tool. She smiled triumphantly.

John tried to keep his tone reasonable. 'Give it a slight push, you'll see that it fits. I've posted the same parcel before as a large letter many times.'

The woman shook her head, causing her unflattering bob to bounce. 'No, I'm sorry, it *must* be sent as a parcel.

If you're happy with that, it'll be four pounds and fifty pence.'

John wiped his hand down his still-wet face and gestured at the blue IKEA bag on the counter beside him. It was filled with small, identical brown parcels. The handful on top were damp from the rain. 'But there's twenty here. It'll cost me an extra fifty pounds to post them all.'

The post office worker shrugged and gave him her best *it's not my problem* stare through her thick-rimmed spectacles. He stared at her name badge: 'Carrie.'

John took a deep breath. What was it his therapist had said? *Focus on the anger. Imagine it as a black ball inside of you. Imagine yourself reaching in and pulling out the ball. You don't need it, it doesn't serve you. Throw it away. Let go of the anger.*

'Fine,' he said, smothering his annoyance with a supreme act of will. 'I assume you don't need to weigh them individually.'

For a moment, Carrie seemed torn between laziness and the opportunity to inconvenience him further. Evidently, laziness won. She calculated the price as John took his bank card out of his wallet. 'May I ask what is in the parcels?' Her tone seemed to suggest it wasn't a question.

'Books,' he replied. Written by him, as it happened. He didn't mention that fact. People were generally a lot less impressed to find out he was an author than he'd imagined they would be, especially when they learned he wrote fantasy. 'Like *Harry Potter*?' they often asked, to which John would reply, 'Kind of, yeah.' In truth, his books were nothing like *Harry Potter*. But it saved five minutes of a pointless discussion neither party really cared to have.

As John finished paying, there came a pained yelp from outside the shop. Remembering Alfie was tied up there, he hurried out into the drizzle to find a couple in their mid-30s standing over his dog. The woman cradled one hand in the other and was trying not to cry while her partner glared at the shih tzu.

'This yours?' he asked as John arrived.

'Yes,' John said. 'What happened?'

'*He bit me!*' the woman screamed. 'I reached down to pet him, and he almost snapped my hand off!'

'He wouldn't…' John began. But then he saw Alfie's lips rolled back, his small, needle-sharp teeth on full display, black eyes narrowed in anger.

The woman held up her injured hand to reveal a pattern of angry red bite marks, tiny beads of blood glistening between drops of rain. John bent down to scold the dog—and flinched back as Alfie snarled at him. A moment later, recognition seemed to dawn in the shih tzu's eyes, and he suddenly relaxed. John reached out a hesitant hand and stroked the dog's head. Alfie licked his fingers, the fury of a moment ago already forgotten.

'I'm really sorry,' John said, straightening. 'He was sick last night. He's never bitten anyone before. He'll growl sometimes when he's picked up or surprised, but never anything like this.'

The woman's partner examined her hand. 'It doesn't look too deep. We'll wash the wound when we get home and put a bandage on it. Luckily, Nikki's had her tetanus jabs.'

'Alfie's had his shots, too,' John said, eager to reassure the couple.

The woman, Nikki, glared at John. 'You should be more careful where you leave your dog. It could have attacked a child.'

He wouldn't, John wanted to say. His anger rose again. He wanted to point out that most children didn't go around petting strange dogs. Even as the thought crossed his mind, he knew that it was a poor defence. He took a deep breath and nodded.

'Look, mate,' said the man with Nikki, his tone firm but calm, 'we're dog people. Got a rottie at home, we love him to bits. Just…keep an eye on him, yeah?'

'Thanks,' replied John. 'I appreciate it.'

The couple left, Nikki throwing one last disapproving look at John and Alfie. 'What the hell is the matter with you?' John scolded, though, in truth, he was beginning to worry something was seriously wrong with the animal. 'Let's get you home.'

Warminster High Street was near deserted as they made their way back toward the house. An ancient market town on the edge of the West Wiltshire Downs Area of Outstanding Natural Beauty, Warminster was notable for its direct rail links to London, as well as the nearby Longleat Safari and Adventure Park.

It was the quintessential small market town, a place where the elderly retired and young couples raised a family when they couldn't afford to live in Bristol or Bath. Maria's job had brought them to Warminster originally. John liked the town well enough, but he missed his family.

The solitary nature of his career kept him in the house most of the time and made him feel like an outsider while Maria was out making friends. With Maria gone, that feeling of isolation increased tenfold. He felt like a lost spirit, moving through an unwelcome reality in which he didn't belong.

He slowed as a familiar face emerged from the café just ahead. He frantically looked around for somewhere he and Alfie could hide, but there was nowhere to run. Elsie would see him trying to avoid her. He tried to appear cheerful as his wife's best friend noticed him. A car roared past and almost splashed him. Though the streets were quiet, the traffic on the main road was as busy as ever.

'Hello, John!' said Elsie warmly, approaching him swiftly. She was a pretty woman, blonde and dark-eyed. She and Maria had met at Zumba class the year after John and Maria moved to Warminster. At first, Maria had jokingly referred to Elsie as 'Paris Hilton' because of her penchant for expensive gym clothes, sunglasses, and designer bags. Once the two got to know each other, Maria discovered she had a lot in common with the Warminster native. They both enjoyed fashion and a glass of wine while listening to Take That. A friendship quickly grew. It always amazed John how quickly Maria made new friends.

When Maria had moved out, she had gone to stay with Elsie and her partner Craig. As far as John was aware, she was still living with them. Not that Maria had to keep him updated on such things anymore.

'Hi, Elsie, how is everything?' John asked. *How's Maria*? he wanted to ask.

'Oh, good, thanks. I just popped out to meet my friend for a coffee. I was waiting for the rain to die off.'

'Crazy weather,' John agreed. He met Elsie's gaze, and she looked away. A small gesture, but it hit him like a slap in the face.

He racked his brain for something to say when a loud *bang* drew his attention to the road. A horse transporter had just come to a stop before a set of traffic lights. The bang seemed to come from within the transporter. The metal trailer shook, as though the animal within was desperate to get out. An equine face appeared in the gap between the door and the roof of the trailer.

John flinched and almost took a step back as he met the animal's gaze. Wild, bloodshot eyes stared at him. He'd been expecting a vacant expression on the horse's face.

Instead, what he saw could only be described as pure hatred.

The horse's lips folded back. Saliva frothed from its mouth, and it head-butted the door so hard it risked damaging its skull. The trailer shook again.

The traffic lights turned green, and the vehicle moved away. John caught one last glimpse of that baleful gaze before the transporter rounded a corner and disappeared.

'What was *that?*' he asked, to no one in particular, trying to shake off the unease within him.

'Sorry?' Elsie seemed to have missed the strange occurrence. She was checking her phone. 'I'd better go. It was nice to see you, John.'

'You, too,' John replied. He hesitated before asking softly, 'is…is Maria okay?'

'She's fine,' Elsie answered quickly, not looking at him.

'Is she planning to come home soon?' He winced, regretting the question immediately.

'I think you'd better discuss that with her.' Elsie put her phone away and gave him a sad smile. 'Take care of yourself, John.'

'You, too.' He watched her walk away—his one remaining link to Maria since she'd stopped answering her phone or replying to his texts.

He considered getting in his car and driving around to Elsie's house to see if he could spot her. Then, he remembered his car was a mangled wreck. Besides, Maria had asked to be left alone. If he couldn't respect that one simple wish, why on Earth would she believe he could change? Why would she even begin to consider taking him back?

With a sigh, John trudged back towards his house. Alfie scampered alongside him, oblivious to his emotional turmoil, oblivious to everything except the next place to take a piss.

Before they could make it home, the heavens opened again and soaked them both to the bone.

3

That evening—after opening a sachet of Hermes' Gourmet Dog Food for Alfie and putting down a fresh bowl of water—John went to the gym. He preferred evening sessions. His sleep patterns made it hard to muster the energy during the day and, besides, he could do without their mutual acquaintances enquiring about the whereabouts of his wife.

The usual half-dozen regulars were deep in their routines when John arrived. He stepped on to a treadmill and then noticed Tom on the lat pulldown machine. He gave the older man a nod in greeting.

'All right, lad?' Tom grunted, in his deep Geordie accent. Silver-haired and over six feet tall, Tom Graves was a powerful presence. When John first met Tom, he had assumed the Northerner was the managing director of some local company. He looked like the sort who drove a Jaguar and owned an impressive collection of well-fitted suits.

As it turned out, Tom was well into his 80s. He hadn't joined the gym until 60, and the reason he was in such good shape was down to a lifetime of lugging bodies around. Before his retirement, Tom had been the local undertaker. His confident manner was less the studied demeanour of a successful capitalist, more the cheerful self-assuredness of a man who had put hundreds in the ground and knew the same fate awaited everyone come the end. Far from being the quintessential Jag owner, he rode a push-pedal bicycle and had never even learned to drive.

Assumptions could be dangerous, John reflected as he adjusted the treadmill to a jogging pace. He was a smart man, but he had been guilty of too many assumptions the last few years. He had assumed a woman who was deeply in love with him would never grow unhappy despite being ignored day after day, week after week.

The books had come first. He and Maria hadn't gone to bed at the same time in over a year. Not since John had developed the habit of writing into the early hours of the morning, the result of unproductive days and the guilty nights that followed.

John increased the treadmill speed until he was sprinting hard. He was forced to concentrate simply to stay on the treadmill. His left leg, the leg that had been badly broken by a motorbike collision years ago, protested only very slightly, the ghost of yet another old trauma he had conquered through persistence and force of will. Though, of late he had sometimes felt as though his entire body was covered in scars he couldn't see.

Once the digital display declared he had run a mile, he hit the 'Stop' button and came to a panting halt. On the other side of the glass that dominated the north wall of the gymnasium, the empty swimming pool below reflected the lights on the ceiling above. The water was perfectly still. The tranquillity was reflected for a glorious moment in John's oxygen-deprived brain before his racing thoughts surged back.

He climbed off the treadmill and wiped the sweat from his forehead with a towel. Then he wandered over to the chest press machine. Mike, a regular at the gym John had chatted with a few times, was a solid-looking guy of similar age to him. He was grunting his way through a heavy set, and there was an angry red pattern of scratches on the dark skin of his face. 'What happened, Mike?' John asked, gesturing to the injured area.

Mike gave a rueful chuckle. 'My cat, mate. She tried to take my face off. She's been acting a bit crazy lately.'

John blinked in surprise, remembering Alfie's out-of-character attack on the young couple earlier, not to mention the angry horse trying to smash its way out of the transporter. 'You should get that checked out. It looks nasty.'

Mike shrugged his powerful shoulders. 'It's just a scratch. What are you benching these days?'

'Around a hundred kilos,' John said proudly. Before joining the gym, he hadn't been able to lift half his body weight. His lack of physical strength had been a constant source of insecurity. John didn't have a university education or a well-to-do family to fall back on. But he had grit and a natural intelligence, and his book deal had given him a measure of confidence he had lacked as an awkward teenager and then as a shy, geeky twenty-something. Getting stronger was another way for him to prove everyone wrong. Of late, it had helped exhaust his body when his mind refused to turn itself off.

'You're catching me up,' said Mike. 'Want to use this machine? I'll be done in a minute.'

'Take your time,' John replied. He thought about saying something else, making some small talk. They probably had interests in common. He'd seen Mike getting ready to hit the badminton court, and badminton was a sport John had loved to play as a kid. But something stopped him.

Instead, he wandered over to the free weights. Adam was there, showing off his impressive physique, his perfect form on the dumbbells. Adam was a little older than John. He was softly spoken, well-mannered, and boasted the kind of body fat percentage a Premier League footballer would be proud of.

Adam and his husband had recently opened a small food shop on the high street. Apparently, business was booming. Adam was a skilled baker, and his partner kept bees. They used the fresh honey the bees produced in all manner of delicious-looking cakes and tarts.

John sometimes wandered past the shop and gazed longingly at the pastries. The idea of encountering Adam outside the gym made John feel strangely uncomfortable, and so he'd never actually entered the shop, but he valued their short conversations in between biceps curls and shoulder presses.

The two men exchanged nods as John selected a pair of heavy dumbbells. Possibly a little heavier than he could manage. 'Late workout tonight?' Adam asked as John struggled them into position.

'Yeah. I'm not sleeping well,' John replied. He waited for the question, cursing his need to speak to someone. Hating how weak it made him feel.

'Any reason?' Adam asked, obliging him.

'My wife left me recently.'

'Oh. I'm sorry.'

'Thanks. It happens, I guess.'

Adam made a sympathetic sound, and the two men continued to work out in silence. On the television sets above the treadmills, the local news channel aired a special report on Longleat Safari and Adventure Park. One of the chimpanzees at the park had brutally attacked a keeper earlier that morning, leaving the poor woman with three fingers on her left hand and several broken ribs.

John stared at the screen, heart pounding. Maria worked at the park. It couldn't be her, could it?

He was relieved when an image flashed up of a woman he didn't recognise. The victim's name was Savannah, and she'd only started working at the park the previous autumn. Had Maria ever mentioned her? Perhaps she had, and he simply hadn't been listening.

'You should stop by the shop,' Adam was saying, tearing John's attention away from the news and the fresh wave of guilt. 'When you need a break from writing, I mean. I have this great new brownie recipe. We serve sandwiches, too. We can make them however you like.' There was a warmth in Adam's voice that made John feel pathetically grateful.

'I'll stop by,' John said, knowing he probably wouldn't, hating himself for it. He checked the time. It was already past 9pm. Alfie had been alone for two hours.

'See ya, laddies,' Tom called, waving at them as he left the gym.

'Cheers, Tom,' John called back. The gym felt suddenly emptier and darker than before, one of his few remaining connections to the world of the living extinguished for the night. John gritted his teeth, put those troubling thoughts aside, and focused on punishing his body.

****

Tom winced as a bump in the road caused the saddle beneath him to jerk suddenly, sending a sharp pain up his arse.

'Sodding haemorrhoids,' he muttered. It was one of the facts of getting old that folk didn't talk about. Aye, your teeth fell out, your hair went grey or disappeared—but it was the constant niggles and pains everywhere that were the real nuisance. Not to mention the inability to pee in a straight line. He needed to go again now, and he'd only just pissed at the gym, feeling a mite guilty about splashing it all over the toilet seat for the next bugger to stumble upon. Still, it couldn't be helped. Some things you just had to accept.

It was like death, Tom reckoned. It might come tomorrow, or it might come a decade from now. Everyone went back to the earth eventually. No point worrying about it.

The streets smelled of rain. The sky was covered by thick, black clouds. The retired undertaker glanced up, hoping he could make it home before this latest deluge hit. Seeking a shortcut, he turned down a road that ran parallel to a stretch of wasteland. A housing development had been planned there years ago, but then the financial crisis of 2008 had hit, and the investors had pulled out.

Damned shame, Tom thought. He didn't envy the young. He was old enough to remember the tough times following the war and the boom that followed. He'd seen the housing market shift through the eyes of his children, and then *their* children. Watching the younger generations struggle to find somewhere to rent, never mind afford a mortgage, had been sobering for a man who bought his first home with two years' salary back in the 60s.

Maybe things would change if the UK voted to leave the European Union. Maybe they wouldn't. Tom was old enough to know that whoever ran the country, the rich generally got richer and the poor generally got poorer, as surely as death follows life.

A fox screamed somewhere up on the wasteland opposite, an eerie sound, like a child's cry of pain. It was joined by another shriek. Despite his old eyes, Tom could make out shadowy figures loping over the wasteland towards the road. Several pairs of glowing red orbs burned in the darkness as they fixed upon him. Tom stared back, confused. Adult foxes didn't usually forage in large groups. They certainly didn't approach humans, not unless they'd been trained with the promise of food by some well-meaning but foolish housewife.

One of the foxes barked at him, a vicious sound that seemed to carry a threat. 'Bugger off!' Tom yelled back, thinking the sound of his voice would startle the animals. Instead, they surrounded his bike, keeping pace with him. Jaws snapped at his ankles as the foxes snarled and screamed.

Suddenly afraid, Tom peddled faster. His legs throbbed with exhaustion, but he didn't ease up until he had opened a considerable distance between himself and the skulk. For a moment, it looked like they would give chase. Then, they melted away into the night, gone as quickly as they had come. 'Bloody hell,' Tom muttered, slowing down and struggling to catch his breath.

This would be a story to tell the grandchildren, and no mistake.

****

John's key clicked in the front door, and it swung open. 'Alfie?' he called, wondering why the dog hadn't greeted him. The house was deathly silent.

He caught sight of the yellow marks on the carpet an instant before the stench hit him. The dog had been sick again.

'I'm tired of this,' he muttered angrily. He found Alfie quivering in the conservatory. John wanted to yell at the dog, to punish him not only for this latest mess but also for his aggressive behaviour earlier that day. A memory came to him: Maria's laughter when they'd first taken the dog home and Alfie had licked his face. How they all had snuggled together on the sofa and John had believed everything was going to be okay.

In truth, Alfie had been the final roll of the die for a relationship that had been in the doldrums for months. Suddenly overcome by guilt, John bent down and wrapped his arms around the trembling animal. 'It's okay. Sorry for leaving you alone. First thing tomorrow, I'm taking you to the vet. Let's get this cleaned up.'

When the carpet was scrubbed and Alfie was finally calm, John showered and went to the kitchen to make himself a cup of tea before bed. It was still early by his standards, but he hoped his labours at the gym, as well as half an hour cleaning up dog vomit, had exhausted him so that he could slip into an easy sleep.

As he turned the cold tap on to fill the kettle, a nightmarish brown shape scuttled over the side of the sink bowl and reared up at him. John flinched back in surprise. It was a house spider—likely the same one he'd washed down the plughole a few days ago. He'd never seen a spider act so aggressively.

The sight of the chitinous arachnid standing on its rear legs filled him with revulsion. He tore away a sheet of kitchen paper and plucked the spider from the sink, squeezing just hard enough to crush it. Then, he dashed upstairs to the bathroom and tossed the tissue into the toilet and pulled the flush.

An hour later, he was finally tucked up in bed. Alfie lay beside him, motionless save for the occasional snore that seemed improbably loud for such a small animal. The quack of a mother duck leading her ducklings came from the stream at the bottom of his garden, an offshoot of the River Were.

The wholesomeness of the image, the natural beauty of it, only magnified his sadness, the suffocating loneliness. The sense that he was an aberration, an invader from another timeline who had somehow displaced the perfect reality of this world and ruined not only his life but Maria's, too. He realised he desperately needed to talk to someone other than his therapist.

Once he had taken Alfie to the vet, he would phone his mum and arrange to visit her in Bristol. That would mean catching the train for the first time in years.

Setting his phone alarm for eight o'clock and dreading the early rise, John Sharrock closed his eyes.

4

The car swerved as bright lights danced around his face like fireflies. He tried to concentrate on the road ahead, but it seemed to twist and writhe. He caught himself drifting towards the kerb and tried to veer away, but it was as though the steering wheel was locked in place.

Nothing made any sense. A car passed him on the right, and he vaguely registered the sound of a horn beeping. He glanced back, taking his eyes off the road for a split second. When his gaze returned, there was something in the middle of the windscreen. It was a moth, a death's-head hawkmoth.

The insect's wingspan was as wide as his hand. The skull pattern on the moth's thorax seemed to leer at him with blood red eyes. He turned on the windscreen wipers, and they flicked it away—but no sooner had it disappeared into the dark night than three more thudded against the glass, followed quickly by another handful, and soon, so many cluttered his windscreen that he could no longer see past them.

He lost complete control then. He was flooded with fear as the knowledge that he was moments from hitting something cemented itself in his mind. Somehow, he heard the crash before he felt it. Reverberating through his bones was a sound like the grinding of metal, the crushing of bone, the dying of a dream—

John awoke with a start. Sweat covered his body. He thrust aside the bed cover and tried to clear his senses. He checked the clock on his phone. *3:50am.* It was strange how often he woke at this precise hour.

The rain was back. It pounded against the windows, a relentless roar. But there was something else: a whirring noise, a bright light from the hallway illuminating the space between ajar door and frame. Alfie wasn't in the bedroom.

John rolled from the bed, almost tripping on Alfie's bone. He cursed and went out into the hallway, wondering if he would find a burglar in the process of looting the place. He didn't keep any weapons around the house, believing, perhaps naively, that he could deal with most potential threats. Besides, Warminster was low on crime. The street in which he lived hadn't recorded an incident in years, until his own recent misadventure.

The bright light was coming from the room opposite. John pushed open the door to the empty room, suppressing the pang of sadness that rose in his chest. This was supposed to have been the nursery for when he and Maria had their first child. Its bare walls and floorboards seemed to glow accusingly in the light from outside.

John crossed to the window and stared out. The whirring sound and the lights were coming from atop Cley Hill in the distance. An Iron Age hillfort, Cley Hill had gained notoriety in the '60s after dozens of locals claimed to have witnessed mysterious objects emanating unusual lights and emitting strange noises throughout the night sky in and around Warminster, as well as a myriad of strange noises and unexplained phenomena such as cars mysteriously breaking down and clocks or their owners losing time. The reports came to be known as the 'Warminster Thing,' and UFO watchers still came to the hill to this day hoping to catch a glimpse of an extraterrestrial visitor.

The fact that Salisbury Plain, a military training area, was right next to Cley Hill should have provided an easy explanation for the sightings. The helicopter hovering above the hill and making a racket at that moment was certainly no UFO, though John had no idea what it was doing at this hour.

He watched the helicopter ascend, and then disappear into the distance, leaving darkness and the soft patter of rain in its wake. In the newly descended silence, John heard something new—a low growling sound. John belatedly remembered that he hadn't seen Alfie since the helicopter had woken him. He left the nursery, calling softly for the absent dog.

He found the shih tzu at the top of the landing. Alfie didn't even look at him. He stared down the stairs, a low growl in his throat. John froze, listening for any sound that would indicate an intruder below. There was a noise coming from the conservatory, faintly audible above the rain and Alfie's growls: a sharp *tap, tap, tap*, like something repeatedly striking glass.

John took a deep breath to steel himself, then descended the stairs. He didn't rush, but neither did he creep. Things might have been different had Maria been in the house, but he didn't care enough for his own safety to feel any real fear. In a strange way, he welcomed a potential confrontation.

The conservatory loomed beyond the living room. The small extension had been there when John and Maria had bought the house. During winter, it was the ideal place for John to write. As spring turned to summer, it quickly grew so hot that it was practically unusable during the day. Dead bugs had begun to build up around the edges of the conservatory, dark spots against the white sealant.

The *tap, tap, tap* got louder as he entered the conservatory. The sound drew John's eyes to the conservatory's outer glass panel and a small, shadowy shape in the garden. John's eyes narrowed as he tried to make sense of what he was seeing.

It was a duck. The waterfowl pecked at the glass, striking it almost obsessively with its beak. Over and over again. When it spotted John, it quacked frantically. It beat its wings and struck the glass even more aggressively. Spots of a darker substance joined the rainwater running down the pane.

'What the hell?' John flicked the light switch on the wall, and the garden lit up. The illumination revealed clumps of bloody feathers and stringy meat on the grass. John recoiled as he realized what he was seeing: Surrounding the mother duck was the remains of the ducklings.

John's immediate thought was that foxes had gotten into the garden, but then he saw the patches of downy feathers sticking to the mother duck's face in gory clumps and somehow knew she had killed her babies.

Beside him, Alfie's growl increased in volume. The dog pressed his nose up against the glass and barked furiously, desperate to get at the bird. So desperate was his desire to get at the bird that the clear glass was soon smudged with drool and spittle.

There's something wrong with the duck's eyes. They seemed bloodshot. Not unlike those of the crazed horse trying to escape the transporter earlier that day.

He considered what to do next. Whatever was wrong with the duck, it clearly wouldn't be able to break into the conservatory. He would have to hope it would get bored and wander off.

He would mention the psychotic duck to the vet in the morning. It was a shame about the ducklings. He couldn't imagine what would possess a mother duck to kill her young. He recalled Maria excitedly telling him she'd found some eggs down by the stream and wanting to show him. He'd told her he was too busy.

Perhaps this house is cursed, John thought. After all, the previous owner had sold up after separating from her partner. He and Maria hadn't made it to a year in the house before she'd left. *A cursed house that drives the local wildlife mad and causes the owners to consume those they love.*

He shook his head forcefully. That was stupid, fantastical thinking, the kind of nonsense he wrote about. In the real world, curses didn't exist. At least not those fantastical, mystical curses. No, the real curses were the poor decisions people made and the consequences that followed.

He reached down to pull Alfie away from the glass.

He stopped, hand hovering in the air above the reflective red collar when the dog suddenly froze mid-bark. Alfie seemed to convulse silently. John noticed spittle bubbling from the dog's mouth. His beloved shih tzu slowly turned its head to stare at him.

John met Alfie's gaze, expecting to see gentle brown eyes. Instead, he stared into crimson pools. Like portals to hell.

John froze. Alfie would never attack *him,* surely. He had known the animal since he was a pup. The dog trembled, his tiny body quivering with rage as though a demon was trying to force its way out—

A cold chill prickled along his spine, a sickening fear rising.

John bolted from the conservatory and slammed the inner door shut an instant before the dog lunged for him. Alfie struck the door with the full weight of his small body. He didn't bark, and neither did he growl. He simply stared at John through the glass with eyes as sinister as infanticide. He smashed into the door again, flecking the inside glass with blood and drool.

'*What the hell is happening?*' John whispered to himself. The world had gone mad.

5

The phone screen displayed 'Mum' in big, accusatory letters. He knew he should answer. It was the third time his mother had tried to call in the last hour, but despite his desire to talk to someone, a part of him was afraid of the direction the conversation might take. He wasn't ready for more bad news.

It was still early, and the sandwich shop on Warminster High Street was mostly empty. John hadn't been able to sleep after Alfie had tried to attack him. By mid-morning, his stomach had begun to grumble. A half-eaten chicken sandwich and a Diet Pepsi rested on the table inches from the phone. Despite his hunger, the gruesome remains of the ducklings in his garden had soured John's appetite.

Perhaps I should have ordered the Veggie Delight.

Alfie was still locked in the conservatory. The little shih tzu had thrown himself at the door for a solid hour. When it seemed as though the dog had finally tired himself out, John made the mistake of opening the door a fraction to bring him a bowl of water. Alfie immediately shot up from the ground and launched himself at the door, resuming his ferocious, single-minded attack. John was fortunate only to spill the water everywhere and not lose several fingers like that poor woman at the safari park.

John had again felt a guilty flood of relief that it hadn't been Maria who had been maimed on the job.

The phone rang once more. With a sigh, John scooped it off the table and answered the call.

'Hello, Mum,' John said in greeting.

'Where are you? I thought you were coming over.'

'I was. But something's happened with Alfie. He attacked me. I think he's unwell.'

'What? Have you tried taking him to the vet?'

'I'd planned to. He won't let me near him. I tried to call to get some advice, but they weren't answering.'

There was a moment of silence. The shop door banged open, and a woman bustled in. John saw it was the jobsworth, Carrie, from the post office.

'Where is he now?'

'At home. I had to lock him in the conservatory. There's something strange happening here. How are things there? What did the hospital say?'

'What do you mean strange*? Everything's fine here. It hasn't progressed since the last visit.'*

John breathed a sigh of relief. He'd been expecting the worst.

'Have you spoken to Maria?'

'No.'

'She messaged me.'

John froze. 'When?'

'A couple of days ago.'

'What did she say?'

The momentary silence seemed to last an eternity. Then: *'She said she's sorry about what's happened. And that she loves us. But she doesn't think things can be fixed.'*

The blackness seemed to rush up to swallow him. There were a hundred things he wanted to say. A hundred things he wanted his mum to say to Maria on his behalf. But all he said was, 'all right.'

'Are you okay?' she asked softly.

'Yes.' Tears prickled the corners of his eyes and he wiped them away angrily.

'Keep trying the vet. If Alfie won't let you near him, you'll have to call someone out.'

'I will.'

'Try not to get too down. Things will work themselves out. I'll talk to you later.'

'Thanks. Talk to you later.' There weren't any "*love yous*" or sentimental parting words: They weren't that kind of family. John hadn't wanted to trouble his mother with any of the drama surrounding he and Maria, and she had been as surprised as anyone when Maria had left him. Ever since the news from the hospital a few months back, he had taken care not to upset his mum.

John finished his sandwich and took another sip of Coke. Carrie was at the counter. She appeared to be complaining about something. The fresh cookies on the side of the counter caught his eye: wholemeal and oat raisin, rainbow chunks, and his personal favourite, the humble milk chocolate chip. He was supposed to be cutting down on sweet treats, but he figured a single cookie couldn't do any harm, especially with his frequent trips to the gym. He needed something to cheer him up.

As he was preparing to queue behind Carrie, he caught a familiar face glancing at him from another table. It was Mike, the big guy from the gym. There was a woman sitting opposite him. She, too, seemed somehow familiar. John noticed the bandage on her hand and knew then why he recognised her. It was the woman Alfie had bitten outside the post office. What was her name? Nikki? She'd been with a different man yesterday.

Mike looked away as John walked past. He seemed faintly embarrassed. Nikki grimaced at him and whispered something to Mike. A moment later, the two of them stood up and left the shop.

John watched them go and shrugged. A town like Warminster was full of small, often tawdry secrets. Whatever was going on between them was none of his business. He just wanted his cookie. Unfortunately, Carrie was still remonstrating with the server behind the counter, blonde bob dancing up and down like a poodle having an epileptic fit as she waved her sandwich in the woman's face.

'I *asked* for tuna with sweet chilli sauce. Does this look like sweet chilli sauce to you?'

The server, an attractive woman of South Asian heritage whom John had chatted with on a couple of occasions, peered at the offending sandwich. 'I'm very sorry,' she said apologetically, with a faint accent. 'Let me make a new one for you.'

'Excuse me? I didn't catch a word you said. Speak slower.'

'I'll make you a new sandwich,' the server—John noticed her name tag read 'Anu'—said very deliberately. 'Give me a couple of minutes.'

Carrie huffed. She swept her gaze over John and everyone else in the shop, checking she had an audience. 'I work at the post office, you know,' she said haughtily. 'We don't have time to make mistakes there.'

'Like I said, I apologise,' Anu replied. The way she gripped the sandwich knife as she viciously cut a new loaf in half suggested she was losing her patience.

Carrie caught John glaring at her and rolled her eyes at Anu, as if assuming he shared her frustration. It was a gesture that seemed to say: *Bloody foreigners, can't do a simple thing right while people like us keep Britain running.*

Anu finished preparing the replacement sandwich while Carrie tutted and checked the time on her phone. When Anu turned to take the sandwich out of the oven, the postal worker snatched a packet of crisps from the counter and shoved them into her bag. John thought about saying something but decided it wasn't worth the hassle. Some people were just arseholes.

'Is there anything else I can do for you?' Anu asked, as Carrie grabbed the sandwich out of her hands.

'No,' snapped the post office worker. As she turned and bustled towards the door, John heard her mutter, just loud enough for Anu to hear: *'How about going back to your own country.'*

'That woman's a bitch,' John said as the shop door slammed shut. 'She gave me a hard time at the post office yesterday. I'm sorry you have to put up with people like her.'

Anu smiled at him and pulled off her plastic disposable gloves. 'You get customers like that. It doesn't bother me.'

'She stole a packet of crisps.'

Anu shook her head and brushed a few strands of black hair out of her face. 'People like her get what's coming to them.'

'You're talking about karma.'

'Yes, karma. Where I'm from, we say what goes around, comes around.'

'Where *are* you from?' he asked, his curiosity getting the best of him.

Anu grinned at him, her dark eyes dancing mischievously. 'Coventry.'

'Ah. Commiserations.' That won a laugh, and it felt good to be able to make someone laugh. Maria used to laugh all the time.

'What can I get you?' Anu asked, her mood seeming to brighten with their conversation.

'A milk chocolate cookie, please. Actually, make it two. All this drama has given me an appetite.'

'Let me grab some fresh ones from the kitchen. Those have been there since yesterday.' Anu went off into the back, leaving the shop floor empty except for John. He glanced at the till, at the various drinks and confectionaries on display. A thief could have a field day.

He wondered if Anu would have left him alone if she'd known he was a soon-to-be criminal. The court case for the drunk-driving incident loomed. By the end of the month, he'd be up before the judges in Salisbury Magistrates' Court. Life had seemed so simple only a year ago. Things had been black and white. There were good people, and there were bad people; there were those who followed the law and those who broke the law.

That had been a naïve way to look at things, John now realised. All it took was a poor decision at the wrong moment to send anyone spiralling.

John Sharrock had learned a lot about himself in the last year.

A terrified scream from the kitchen shattered his contemplations like a fist through a glass window. There came the sounds of a brief struggle, and then Anu stumbled back into view. John saw the black shapes clinging to her and froze momentarily in shock. Two large rats had their jaws latched on the employee. They were trying to climb her body, desperate to get at her throat.

'Get them off me!' Anu screamed frantically, flailing around desperately, knocking bread rolls and packets of crisps and bottles of fizzy drink from the counter. One rat hung from her arm. The other sank its incisors into her thigh.

John sprang into action. He vaulted the counter, picked up the knife Anu used to cut sandwiches and slashed at the rat on her thigh. The vermin released its grip and turned to him, yellow teeth snapping at his hand. He stabbed again, and it jerked spasmodically, skewered by the blade. John hurled both knife and rodent across the shop and turned his attention to the other rat.

The bloodthirsty creature seemed to narrow its red eyes at him as he reached for its tail. Suddenly, it leapt from Anu's arm straight at John, who managed to backhand it away in mid-air. The rat landed in the mayonnaise tray under the glass counter. It disappeared, submerged in the creamy condiment. A moment later, it scuttled free, now slimy with mayonnaise, like some tiny alien still dripping with afterbirth.

Before John could act, Anu grabbed the rat by the slimy scruff of its neck and shoved it inside the bread toaster. She slammed the metal door shut as it launched itself towards the opening. Her hands shook as she set the oven timer to sixty seconds. John and Anu waited in horrified silence as the rat scrabbled to escape, its efforts growing weaker as the timer ticked by a minute. The toaster alarm rang. Anu cautiously pulled the door open.

The dead rat was curled into a ball. Smoke rose gently from its blackened, crispy body.

'Are you hurt?' John asked, trying to ignore the smell of the charred remains. He examined Anu's arm, winced at the bloody wound where the animal's sharp teeth had done their wicked work. Anu's thigh seemed uninjured, though her jeans had a hole from where the rat had tried to get to the flesh beneath. 'What just happened?' he said, as much to himself as to the woman opposite him.

Anu seemed remarkably calm in the circumstances. 'I was sorting through this morning's delivery when they attacked me. They came out of nowhere! We were audited by the Food Standards Agency just the other week; they awarded us five stars. We've never had a rat problem before.'

'I believe you,' John said. 'But don't worry about any of that right now. You need to get that wound checked out.' Something about this woman being so earnest and eager to reassure him after having just suffered a vicious attack made him warm to her immediately.

Anu looked him up and down. 'They didn't bite you as well, did they?'

'I don't think so.'

'Do you make a habit of saving young women from bloodthirsty beasts?' Anu asked. She smiled at him.

'I try not to,' John joked.

A memory came to him then. He was a young boy, four or five years old. His aunt and uncles were telling him that he had to be strong, that he had to look after his mum. Something terrible had happened, and it was his responsibility to make sure she was okay. He had forced himself to become like one of the mighty dinosaurs in the picture books he liked to read: fiercely aggressive and ready to fight anyone to protect his mum. She had eventually grown so concerned by his behaviour she arranged for him to be seen by a therapist.

'Everything all right? You seem distracted.' Anu was looking at him with a concerned expression.

'Huh? I'm sorry, I was remembering something that happened a long time ago.' He blinked away the cobwebs of ages past. 'Have I even introduced myself? I'm John.'

'Well, John,' Anu said wryly. 'I'm afraid we've made a bit of a mess.'

John stared around the restaurant. Food and drink were strewn everywhere. A bottle of Pepsi had exploded, and the brown, syrupy liquid was spreading over the floor. The skewered rat was still twitching by the entrance to the toilets. 'You know,' he said. 'This isn't the first time I've seen animals behaving strangely of late. My dog has gone crazy.'

'Really?' Anu said. 'You should tell me about it while I clean up this mess. I'm so sorry for all this.'

'Don't be sorry on my account, it's not your fault,' said John. 'And forget about the mess. We need to get that wound seen to.'

'I'll call my papa,' Anu said. 'He's a doctor at the surgery here in Warminster.'

John nodded. 'We can go together, if you like. I can't be gone too long, though. Someone needs to check on Alfie.'

'Alfie?' Anu asked. She pressed a paper towel against her bloody arm and winced slightly.

'My dog.'

'Ah. Cute name. Let me lock up here, and we'll head straight to the surgery.'

As Anu busied herself cashing up the till, John popped out of the shop to get some air and warn passers-by not to come in. He'd been a lost soul since Maria had left, stranded in an emotional wasteland in which only guilt and flashes of anger occasionally pierced the malaise. Leaping to Anu's defence seemed to have snapped him out of it, at least temporarily. It had reminded him of who he was.

A sudden gust of wind blew down the street. It carried the smell of more rain to follow, but something else lurked on the breeze, too: a brooding threat, a dark promise of bad things to come. The animal attacks, the strange dreams…there was a palpable sense that *something* was happening. Something sinister.

Across the road, Adam was just leaving his shop. He saw John and gave him a cheery wave. If his gym buddy judged him for buying a sandwich at a fast-food franchise instead of at his own bakery, to which he'd personally extended John an invitation, he didn't let it show.

Somehow, that didn't make John feel any better.

6

Nikki Glass groaned with pleasure as she felt him enter her. She was bent over the marital bed, staring down at the duvet covers her mother-in-law had gifted Nikki and Kevin on their wedding day. That had bothered Nikki at first, but six months into her affair with Mike Skinner and she was past caring about decorum. She didn't even bother to hide Kevin's photos when her lover was over at the house anymore.

'Fuck, Nikki, *yes*,' Mike grunted behind her. His powerful arms gripped her thighs, forcing them apart, and she moaned in excitement. Kevin was a nice enough guy, polite and helpful and caring—but God was he *boring*. He wouldn't know how to please a woman sexually if she came with an instruction manual, whereas Mike was like a wild animal. He knew what he wanted, and he took it.

It thrilled her, to be desired that way. She'd put on some weight since the wedding three years back—between her busy job and looking after the home, how could she be expected to obsess over her figure? —and Kevin's sex drive, which had always been low, had all but disappeared.

Oh, he'd made the effort on a few occasions. Just this Christmas gone, he'd booked a hotel getaway in Edinburgh for the two of them. He'd bought her some naughty underwear from Victoria's Secrets but got the sizes wrong. That had annoyed her from the off. Then, when she had encouraged him to put his hands around her throat and tried to introduce something new and exciting into their boring routine, he had said he felt uncomfortable. They barely spoke for the rest of the trip.

She'd already told her mum and closest friends that she and Kevin were unhappy. That she didn't feel valued or loved, and that she was thinking of leaving him. They didn't know about Mike yet—she was determined that he dump his girlfriend before they announced their relationship. Mike wanted to wait until his newborn was older before cutting her loose, which was a constant source of annoyance for Nikki. He was so decisive in every other way!

He was gaining momentum now, pounding her with a strength and rhythm Kevin could never hope to match. She tried to shift position so that he could get even deeper inside her but accidentally banged her wounded hand against the bedside table.

'Shit!'

Mike stopped his thrusting and hovered behind her uncertainly. 'What's wrong?' he asked.

'I knocked my hand. Bloody stupid shih tzu. Who has a dog like that anyway? What are they good for?'

She felt Mike's fingers enter her and gasped. He had thick fingers, rough and manly. Kevin's were long and thin, almost womanly. The hands of a man who spent all day tapping away on a keyboard and leafing through boring accounts. He was away now in London, meeting with some client or another. He wouldn't be back for a few days. Nikki didn't mind. It gave her more time with Mike.

His fingers withdrew, and Nikki turned to regard her lover. The scratches his cat had left on his face were healing. He was frowning over at Charlie, who watched them from the corner of the room. Her beloved black-and-tan rottweiler was a *real* dog—not like the pathetic, teddy-bear-looking mutt that had taken a chunk out of her hand. 'You said you knew the owner?' she asked.

'Yeah,' said Mike, distractedly. 'We go to the same gym.' His naked chest glistened, dark and strong and muscular. Kevin was ten stone dripping wet. Mike could have crushed him with one arm.

'I wish it had been you with me,' Nikki said, reaching out with her good hand to stroke his cheek. 'Kevin just stood there like a twat. We argued about it for an hour when we got home. He barely said a word to the owner.'

'I'd have decked him,' Mike said. He seemed preoccupied with Charlie. The dog didn't like him, she knew. Despite all the attention she gave him, the big rottie had always favoured Kevin and seemed to resent Mike's presence.

'You promise?' she said. 'You'd protect me?'

'Of course I would.'

Nikki felt herself getting wetter by the moment. She gave Mike her best sexy look. 'Fuck me,' she demanded.

Mike fumbled around behind her, his drooping member poking at her private parts but failing to bury itself in the moistness beneath her thighs. 'What's wrong?' she asked, slightly impatient.

'It's your dog. He won't stop staring at me. It's putting me off.'

'Fuck, Mike! He's a dog! I can shoo him out if it bothers you that much.'

'Yeah, okay.'

Nikki pointed to the bedroom doorway with her injured hand, balancing herself on the bed with the other. 'Charlie! Out!'

The rottweiler didn't respond to her command, which was odd. He was generally an obedient dog. Less so with her than with Kevin, but still. 'I said OUT!' she barked, more forcefully this time.

Charlie still didn't move. He was watching the pair of them with an intensity that made her uneasy. There was something strange about his eyes…

'Nikki…' Mike began, sounding worried. He never got to finish his sentence.

With a bone-curdling howl, Charlie launched himself across the room. The dog's slavering jaws closed around Mike's forearm, causing him to cry out in pain. Nikki jumped off the bed and screamed at the dog to stop. It ignored her, snarling like a thing possessed. She realised then what was wrong with Charlie's eyes. They were bloodshot, as though something in his brain had burst.

Mike punched the dog twice in the face, surely hurting it but not badly enough for it to release its grip. With his free arm, he grabbed it around the neck in a choke hold, forcing it down, attempting to strangle it.

'Stop!' Nikki screamed. 'You'll kill him!'

‘He’s trying to kill *me!*’ Mike roared back. The dog finally released its hold on his arm, and he thrust the raging animal aside. Blood poured from the wound it had left. The dog backed away, more cautious now, understanding this powerful human could match his strength. ‘What the hell’s wrong with him?’ Mike shouted, an accusatory edge in his voice.

‘I don’t bloody know!’ Nikki yelled back. A thought occurred to her. ‘Let me try something,’ she said. ‘Kevin’s slippers. Charlie loves them. I think they comfort him when he’s away.’ She bent down and snatched up one of her husband’s slippers. ‘Here, boy,’ she said, making her voice as soothing as possible. ‘You know who this belongs to, don’t you? It’s daddy’s slipper.’

Charlie sniffed it. Some of the tension drained out of him. The rottweiler shook his head wildly, as though trying to defy whatever madness afflicted him. He gave a small whine. Nikki took that as her cue to go to him, ignoring the bleeding Mike, who clutched his arm.

She knew instantly she’d made a mistake.

Charlie jerked once. His teeth reappeared, black lips folding back to reveal razor-sharp canines. Bloody spittle dripped from his mouth. Before Nikki could open her mouth to scream, the dog’s jaws clamped around her throat. The pain was overwhelming, and she blacked out for a moment as the animal bore her to the ground.

The pressure in her neck was so great she thought it might snap. She tried to suck in breath. Attempted to cry out for help. Nothing filled her mouth except the coppery taste of blood. She beat at the dog with her hands, but her blows were weak, pathetic.

She saw Mike staring down at her in horror, his flaccid penis hanging uselessly between his quivering legs. He hesitated for a moment. 'Help me,' she tried to gasp, but the pressure around her throat turned her words into a wet, unintelligible gurgle.

'Fuck this,' Mike said, eyes wide and dark face paler than usual. He turned and bolted out of the door. She heard his footsteps thumping down the stairs as he fled.

Charlie suddenly tore at her throat, his great jaws ripping a jagged hole in her flesh. Warm blood sprayed out in a fountain. Nikki watched dully as it splashed over the carpet, the newly painted walls, the bedding her mother-in-law had bought for her and Kevin.

Her vision dimmed as her strength fled. She hardly felt it when Charlie's jaws closed around her neck again, her beloved pet rottweiler ravaging her with the same relish with which he'd devour the leftover beef after a Sunday roast. Her fading gaze settled on the dresser on the far wall.

The last thing Nikki saw before death claimed her was a bloodstained photo of her and Kevin smiling at the camera on their wedding day.

7

The small general practitioner surgery on The Avenue was heaving with patients when John and Anu arrived. The practice was busy at the best of times, with Warminster's ageing population and deep cuts to the National Health Service placing more strain than ever on the doctors and nurses.

John was staunchly against leaving the European Union, afraid of what it would mean for Maria and her family, but he had to admit that the extra £350 million a week for NHS funding promised by the pro-Leave campaign made for a compelling argument. Perhaps by 2026 the United Kingdom would have the most comprehensive and efficient health service in the world.

In the here and now of 2016, things were decidedly less utopian.

'Excuse me, I was here first,' said an elderly woman as Anu pushed her way through the queue outside the surgery to the reception desk within. The older woman wore a scarf covering her face and had a nasty-looking bite on her arm. John noticed that most of the other people huddling miserably in the rain outside bore similar-looking injuries on their bodies. All had their hoods pulled up to keep the weather at bay, a line of faceless wraiths in the downpour.

'You'll need to wait your turn like everyone else,' said the large, softly spoken woman on reception. She looked flustered, sweat glistening on her face as she glanced nervously at her computer screen, and then back at the bad-tempered crowd outside. Her name badge said, 'Rachel Hurt.'

'I need to speak to Doctor Sutra,' Anu said. 'He'll want to see me immediately.'

The receptionist, Rachel, stared at Anu, blinking slowly as she took in the uniform, the bleeding wound on the young woman's arm, the hole in her trousers from where the rat had tried to feast on her leg. 'And you are…?'

'I'm his daughter.'

'Ah. Um, I'll just go fetch him. Wait here a moment.'

The receptionist hurried off with surprising speed, leaving a gaggle of annoyed townsfolk to glare at Anu and John. Most weren't close enough to have heard the exchange, but the appearance of these two queue-jumpers had obviously caused the receptionist to disappear and further disrupted the dysfunctional system. It was therefore open season for muttering, tutting, and—worst of all, to John's mind—the long, drawn-out sigh.

He studiously ignored the cacophony of passive-aggression, eyes settling on a poster on the far wall. '*Have you been screened recently?*' queried the bright, pink text. '*Cervical screening can stop cancer before it starts.*'

John had taken Maria to Salisbury Hospital to get screened the year just gone. It had been the first step towards receiving treatment to get pregnant. John's struggles with his book, and the subsequent breakdown in his and Maria's relationship, had disrupted that dream and turned it into a nightmare.

He thought again of the nursery, as empty as a tomb. What was once a nursery-in-waiting had become a shrine to his failure. Other than investigating last night's strange helicopter visit, he only ever ventured into the nursery to cut his hair in the wardrobe mirror.

Perhaps being alone with his own reflection in that particular room wasn't the wisest idea. It was funny how moments of clarity could strike from nowhere, like a snake in the grass.

'John? Are you coming?' Anu's question jerked him back to the here and now. She gestured down the hall to where one of the surgery doors stood open. A distinguished Asian man in his late fifties whom John vaguely recognised poked his head out and stared at Anu with a concerned expression.

'Yes, sorry. Lead on.'

****

Doctor Arjun Sutra closed the door to his surgery and went immediately to Anu. The armour of calm professionalism he donned for his other patients was shed in an instant when faced with his own wounded daughter.

'Rani, what happened?' he demanded, pulling up her sleeve and inspecting the bite marks on her arm. The wounds were still bleeding, though the flow had slowed. 'Something bit you?'

'A rat,' replied Anu, tolerating her father's ministrations with only a slight grimace. 'I was fetching something from the kitchen at work when a pair of them attacked me. My friend John got them off.'

Doctor Sutra glanced at John, who remembered then why the man seemed familiar. Anu's father had performed a prostate examination on John a couple of years ago, after John had suffered a prolonged bout of prostatitis. As it turned out, sitting in an uncomfortable office chair for countless hours and then resting heavy dumbbells on one's groin at the gym could have a negative effect on certain delicate parts of a man's anatomy. John recalled being very embarrassed to drop his trousers, though he knew Doctor Sutra must have performed the procedure a hundred times.

If the doctor recognised him, he gave no sign. 'Thank you for helping my daughter,' he said simply.

John nodded. In the fantasy novels he wrote, aggressive rats were a common enemy for would-be heroes to practice their skills against before tackling more dangerous adversaries. Until an hour ago, he'd always thought their reputation to be ill-deserved.

'This isn't the first animal attack today,' Doctor Sutra continued. His face was grave. He rubbed at his greying beard and adjusted his gold-rimmed spectacles. 'I've seen four dog bite victims and three patients clawed by their cats, and it is barely midday. One man was bitten by his ferret.'

'My dog attacked me in the night,' John said. 'He went crazy. Just turned on me out of the blue. There was a duck, too. Outside. She was pecking at the glass. I think she killed her ducklings.' John felt suddenly foolish. Rat bites and dog attacks were one thing, but a crazed, infanticidal duck going on the rampage sounded too silly to be true. Doctor Sutra didn't laugh or sneer, however. He simply watched him.

'There is something very strange happening in this town,' he announced finally. 'I've never seen anything like it. Not in my fifty-eight years.'

'Could it be some kind of virus, Papa?' Anu asked.

Doctor Sutra frowned. 'It is the most likely explanation. But I don't know of any virus that could infect cats and dogs, ferrets, horses…ducks.'

John remembered the frenzied horse and the way it had stared at him—as though it wanted to crush his skull beneath its hooves and smear his brains over the road. 'I read online that there's a high concentration of radon in the ground in the local area. Could there be some kind of gas leak? Would that cause animals to act strangely?'

'Unlikely, but who knows? I am a general practitioner, not a virologist nor a geologist nor even a veterinarian.'

John had the sense he'd annoyed the doctor. It was the superpower of writers, he reflected, to appear as omniscient creator gods through the power of carefully chosen words on a page. An actual conversation with a professional? That could make even the best writers appear dull and foolish if they lacked sufficient time to prepare. Even then, natural charm was nine-tenths of a successful conversation. John was almost certain he lacked what most people thought of as 'charisma', and he was beginning to doubt he even possessed a skill with words. Perhaps he had simply enjoyed a run of good luck, a run that was well on the way to balancing itself out.

He was relieved when Doctor Sutra smiled at him. 'Whatever the case, I'm sure the experts are already investigating the situation. The local council leaders have been alerted, and the Environment Agency has been informed. Where is your dog now?'

'I locked him in the conservatory.'

Doctor Sutra nodded. 'For now, we are recommending that all pets are kept in separate parts of the home and allowed no access to humans. Animal contact must be kept to a minimum until we find out what is going on.'

'What about Tango, Papa?' asked Anu. She looked crestfallen.

'Your mother locked her in the attic. Don't worry, *rani*. We have enough tins of Hermes' cat food to survive a nuclear war. That reminds me,' he continued. 'John. When you leave here, would you please head to the police station and report everything that has happened? The police are keeping a record of all incidents in the area.'

The police station. John suppressed a wince. That wasn't a place he wanted to see again in a hurry. But what he said was, 'Sure.'

'What about me, Papa?' Anu asked. 'I can go with John.'

Doctor Sutra shook his head firmly. 'You're hurt, daughter. The nurses will need to clean and stitch this wound. I don't want you out of my sight.'

'I'm not a child, Papa!' Anu protested. She glanced at John, colour rising in her cheeks.

'You are not,' Doctor Sutra agreed. He reached out and placed a hand on his daughter's shoulder. 'But you are my *rani*—my princess. I could not stay here and help my patients without knowing you are okay.'

Anu's resistance melted like warm butter. She leaned into her father, and he gave her a comforting squeeze. John watched it all with a strange ache in his chest. His own father had died in a car accident when he was four years old. It had left an emptiness that he couldn't begin to describe, but moments like these gave him a fleeting sense of what might have been: the strength and security only a father could provide.

His aunt and uncles, his father's siblings, had promised to be there for him in his father's absence. They had ceased contact while he was still a teenager. Disappeared without explanation.

'If I may ask another favour,' Doctor Sutra said. He went to the coat hanging on a peg on the door and withdrew an expensive-looking leather wallet from a pocket. 'Would you mind bringing us something to eat? Sandwiches, perhaps? No pork, please. I didn't have time to prepare lunch. Normally, my daughter would bring me something, but…'

Anu smiled. 'No sandwiches! I'm sick of them! Fish and chips would be perfect.'

Doctor Sutra grinned. 'Fish and chips it is! Please, buy yourself some, too.' He handed John two crisp, twenty-pound notes. John took the money and turned towards the door. 'One last thing,' came the doctor's voice from behind him. 'How is everything down there? No more discomfort?'

John paused, hand on the door handle. He didn't turn to see the look on Anu's face. 'I'm good. The pills you prescribed did the trick.'

Now, if only someone could invent a cure for a broken heart, he thought.

8

The squirrels were driving her insane.

Carrie Splint took an angry sip of her wine and stuffed a handful of the crisps she'd stolen into her mouth. She tried to concentrate on the daytime TV show she was watching while scrolling her phone, but the sound of tiny footsteps skittering across the loft made it impossible to concentrate. This was her day off! How was she supposed to get any rest with this racket going on?

She heaved a sigh and placed the wine glass down on the bedside table. The exterminator was supposed to have taken care of the squirrel infestation weeks ago. The Polish fellow had spoken good English, and she generally didn't mind the Eastern Europeans; they worked hard and paid their taxes.

She'd agreed to give him the job after knocking him down to a price she was begrudgingly willing to pay. If she'd known he would prove so bloody *useless,* she would have hired a proper British exterminator instead.

She rose from the bed somewhat unsteadily. The bottle of Chardonnay had been full when she'd returned from the shops earlier that day. Now, it was nearly empty. Carrie had only intended to enjoy a small glass with her lunch. All that business with the uppity brown girl at the sandwich shop had triggered her anxiety, and her fibromyalgia had begun to act up.

She could hardly be blamed for needing something to take the edge off. Perhaps if the fellow behind her in the sandwich shop had shown her some support, she wouldn't have needed to pour herself a stiff drink afterwards. After she had helped him post his books at the post office, too! Some people were just bloody ungrateful.

The scratching of clawed feet reverberated through the floorboards above, and Carrie snarled in annoyance. 'Shut up!' she yelled at the ceiling. She half-marched, half-stumbled to her bathroom and grabbed the old mop leaning against the shower cubicle. She dragged the mop back to the bedroom and slammed the handle into the plaster above. There was a moment of blissful silence, and then more skittering as the squirrels raced around in confusion.

Bloody squirrels, she raged. They weren't even proper British squirrels. The grey ones were foreigners, immigrants from the United States that had invaded the native red squirrel population and made them an endangered species with their excessive breeding and nasty diseases. How she would love to round them all up and wring their necks!

The TV show she'd been watching returned following the ad break. A panel of guests were debating the merits of leaving Europe. This was followed by a report in which workers from several European countries were interviewed about what a vote for 'Leave' would mean for their futures in the United Kingdom.

'Send them all home!' Carrie hissed at the television, as a Greek barista and a Romanian caregiver spoke of their fears. She might've been talking about the grey squirrels or the migrants. In the midst of her righteous fury, they were one and the same.

The buzz of her mobile phone vibrating snapped her attention back to the bed. She scooped up the device and squinted at the screen while the lyrics of Kelly Clarkson reminded her of just how empowered she was.

It was the solicitor's office. Carrie had been waiting on this call for over a week. She had phoned on three separate occasions to demand an update. The receptionist had fobbed her off, saying everyone was working as quickly as possible. That had done little to appease Carrie, who had left an anonymous one-star review for the firm a couple of days ago.

'Hello, is that Mrs Splint?' asked a male voice in a strong Welsh accent. 'It's Mr Davis here, from Davis, Davis, and Co.'

'*Speaking,*' Carrie replied in her best faux-posh telephone voice, trying not to slur. The wine was stronger than she realised.

'Ah, good afternoon, Mrs Splint. I've had the opportunity to review your claim against your ex-husband, Mr Philip Splint, and I'm pleased to say you have a case.'

Carrie felt a thrill at the solicitor's words. This was it, vindication at last! 'How much?' she demanded, unable to control her volume in her excitement. 'How much do you think I can get? I ought to be entitled to at least half. We were together twenty years.'

Mr Davis chuckled politely. 'I couldn't give you an immediate figure, I'm afraid. But I suspect we could secure a substantial percentage of your ex-husband's pension.'

'I should think so. That man put me through hell. This is the least I deserve! I'll text him now to let him know, that bloody tool.'

There was a moment of silence on the other end of the phone, and then, 'I would advise against that, Mrs Splint. It's best if I handle all communications pertaining to this claim.'

'Fine,' Carrie replied sulkily, annoyed at having the opportunity to gloat stolen from her. 'How much is all this going to cost me, anyway?'

'The initial consultation is three hundred and fifty pounds. I should be able to draft the letter presenting evidence to support our claim for an additional three hundred and fifty pounds.'

'That's disgraceful!' Carrie exclaimed, righteous indignation giving her voice a shrill edge. 'I barely earn that in a month!'

Mr Davis's voice took on a sympathetic tone. 'We offer a variety of payment plans. I think you'll find our rates among the most competitive in Wiltshire. Are you happy for me to proceed with the claim?'

'I suppose I'll have to be,' Carrie answered bitterly. She sank sullenly into her chair. It was shameful, how a part-time post office worker with a debilitating health condition was being forced to pay out the nose just to receive what was rightfully hers!

'Wonderful,' replied Mr Davis, though his tone seemed to suggest it was merely satisfactory. From somewhere in his office came the sound of another phone ringing. 'Please excuse me a moment,' he said, apologetically.

Carrie listened to the solicitor take the other call. His voice quickly grew agitated, and she heard him say, '*Are you sure? Her hamster bit her? No, I'll come home immediately. See you soon, love.*'

'I'm so sorry, I must go,' Mr Davis suddenly announced, his voice louder and clearer as he returned to his conversation with Carrie. 'Something has come up. I'll send the paperwork over shortly. Have a great day, Mrs Splint.'

Carrie ended the call without returning the farewell. She hesitated a moment, then poured herself the last of the wine. Despite the solicitor's frankly *criminal* fees, this was good news. Phil had earned a very decent salary before their separation, and his pension was surely generous.

It wasn't her fault she'd lost her attraction to him, any woman would, seeing him depressed day in, day out. Thanks to him, she'd lost her lovely home and now lived in this squirrel-infested flat. She deserved so much better.

Fury once more rising within her, Carrie Splint unlocked her mobile phone and navigated to her Facebook page. She searched for Phil—he still hadn't blocked her—and tapped on his name, intending to ignore her lawyer's advice and send him a text via Messenger. She stopped when she saw the most recent photo he had uploaded.

'*Who's this bitch?*' she hissed to herself. Standing beside Phil, who looked tan and handsome in the white, crewneck tee she had bought him a few Christmases past, was an attractive blonde woman some ten years his junior. 'Sophie Ward,' Carrie read aloud, something dark and ugly twisting inside her. She clicked on the woman's profile.

Education: Studied Nursing at the University of the West of England. Graduated 2010. (Ten years? Make that twenty.)

Work: Nurse at the NHS, Salisbury Hospital.

Relationship status: In a relationship.

Eyes narrowing, Carrie scrolled down the blonde bimbo's Facebook page. Sure enough, there was a photo of her and Phil sitting at a bar. Another one of them at a barbecue, faces Carrie had known for years smiling at the happy couple, just like they had at Carrie and Phil when they were together. None of their mutual friends had kept in touch with *her* after the separation. It was as though she had ceased to exist.

Finally, the photo that was the dagger through Carrie's heart. Phil and his much younger lover in *her* kitchen. The house she and Phil had lived in together for years. He looked happy.

Carrie hurled the wine glass at the wall. It shattered, spraying sticky wine over the cheap carpet, but she paid it no mind. As though possessed of a life of their own, her fingers carried on scrolling until she found a photo of an older, dark-eyed woman who bore a striking resemblance to Sophie Ward. Sophie had commented under the photo: 'It's been a year since you left us, Mum. You fought so hard. We'll never forget you.'

Another post below linked to a successful fundraising campaign for Cancer Research UK. Sophie had managed to raise £5,000 for a sponsored half marathon in memory of her mother.

Carrie Splint tapped on 'Send Message.' The conversation window opened. A tiny voice inside her head told her to stop, to put the phone down, but she couldn't stop herself.

'Hi Sophie. It's Phil's ex. The two of you look so happy together. Shame he never took me to any posh bars. I would ask what he sees in you, but I think it's quite obvious. You're young enough to be his daughter. Guess that's not important when you're only after his wallet. Enjoy sitting on my sofa and sleeping in my bed. Hope you realise they were paid for with my hard work.

P.S. I hope you die of cancer just like your mum. Bitch.'

She sent the message and put her phone away. The brief spark of satisfaction at standing up for herself quickly faded. She stood there for a long while, staring at nothing. It was all so unfair.

The sounds of scratching once again came from the loft above. The squirrels were back at it again.

Carrie snapped.

She bent down and reached under the bed. Picked up the hammer she kept there in case a burglar ever tried to break in. She hurried out to the hallway, snatched up a hooked pole and used it to open the loft hatch. The flimsy metal ladder dropped down with a *clang*.

She climbed up it, one hand clutching the hammer, the other guiding herself into the darkness above. She fumbled around, searching for the light switch. Her questing fingers brushed aside stray cobwebs before finding the switch. She pushed it. A second later, the old halogen bulb hanging above the central support beam illuminated the loft in an eerie orange glow.

Carrie blinked in surprise. She had expected the squirrels to try to flee once she began climbing into the loft. Instead, a half-dozen pairs of beady eyes stared back at her. They seemed to shine a sinister red in the light of the flickering bulb.

The insulating foam that coated the base of the loft was covered in squirrel shit. The alcohol coursing through her veins and the rage she felt at Phil's betrayal lent her courage. Carrie pushed herself up into the loft, heedless of the small brown droppings. She lifted the hammer. 'Right, you little bastards,' she hissed. 'I'm going to do what that bloody Pole ought to have done—'

Her words caught in her throat as six furry shapes launched themselves at her. Razor-sharp incisors pierced her face, sinking into her flesh. One squirrel nipped painfully at her nose. She screamed and waved the hammer around ineffectually, hitting empty air.

'*Get off me!*' she shrieked. The right side of her face exploded in pain as one of the crazed squirrels sank its teeth into her eye. Carrie dropped the hammer and grabbed the squirrel, tearing it from her face, smashing its body into the floor. The effort unbalanced her, and her feet slipped on the ladder.

With a terrified cry, Carrie Splint toppled backwards out of the loft.

There was a moment of weightlessness—the feeling of the earth rushing up to meet her.

She struck the hallway with a sickening *thud.*

The last thing Carrie Splint remembered was the horrific sensation of something breaking inside her. And then only numbness, spreading from her back up to her neck and down through her shattered legs. As consciousness drifted away, she felt nothing. Nothing besides the methodical gnawing of several mouths full of tiny, sharp teeth as the squirrels devoured her face.

9

The police station was a run-down building close to the GP surgery. It was just south of the railway station, opposite a retail park and the recently opened German supermarket where John and Maria would sometimes grab their weekly shopping.

John stared at it as he made his way towards the crowd of people gathered outside the station. It was strange, how something as mundane as a supermarket could dredge up feelings of guilt and loss. In his mind's eye was a snapshot of a happier time. The sense of comfort in their weekly routine. The warmth of a loving smile as he carried bags of groceries and loaded them into the boot of the car.

Both gone now, as surely as the car itself.

The wail of an ambulance siren cut through the murmur of townsfolk outside the police station. The crowd turned with John to watch as the van raced down the road, flashing blue lights denoting a state of emergency. It roared around a roundabout and disappeared.

John used the temporary distraction to edge through the mass of people towards the station door. Just as he reached the entrance, a police officer in full uniform stepped out. John froze.

‘Hello there, Mr…Sharrock, is it?’ said the blonde-haired woman opposite him. ‘I hope you’ve been keeping well since your previous incident.’ She gave him a pleasant smile. The earnestness in her dark eyes made him feel even more ashamed.

‘I’m fine,’ John said sheepishly. He remembered standing drunkenly in his bedroom with only a pair of briefs covering his modesty as the police thundered up the stairs. He recalled the surprise on the face of the woman opposite him as she and her colleague barged into the room, Maria still in bed, a mortified expression on her face.

The collision with the parked vehicle had left a trail of debris all the way back to John’s house. Someone had phoned to report the incident, and it had been a trivial task for the police to track down the perpetrator, particularly with John’s ruined convertible haphazardly parked outside.

‘About that night—’ John began, searching for something to say to assuage his embarrassment.

‘It’s in the past,’ the police offer cut in gently. ‘That matter will be dealt with in due course in the courts. The important thing right now is keeping everyone safe from whatever is happening in this town. Do you have an incident to report?’

‘Yes,’ John replied, grateful to change the subject. ‘A couple, actually.’

‘Come on in,’ the officer said. She turned and went back inside the station. John hesitated for a moment and then followed her.

The main reception was just as busy as the street outside. John counted thirteen concerned locals, some bearing bites or other injuries from animal attacks. Strangely, all but one was holding their head in their hands. Mike, his fellow gym-goer, was instead clutching his arm. It appeared to have been badly shredded by the jaws of some huge dog.

Mike was naked from the waist up, and his trousers looked too small for him, as though they'd been borrowed from somewhere. They were covered in dark red splotches. John half-heartedly raised his hand in greeting, but the larger man quickly averted his gaze.

The police officer led John around the side of the reception counter to a waiting room that contained several desks. Officers were seated at each of the desks, all with their backs to John, tapping away at laptop keyboards as they interviewed local victims of hostile animal activity. John tried to catch a glimpse of the faces of some of the victims, but he couldn't seem to peer past the backs of the interviewers.

'Take a seat,' the police officer said, gesturing to an empty desk. John noted the name on her badge: Rachel Burns.

'Shouldn't the people in reception be seen first?' John asked. 'They were here before me.'

Rachel appeared not to have heard him. 'You mentioned two incidents? Please, describe the first to me. Include as much detail as you can.'

John did as the police officer asked, describing how a crazed duck had killed her young and attempted to break into his conservatory. He revealed how Alfie had gone mad and attacked him. Once he had finished relaying the events of the previous night, he told the story of how a pair of rats had attacked Anu at the sandwich shop earlier that day.

Halfway through telling the story, he spied another familiar face across the room. It was the woman whose car he had collided with. He had knocked on her door the day after the incident, clutching flowers and a handful of shopping vouchers by way of apology. She appeared to have received them in good grace. Later that same night, another police officer had turned up at his door saying she had filed a complaint. His actions could be construed as witness intimidation. John's mouth had dropped open, aghast that his gesture could be misinterpreted so badly.

The police officer had seemed to empathise with him, saying that he would take no further action, and telling John to keep clear of the woman. He'd heard nothing more from her since, but that interaction had drummed home his fall from grace even more than being arrested and placed in handcuffs.

'Is that everything?' Officer Burns asked, looking at him expectantly. John blinked, trying to focus on the woman opposite him. His therapist had stressed the importance of being present in the moment. The past had already happened, and the future was an infinite series of possibilities. The only thing he could affect was his *now*.

'That's all,' John confirmed. 'Do you have any idea what's going on?'

Rachel shook her head, apparently frustrated. 'We're still trying to get to the bottom of it,' she said. 'I've heard all sorts of theories. A virus. Some military experiment at the nearby Warminster garrison gone awry. You've heard of the LHC?'

'The Large Hadron Collider?' John ventured.

'Yes. The scientists were experimenting with dark matter. Something to do with light particles.'

'That's right,' John replied. He recalled a sensationalised report in the newspaper some years ago. The columnist had been speculating about the possibility of scientists accidentally opening a black hole and bringing about the end of the world.

'An older gentleman swore that the LHC had broken reality. Created a sort of alternate universe,' said Rachel. She snorted softly, demonstrating what she thought of that idea.

'I've felt a bit like that recently,' John said. He risked a rueful smile. 'Like nothing is how it's supposed to be.'

'I think we all feel like that sometimes,' Rachel said, returning his smile. 'Anyway, all we know for sure is that animals of all sorts have begun attacking people without provocation. A Local Emergency has been filed and we're awaiting instructions from Westminster. There's a COBRA meeting underway as we speak. For now, we want everyone to return to their homes. If you have pets, place them in a separate room with food and water and lock the door. Do not approach any animal for any reason. You have somewhere to go, yes? I have to ask,' she added, apologetically.

'Yes,' John replied. 'You'll be pleased to know I fixed the door.'

The police had kicked in the door to John's house the night of the arrest. In truth, they'd hardly caused any damage, only bending the PVC slightly as they forced it open. They said an Englishman's home was his castle, but if that was the case, his was a castle that could be breached by anyone with a well-placed boot. The average person had no idea how vulnerable they were even within their own four walls.

'Good to hear,' Rachel replied. She closed her laptop and rose from the desk. 'Shall I show you out?'

John followed Rachel into the reception area. Just as they arrived, a heavy door opposite swung open. It was the door to the holding cells. Another snippet of memory poked at John, of being marched down that corridor and placed in an overnight cell until he was sufficiently sober to conduct an interview. He remembered his sheer panic at being imprisoned, even only for a few hours. Like good health, liberty was something people took for granted until it was taken from them.

A line of offenders was led down the corridor and into the reception area. A few looked sheepish. Others appeared gleeful. Almost all of them looked relieved in some way.

'Best give them space,' Rachel said beside him, guiding him gently to the side to allow the freed detainees to pass. 'We're having to clear the cells until this crisis is over. We have a rat infestation problem, and several detainees have already been bitten. Our liability insurance doesn't cover us for bite wounds from pests. Most of the detainees are harmless, but you can never be sure.'

One of the men turned to John and grinned. His teeth seemed too large, even predatory. Though the cap he wore cast a shadow over his face, hiding his features, John thought the man was of a similar age to him. Similar age and similar build, too.

A chill passed through John. He sensed this stranger was dangerous. Even so, there was something about the man that made John angry. He felt his fists clench. Before he could do anything else, the man was led into the waiting room. He was followed by a thin, scruffy-looking fellow in grey tracksuit bottoms. This prisoner's face was drawn, his balding head and face bristling with unsightly fuzz and his eyes tired. Nonetheless, he leered at the woman beside John. Suspicious stains covered the bottom of his tee and top of his trousers.

'Is something the matter?' John demanded, already angry, now filled with disgust at this degenerate.

The balding lech leaned in close to him. 'Suck my cock,' he whispered. He reached down and grabbed the bulge beneath his slacks, gave it a squeeze.

'The fuck did you just say?' John surged towards the man, but Rachel quickly inserted herself between them.

'*Relax*,' she commanded as the pervert seemed to cower behind her. John blinked slowly before taking a step backwards and visualized untangling the ball of his anger. 'Go home, John. You've had a long day.'

John hesitated, torn between the desire to punish this pervert and fear at landing himself in yet more trouble with the police. He took a deep breath and tried to clear his mind. The anger subsided. With a final glare at the vulgar arsehole, he bid Rachel an abrupt goodbye and left the station.

10

Adam Gurney closed the door of his new Tesla and grinned across the car at Justin, who raised his eyebrows in mock annoyance. His husband had had his heart set on a Ford Mustang. Adam's arguments about fuel efficiency had succeeded where his appeals over the environmental benefits of owning an electric vehicle had failed. Justin's fondness for American muscle cars was surprising in such an unassuming man, but quirks like these were one of the many reasons Adam found him so endearing.

'I have to admit, it is a smooth ride,' Justin allowed. 'Now, give me a hand with the shopping.'

The two men unloaded the contents of the boot, Adam's muscles bulging out from his tight vest as he carried three heavy bags in each hand. Justin was a good six inches shorter than his partner, soft in the places Adam was as hard as iron.

They reached the front door. Justin fished the house keys from his pocket and let them in. Adam went straight to the kitchen and began unpacking, starting with the refrigerated items: butter and jam, several bottles of milk, cream (whipped, clotted, pouring), as well as a dozen varieties of vegetables, fruits, and salads. By the time he had finished, the fridge was bursting with all the ingredients the pair needed to produce the homemade sandwiches, bagels, soups, tarts, cakes, and pastries they would serve their hungry customers tomorrow.

Justin joined him in the kitchen. The two men busied themselves with the familiar routine they had performed so many times. It gave Adam a deep sense of inner calm to watch his husband fussing over the proper location for the all-bran cereal, lentils, protein bars, and other worthy foodstuffs Adam added to their basket.

He never complained about the cost. Justin knew how important it was to his husband to maintain a healthy lifestyle and keep in shape. If he knew the reasons for Adam's focus on his physical exceptionalism—the years of bullying, first for being too small, too soft, and then for never quite fitting in with the rowdy, expensively educated public schoolboys he'd grown up with—he never spoke of them.

Of course he knows, Adam thought. Justin was the most insightful and empathetic person he knew. He was also the kindest. When they argued, which was rare, Justin would rather bite his tongue than utter something intentionally hurtful. He was Adam's rock, a place of absolute safety in a world that had given Adam plentiful reason for developing the anxiety disorder he struggled with.

His husband turned to see Adam watching him and smiled. 'Cup of tea?' he asked. 'I want to try some of the honey from last month's harvest.'

'It'd be rude not to,' Adam replied. 'Hey, I'm going to hit the gym this evening.'

'Again? You went last night.'

Adam grinned. 'I need to work off all these pastries we've been testing.'

Justin smiled back. 'Fair. One day, I'll join you.' He patted his stomach ruefully.

'You're fine the way you are,' Adam replied. He took a seat at one of the kitchen diner chairs as Justin finished brewing their tea. 'I spoke with John at the gym yesterday evening,' he volunteered

'John?' Justin queried, stirring a generous spoon of honey into each of their cups.

'The writer. He and his wife have separated.'

'That's a shame,' Justin said.

'Yeah,' Adam agreed. 'He's a nice guy. A little odd, but nice. I invited him to the shop. If he shows up while I'm not around, give him something on the house, will you?'

Justin nodded and brought the cups over. Adam blew on the steaming, golden liquid within and took a careful sip. 'Well?' Justin asked.

'Delicious,' Adam replied. 'Perfect, even.'

Justin's beaming smile could have lit up the darkest room. 'We'll keep half the honey to sell in the shop. It should pay for our next holiday. Or at least cover the spending money.'

'Tuscany?' Adam said with a cheeky smile.

Justin gave a mock sigh. 'That wasn't the agreement. You got the Tesla, I got to choose Paris. You'd better start brushing up on your French.'

'*Oui, mi amor*,' Adam replied mischievously. Justin raised an eyebrow.

'I know you're teasing me. You're confusing Spanish and French.'

'I guess we need to take more holidays, then.' Adam grinned. 'First Paris, then Ibiza. Perhaps Tuscany afterwards?'

'Sounds great, except the shop won't run itself.' Justin's eyes were bright with amusement. 'On that note, I'd better go check on the bees.' He squeezed Adam's arm and departed the kitchen to the garden outside.

Adam sat in his diner chair, sipping his tea and humming the tune to "Save Tonight" by Eagle-Eye Cherry. He remembered listening to the song on a cheap pair of headphones while on a flight to Spain as a boy. The track always made him think of holidays: of warmth and laughter and carefree days in the sun.

Many of Adam's earliest memories were rooted in holidays abroad with his family, as well as a year spent as a rep on the Balearic Islands in his early twenties. That was the time during which he had finally found himself. It saddened to him to think that future generations might not have the same opportunity, depending on the outcome of the vote.

Adam thought of John, the author who had separated from his wife. There was always a slight sadness about him. Perhaps it was the curse of the creative, doomed to be eternally preoccupied with their own thoughts. Perhaps he was just awkward around people he didn't know well. Adam knew how it felt to be an outsider. It had taken him a few months to get comfortable dealing with customers. Justin, of course, had taken to it like a duck to water.

'Hun?' he called out, wondering what was taking his husband so long. There was no reply. Adam sipped his tea and frowned. There was something odd. It took him a moment to realise the cause of his growing disquiet. It was just there, right on the edge of hearing.

A buzzing. Thousands of bees. The furious sound of a colony turned hostile.

Adam jumped from the chair, knocking over the cup and spilling lukewarm tea over his jeans. He raced outside but stopped in horror when he saw Justin writhing on the grass.

His husband was barely visible beneath the crawling, stinging mass of black and yellow that covered him from head to foot. Justin managed to turn his head and met Adam's gaze, his eyes bulging in terror. He opened his mouth to scream. The scream came out as a strangled cough. Bees spewed out of his mouth, some of them half-masticated, others still alive, still stinging furiously.

Adam shook off his horror and bolted towards Justin, screaming in fury, batting at the bees that detached themselves from his husband and swarmed towards him. He was stung once, twice, three times, but the pain meant nothing, hardly registered. He saw the empty beehive at the bottom of the garden, Justin's phone on the grass where he must have dropped it when he turned and fled.

He stared around wildly, desperately seeking a way to get the bees off his husband. He caught sight of the shed and raced across to it, flinging open the creaking wooden door and knocking over half-empty cans of paint in his rush to find what he was searching for. He yanked an old bucket from the corner of the shed and snatched a plastic container filled with liquid soap from a shelf. Then, he sped out of the shed and turned on the tap beside the kitchen wall. The tap gurgled for a second or two. To Adam, it seemed an eternity, his eyes darting wildly between his suffering husband and the dry tap. The tap shook and water finally jetted out.

Adam thrust the bucket under the faucet. He unscrewed the cap from the container of liquid soap, half wrenching it off in his haste. Then he poured the entire contents into the swirling water. Every beat of his heart seemed to last a lifetime. Justin was still groaning weakly in the middle of the lawn. Some of the bees had fallen off him and were twitching on the grass, their lives and venom spent. Hundreds more bees still crawled over his body.

With a cry, Adam Gurney upended the bucket of soap water over Justin. Within seconds the remaining bees dropped away from their victim, exoskeletons flooding from the surfactant, drowning them from within. Adam took hold of Justin's feet and dragged him down the garden towards the house, screaming in pain and sheer terror. He had been stung dozens of times, was still being stung, but the burning bee stings were nothing compared with the agony in his chest.

The thought of losing Justin was worse than any pain. Worse than dying. Adam pulled Justin to the safety of the kitchen and slammed the door. He raced to his phone and dialled 999 with shaking hands already swollen from repeated bee stings. The call seemed to take forever to go through, every harsh ring that went unanswered like broken glass against his skin.

When the responder's voice finally answered and asked him which service he required, Adam collapsed to his knees, his eyes weeping tears down puffy, venom-engorged cheeks.

11

Alfie was fast asleep when John returned to the house. Anu and her father had been too busy caring for the injured to spare him more than a quick glance and thank you for the delivered lunches. He decided to take his fish and chips back to his house, not wanting to get in anyone's way in the busy surgery.

There was no sign of the duck, though the bloody smears on the glass were still there. Cautiously, half-expecting the dog to awaken and lunge at him at any moment, John opened the inner conservatory door a crack and placed a fresh bowl of water just inside. Then, he returned to the living room and sat down on the sofa.

What a crazy day, he thought. The kind of unlikely series of events he might write about in one of his books. Maybe he should write something like it, he thought with a yawn, suddenly tired. He must have dozed off, for the next thing he knew, it was night and everything was black.

He got up with bleary eyes and flicked the light switch on. The darkness was instantly dispelled, 60 watts of electricity illuminating every corner of the lounge. John winced and blinked rapidly to acclimate his eyes to the light.

A huge house spider froze in the middle of the carpet, caught halfway between hiding places.

John stared at it. As he watched, the spider danced around on the spot, swivelling like a dancer until it faced him. It reared up on its back legs.

The spider raced towards him.

John flinched, quickly mastering a rising panic before bringing his size 9 Nike down on the tiny predator, crushing it into the carpet. Given the circumstances, he didn't feel any remorse over the death of another spider. It had clearly been planning to attack him first.

He had once read that the average person was no more than six feet from a spider at any given time. *Did I read it...or did someone tell me?*

His thoughts felt sluggish and confused. His head hurt. He shook it and tried to relax. The stress of recent events was getting to him.

He supposed he was fortunate the recent bizarre outbreak of hostile animal activity was happening in sleepy Wiltshire and not somewhere in Australia or Brazil. The most dangerous arachnid in the UK was the noble false widow, the bite of which was said to be little worse than a bee sting. So long as nothing attempted to crawl into his mouth while he slept, John wasn't overly worried about spiders. Maria, on the other hand—his wife would flee to another room at the mere sight of an arachnid.

It was like clockwork, the way his thoughts always returned to his estranged wife. He tried to stop thinking about her, but it was like trying to hold back the tide with one's bare hands: a trifling flash of defiance before the memories rose to drown him completely.

John fetched the vacuum cleaner and lost himself in the white noise as he sucked up the crushed remains of the arachnid. He turned on the television and flicked between channels, anticipating a special report on events in Warminster, or at least some mention of it in the regional news.

Strangely, there was nothing. Perhaps the government was suppressing the story until they had a handle on a situation. He changed the channel once more. The signal was scrambled. He thought he could make out figures in blue through the static, but there was no sound save for a sharp beep.

Beep. Beep. BEEP.

John suddenly remembered the food he had put in the microwave oven. It wasn't the first time his memory had been fuzzy of late. The lack of sleep was doing him no favours.

He returned to the sofa with a bowl of warm soup, keeping a wary eye out for more eight-legged intruders. He tried to change the channel but found the clicker had suddenly stopped working. With a sigh, he finished his soup to the strange static of the channel, rose from the sofa, and switched off the television via a tiny button on the underside of the set. He made himself a cup of tea and checked on Alfie.

The shih tzu was still dead to the world.

John turned off the lights and went upstairs. He was preparing to use the bathroom when he heard a faint thudding sound from the nursery. He placed a hand on the door. Hesitated. Finally, he mustered the courage to turn the handle and stepped inside.

The window was somehow open, the cold air blowing in from outside making him shiver. Perhaps he had left it open the previous night while staring out at the helicopter? From behind him, there came the faint thudding sound again.

He turned on the light. Taking care not to look at the walls, he located the source of the sound. It was a moth. A death's-head hawkmoth. Just like those from his dream.

It was flying into the mirror on the wardrobe. Over and over again, like a YouTube clip stuck on repeat.

Thud. Thud. Thud.

As though in a trance, John approached the moth and held out a hand. Some instinct compelled the insect to change its behaviour, and it landed upon John's outstretched palm. He stared at the skull pattern on the creature's abdomen, mesmerised.

A beeping rang in his ears. Hadn't he turned the microwave off when he grabbed his soup? He listened, straining to hear it again. Nothing. He must have imagined it. The moth remained motionless on his palm.

John crossed the room and stuck his hand out of the window. He shook it. After a second's hesitation, the moth took off, fluttering away into the night.

John closed the window. He caught a glimpse of the nursery wall on his way out of the room, squeezed his eyes shut and ignored it. He turned off the light and pulled the door firmly shut behind him.

He went to the bathroom and brushed his teeth. When he spat out the paste, he saw that it was tinged with red. Were his gums bleeding?

He was poking around in his mouth for the source of the blood when the doorbell chimed.

John froze, fingers slick with saliva. Sudden dread filled him. He waited. The doorbell chimed again. He wiped his hand dry on his shirt and made his way downstairs to the hallway.

He could see a shadowy figure through the frosted glass near the top of the door. The doorbell chimed one final time. This close, it seemed to cut through his very soul. A funerary toll to signify approaching doom.

He opened the door and stared in surprise. Dark eyes he had seen just a day prior looked back at him.

It was Maria's best friend, Elsie. Her voice was uncertain. 'John…I'm really sorry to bother you at this hour. I wasn't sure if I should, or if I'm just being daft…'

'What is it? What's the matter?' John asked. But, deep down, he already knew.

'It's Maria. She's not answering her phone. She didn't come home from work today.'

12

John felt as though the earth had suddenly shifted beneath him. 'What do you mean she didn't come home?' he asked, dread worming through his heart like some hungry parasite.

'She worked the night shift at the park. She should have been back by midday. I thought she might be working overtime, so I tried to call. Her phone is switched off. Then, Lizzie had an incident with Pepsi, our rabbit, and I spent all afternoon trying to get through to the doctor. When Craig got home from work, he told me about all the animal attacks happening across town. I'm worried something happened at the park.'

'Have you called Longleat?' he asked, trying to keep calm.

Elsie nodded. 'Three times throughout the afternoon. No answer. I even tried to drive down there, but the roads are blocked. The army's not letting anyone through to Longleat.'

John blinked in surprise. 'But there was nothing on the news!' he exclaimed. 'Now the bloody *army* is involved?'

'I didn't know what else to do, John,' continued Elsie, as though she hadn't heard him. 'Maria's family is hundreds of miles away. There's no one else I can go to for help.'

John checked his phone. It was 9:30pm.

'Thanks for letting me know,' he said. 'I need to grab my coat and a bag, pack some supplies. If I hurry, I can be at Longleat in a few hours.'

Elsie's mouth dropped open in disbelief. 'You're not serious? You're planning to go there on foot? John, it's crazy out there! You could get hurt.'

'I won't. There's a trail that will take me along the edge of Lake Shearwater as far as the woods. I can cut through them, avoid the roads until I'm at the park.'

'What about the army?' Elsie demanded. 'They won't let you through.'

'I'll figure something out,' John replied. He met her doubtful gaze, and something inside him seemed to flare in anger. 'I made a promise to her father,' John rasped. 'Before she visited England the first time. I promised I would protect her.'

Elsie said nothing, merely stared at him.

'Say hi to Craig,' John said, forcing his simmering anger to calm. 'And Elizabeth. I miss her.' Lizzie was Elsie's daughter, three years old and a bubbly force of personality. Maria doted on her. Before the cracks had appeared in their relationship, John and Maria would often talk excitedly of having their own little Elizabeth running around. Or rather, Maria would.

John had harboured some anxiety about how a baby would impact the peace he needed to write, the freedom they had to hop on a plane to somewhere warm when Maria was feeling unwell.

'How is Lizzie?' John added. 'You said there was an incident with Pepsi.'

'She's fine,' Elsie replied, 'He bit her, but it was just a small cut, she'll be fine. Please be careful out there, John.'

'I will,' he replied. 'Thank you for coming to me, Elsie.'

Once Elsie had left, he dug his mobile phone out of his pocket and tried to call his mum. He wanted to talk, if only briefly, just in case something happened to him outside town. His mum would sometimes tell the story of the last night she had seen his father alive and well. How they had both bathed John together, his dad splashing her and laughing and seeming so happy.

They had scrimped and saved to get their first home together. John's father had just started a new job. His own upbringing had been tough, an alcoholic mother and an emotionally absent father. Now he had the chance to give his young family the kind of love he had always yearned for.

The following day, his car hit a truck.

He had been giving his friend a lift to work. Unbeknown to either of them, the mechanic who recently replaced one of the wheels on John's father's car had botched the job, and the wheel came loose while they were taking a corner. The car careened across the road into an upcoming truck. The impact caused catastrophic brain injury to John's father.

After a week in a coma, John's mother had, with the hospital's recommendation, made the heartbreaking decision to turn off the life support machine. The passenger in the car, as well as the driver of the truck, had come away relatively unscathed.

John couldn't recall the last words he and Maria had spoken to each other, but he knew they were angry ones.

The phone seemed to resist his efforts to make a call, and he fumbled with the controls for what seemed like an eternity before it rang. John tapped his foot impatiently, waiting for his mother to answer. It seemed she wasn't picking up, and the phone eventually went to voicemail: the somewhat ingratiating Estuary English of the service provider woman rather than his mum's West Country accent. She'd never been great with technology and probably hadn't figured out how to leave a personalised voicemail greeting.

John was preparing to leave a voice message of his own when sudden static on his phone's receiver made him recoil slightly. He stared at the phone in consternation and ended the call. Then, he quickly used the bathroom and put his phone charger, a change of clothes, some food, and a bottle of water into his backpack. He checked on the slumbering Alfie one last time and left the house.

13

There was not a soul in sight as John made his way through the dark and empty streets. He passed the Old Fire Station on his left. The red brick building had been built in 1905 and used as a fire station until the 1960s, when it was no longer large enough to support the new breed of fire engine. It was then used by the St John Ambulance charity until a local property owner bought the building. Two years ago, it had relaunched as a café and pizza restaurant.

John and Maria had eaten there only recently. The décor had been cleverly chosen to evoke memories of the building's former purpose: ladders, hoses, pipes, bells and other memorabilia complemented the bright red bay doors on the exterior, which had been flawlessly preserved, save for the tasteful addition of a pair of customer entrances.

Despite the excellent food, dinner had been a disaster. The distance between John and Maria had felt like the space between stars. Their relationship was burning down around them, and no fire station full of engines could ever put out those flames.

As John glanced through the glass panel door at the darkened interior, he could have sworn he saw the pervert from the police station sitting at one of the tables, hunched over and looking pathetic. He blinked and the apparition was gone. It was just a trick of the light, fuelled by his anxieties and lack of sleep.

Clouds the colour of old bruises obscured the night sky, threatening more rain. In his haste, John had forgotten his coat again. He passed a flickering streetlight, the lamp fighting desperately to survive, to keep the shadows at bay. The roads were desolate passages into the unknown.

John remembered what Elsie had told him about the army patrolling the roads. Whatever was happening in Warminster and the surrounding area, it made sense the authorities would want to keep it contained until someone figured out what the hell was going on.

He hesitated. Then, he left the road leading south out of town and instead cut through Warminster Pleasure Lake Grounds. He and Maria would picnic there in happier times, enjoying a pizza while watching the ducks and swans and the grey heron that occasionally visited. Recently, he had begun jogging around the pleasure grounds when the prospect of human interaction at the gym seemed too much.

As he neared the lake, John saw dark shapes floating in the water. His heart broke a little when he saw that the shapes were dead birds: ducks and geese and even swans, magnificent animals he and Maria used to feed in the summer months. They had been shot and left to bleed out in the lake. The bodies of some of the waterfowl had drifted together at the southern end of the lake, forming a grisly tapestry of feathers that resembled some grotesque monster.

It seemed the military had taken no chances. Had they destroyed every animal in town capable of causing harm? Or maybe a farmer had decided to take matters into his own hands and fetched his shotgun. Whatever had occurred earlier that day, the lake grounds were deserted now.

Almost deserted.

John saw the figure then, sitting on the bench across the lake. It appeared to be a large man, his head in his hands, elbows resting on his knees. It was unclear if he had seen John.

John carefully approached. As he got closer, he saw that it was Mike. John remembered Mike's bare chest and savaged arm from the police station earlier that afternoon, how he had leaked blood over his too-small trousers. Mike's arm was wrapped in thick bandages now, and he had found a thick jacket to wear over his jumper, the sleeve of which was rolled up around the wound.

Mike looked up, finally noticing John's presence. His eyes were red from crying. 'You,' he said. His voice was raspy, the word forced through a throat raw with grief.

'Mike,' John replied, uncertain. 'What are you doing out here alone?'

'I fucked up, mate. *I fucked up.*' Mike's words came slowly, as though he were in a daze.

'What do you mean?' asked John.

'I was with her. Nikki, I mean. Should have been home with my missus and the kid. Charlie, Nikki's rottweiler, he went nuts. Attacked me and savaged Nikki. I couldn't… I couldn't protect her. I fucking *ran.* She's dead. She's *dead*, mate. Got her throat torn out.'

‘I’m…I’m sorry, Mike. Jesus. That’s awful.’ John stood there in silence, unsure what to say. Mike sniffled and wiped his face with the back of one meaty hand. John stared in confusion. For a split second, he thought he saw his own features reflected back at him.

‘I told Hannah everything once I got home. What other choice did I have? We argued— I mean, she screamed at me. Then, she kicked me out. I’ve got nothing. I had everything, and I threw it all away. I’m done.’

John closed his eyes for a moment, steadied himself as the world seemed to rock around him. Mike’s words had hit much too close to home. He felt a sudden whirlwind of emotions. Guilt. Anger. Disgust at the man opposite him, at himself. ‘We all make mistakes,’ he said at last. ‘There’s nothing wrong with you. You’re human. Listen, I’m heading out for a bit. You can have the keys to my place. Make yourself comfortable while I’m gone. Things will get better. You will heal from this, Mike.’

Mike stood up suddenly. ‘It’s too late for that,’ he said. There was a strange look in his eyes. ‘You can’t heal when there’s nothing left *to* heal.’ The big man took a step towards the lake.

‘What do you mean? Mike, what are you doing?’ John reached out a hand to grab Mike’s shoulder and pull him back. Mike turned, pushed his hand away.

‘Don’t,’ he said coldly. His voice thawed a fraction. ‘You’re a good man, John. I don’t want to hurt you. No more than you’ve already been hurt. Some things can’t be undone.’

John stared at the larger man. ‘Why, Mike?’ he managed.

‘Because it’s what I deserve,’ Mike said. He took another step. And another.

‘Mike!’ John tried once again. But Mike was at the edge of the lake now.

The muscular man glanced back, gave John a small nod. ‘Bye, John,’ he said. He stepped into the lake with a splash.

A shadow passed overhead. A heron landed where Mike had been standing but a moment before.

I know you, John thought. He had occasionally seen the huge bird standing imperiously on the stone platform that extended a small way into the water, surveying the pleasure grounds like a king gazing out over his dominion. Whomever had culled the other birds had missed the true master of the lake.

The heron stared at John, its sharp bill twitching, probing the night air like a knife. Then, it turned towards the water and the man struggling beneath the surface.

Like a spear, the heron dove at him, stabbing down into the water. Mike tried to rise, stumbled as the bird’s beak punctured his cheek. The wicked bill darted forwards again, stabbing at his eyes, darting into Mike’s ears, driving up his nose and leaving him choking on blood as well as filthy lake water.

John watched in horror. Despite Mike’s warning, he was about to jump in and attempt to help when torchlight suddenly materialised at the end of the lake. A trio of shadowy figures appeared, their outlines a dark stain in the night. A Northern voice carried across the water, magnified by the harsh acoustics of a megaphone.

'This is the army. All citizens are to return to their homes immediately.'

Mike had stopped struggling. Only ripples of water hinted he had ever been in the lake at all. The heron dipped its head. Bloody strips of flesh and glistening sinew dangled from its bill. It flapped its mighty wings, took to the air, and was gone in the blink of an eye.

Maria, John thought desperately, watching the torch's probing beam slowly illuminate the horrors of the lake, ever closer to exposing his own presence. If the army discovered him there and forced him to return home, who would make sure she was safe?

John Sharrock backed away. Then, he turned and ran.

14

Lilith Von Goth stared at the fresh, paper-thin line on her arm and waited. This was her serenity, her brief moment of respite from the emotions raging around her fucked-up brain. She placed the surgical blade on the desk beside her. A moment later, blessed release. The sudden red was the beauty of a blossoming rose. The flames of a cleansing fire. The birth of a new day, the conceit that things would go differently under the bleeding light of another dawn.

They never did. She was locked in the prison of her own mind, and it was not a merciful jailer.

She heard the creak of stairs outside her room and quickly put the blade away in her desk drawer. Then, she grabbed a long-sleeved cardigan—black, like most of her clothes—and pulled the sleeve down over her arm, hiding the evidence of her latest act of self-harm.

The bedroom door banged open a moment later and her mum staggered in. 'Three hours,' she slurred, waving the flute glass in her hand around to emphasise her disgust. Prosecco splashed over the side and onto the carpet. 'He's three hours late. What do I do, Kim? I told him the last time I'll kick him out if he does this again. He's got no respect for me. No respect for you, either.'

Lilith jumped up from the bed, grey eyes narrowed in fury, cheeks red with anger. 'I told you not to barge in here,' she shouted. 'This is *my* room, Mum! I don't care about your drama! Don't involve me! I'm sick of it.'

Lilith's mum blinked in surprise. She hovered uncertainly in the doorway for a moment Then, her face twisted, her drink-fuelled rage finding a new target. 'But it *is* your problem, Kim. This is my house, in case you forgot. If I kick Steve out, who do you think will pay the bills? I already work all the hours God sends. We can't all spend our lives in school.'

'I'm studying for a PhD!' Lilith screamed. 'I'm studying so that I can become a wildlife biologist! I want to do something worthwhile with my life. I don't want to be like you.'

She saw the hurt in her mum's eyes and knew that she'd gone too far. She had been the first member of the Grimes clan ever to earn a degree, never mind achieve a grant to study for a doctorate. But despite her keen intelligence, she had inherited the quick temper of her ancestors. The susceptibility to mental health issues, too. Generational trauma had deeper roots than the mightiest trees. And it was harder to eliminate than Dutch elm disease.

'Mum—' she began, but it was too late. Her mother turned and closed the door behind her. Not with a slam, but slowly and carefully. That was bad. It meant her mum was *really* upset.

Lilith stared at the journal on the desk. It was one of many journals she had collected over the years. Making notes at the end of each day helped her organize her thoughts and emotions. This one was from her final year at secondary school, 'Kimberley Grimes' written in neat cursive on the black leather cover. Above her name, a purple unicorn rode a rainbow from the spine to the edge of the cover, its face a picture of determination. An impossible creature doing the impossible.

She picked up the journal and flicked to one of the early entries. It contained a note written during one of her worst episodes, a sobering fact to remind herself just how insignificant she and her troubles were in the grand scheme of the cosmos.

There are over 8 million animal species on Earth. For every one human, there are seven birds, 500 fish, and 2.5 million ants.

Intellectually, she knew that to be true. But emotionally, it did nothing to slow the abyss that was unfurling within her. A void that swallowed everything, even her identity, until she was nothing but a tiny, quivering ball of anxiety huddling in the vast blackness of a predatory universe.

She could feel herself dissociating again.

She grabbed her phone and desperately tried to call him. The cut on her arm had begun to hurt, but it provided no relief. Only he could. His voice was the lifeline she could cling to, her tether to reality.

There was no reply. He hadn't answered her in days. She put the phone down and stared at nothing for an uncertain period. Wetness on her arm, wetness on her cheeks.

Eventually, she rose and went to her wardrobe. She selected a royal purple corset and a black lace dress. Then, she retrieved a pair of boots from the plastic container stashed at the bottom of the wardrobe. The boots were ornate wonders, leather straps and silver buckles and spikes and five-inch heels that transformed the wearer into one of Lucifer's very own wives, summoned to the mortal plane to tempt men into hedonistic acts all desired but few would admit.

Kimberley Grimes retreated into the place young girls go to hide, and Lilith Von Goth fully emerged. In search of distraction. In search of obliviousness. In search of connection.

15

John had been jogging for almost half an hour. His lungs burned from the effort. Warminster was well behind him now, the lights of the town suburbs mere specks in the distance. The A350 road was as dead as old bone, no traffic passing in either direction since he had been following it south. It was as though the world had come to a standstill.

Trees lined either side of the road, dark fields visible beyond. Occasionally, an animal would grunt or cry or howl nearby, and John would slow a little, half-expecting some nightmare of claw and fang to come charging out of the undergrowth and attack him. But nothing did. Eventually, he slowed to a walk, trying to keep his breathing under control, to avoid making too much noise.

He couldn't get the image of Mike walking into the lake out of his mind. The hopelessness on the man's face. John had failed to protect him. Just like John, Mike had always seemed so strong, so unshakeable. There had been times when John's emotional state had grown so dire that dangerous thoughts had briefly occurred, but the invisible wall within him had always held.

When pushed, John would push back. When knocked down, he would rise stronger than before. Would-be bullies at school had learned that the hard way. At the age of 21, he had been hit by a motorbike that had broken his leg in two places and almost fractured his skull. Five months later, still not fully able to walk, he had taken a flight abroad, alone, to meet a girl he had met in an internet chat room just before his accident, then fallen in love with while recovering from his injuries.

That had been the first time he had met Maria in person. The odds had been stacked against their relationship—the distance, the cost, the mistakes of youth—but they had made things work. He was not the sort to give up. No matter how difficult things became.

To his left, the road turned into Crockerton Furniture Centre: a vast showroom filled wall to wall with sofas, cabinets, dining tables, bookshelves, and other interior furnishings. John and Maria had ordered their bed and three-piece suite there shortly after moving into their new home. He remembered he had been distracted, irritable at this interruption to his work, consumed with the need to finish his book by the deadline. Maria had been so happy that morning. By the time they had returned home, she was visibly upset.

Opposite the Furniture Centre was the Garden Centre. John had rebuffed Maria asking if they could look at outdoor fittings with an abruptness that left no room for argument. They needed somewhere to sit and somewhere to sleep. Everything else could wait until the book was finished.

He thought he felt rain on his cheek and looked up. He was surprised to see the night sky had cleared and the stars were out. There was the North Star, Polaris, which his mum had always claimed was his father looking down on him. There was Ursa Major, the Great Bear.

As he focused on the night sky, he heard a strange whispering sound, as though a soft wind had sprung up, though there was no sensation of it against his skin. He paid it little mind, his attention instead focused on something much more disturbing.

There was a strange star he had never before seen. He was no astrologer, but this particular star was nothing like the others.

For one thing, it was red. The angry crimson of fresh blood.

John stared at it. As he watched, the red star disappeared, then reappeared. He waited, and it happened again. It was as though the star was blinking at him.

He felt a sudden stab of pain in his skull and gasped. He reached up to his head, felt a gentle swelling on the side of his temple and probed it with his fingers. It hurt like hell. Had he somehow bruised himself? He tasted copper in his mouth and spat. There wasn't enough light to be sure, but he thought his spit was dark with blood. He grabbed his phone and activated the torch, intending to inspect it more closely.

He heard a sudden hiss from a bush just behind him. He turned his head and saw something slither over the grass. John held up his phone with nervous fingers, the weak light illuminating the road, the predator beside it.

It was a snake. Thick-bodied, about two feet along, with a distinctive zig-zag pattern over its grey body. Red eyes stared at John above a wide snout, its mouth containing fangs with venom sufficient to demand immediate medical attention in a healthy adult.

Vipera berus—more commonly known as the adder.

How do I know that? The information had just come to him from nowhere. Maria worked at the park and knew much about animals, but she was no expert on Latin. The more he tried to remember the source of his knowledge, the foggier his brain seemed to become.

John watched in numb horror as the snake slithered towards him. There was a hiss closer to where he was standing, and another adder detached itself from a rock near to his feet. It coiled, preparing to strike.

John finally shook himself free of his confused stupor and leapt back, evading the lunging snake. He looked around wildly, seeking some weapon with which to fend off the serpents.

Only then did he realise that what he had taken to be the whisper of wind was in fact the susurration of hundreds of snakes. Waves of wriggling, slithering ophidians, moving in unison over the fields on both sides of the road, their movements strangely hypnotic.

Two streams of reptilian malice, moving towards him with laser-like focus. He was caught between them.

John did not particularly fear snakes, but the sight awakened something in his mammalian DNA. Some primitive ancestral fear, learned over countless generations of nights spent under clear skies and in dark caves, where a hand or foot in the wrong place could mean agonizing death.

He broke into a sprint. Longbridge Deverill was less than a mile ahead. The village straddled the A350 and was once the site of Neolithic activity in ages past. John had driven through Longbridge Deverill on many occasions. One place in particular was familiar to him, an old coaching inn. That was his destination in this life-or-death race against another prehistoric holdover.

The snakes were fast. The leg he had broken years ago throbbed. His head still hurt. His punishing hours in the gym proved their use by allowing him to grit his teeth and push even harder. The trees on the sides of the road blurred together. Somehow, he outdistanced the serpents.

Finally, John reached the village outskirts. The scattered houses were as dark as a tomb. It was as though Longbridge Deverill had experienced a power cut. Perhaps the villagers had been instructed to turn off their lights in order to avoid attracting attention from the local wildlife.

Like the outstretched arms of a loving parent, the welcoming walls of The George Inn appeared, offering succour from the horrors of the dark. The waters of the River Wylye gurgled nearby. Though the curtains were drawn, a soft light bled out from beneath the inn's entrance.

Gasping with effort, John reached the doors. They were locked. He banged on them desperately, risked a look back at the road. The serpentine wave was still there. Still approaching. Still whispering its dark promises.

'Let me in!' he yelled, hammering at the door with his fists. 'Please.'

'There's someone out there,' said a voice from inside. A young woman. An anxious moment passed.

There was a rattle, the sound of a bolt sliding across metal. The door opened a fraction. An older man's face squinted through the gap at John, grey moustache twitching nervously. 'What are you doing out there?'

demanded the man in a gravelly Welsh accent. 'Get inside, quick. There's death on the roads this night.' The door swung open.

Just as he was about step through, the sudden high-pitched beep of a car alarm startled him anew. With one final glance back at the lifeless village, John entered The George Inn.

16

The Welshman's name was Bill. He was the current owner of The George Inn, and as John ate the hasty meal of bread and cheese Bill had generously prepared for him, the inn's proprietor took great pains to tell his guest how foolish he'd been to venture out into the night by himself.

'You must have a death wish,' Bill was saying now. He leant on the bar, a pint of ale clutched tightly between his gnarled hands. 'I tell you, I ain't never seen the like. A whole flock of sheep escaped the Pillman farm and came marauding down the road. They were charging at everyone in sight. One poor kid got his ribs broken. Old Steve Pillman had to shoot them all.'

Bill's daughter, Rosie, sauntered into the bar area from the kitchen. It was she who had heard John banging on the door after Bill had retired for the night. She was a pretty girl, around twenty years old and curvy in all the right places. John caught himself staring and lowered his eyes.

'I was outside serving when the swans began attacking our guests,' she said. 'We had to evacuate the garden and close the pub. The army showed up a couple of hours later, two soldiers in full uniform. They went outside and…took care of the swans.'

'Ordered everyone in the village to stay inside, they did,' said Bill. 'Said they'd be back tomorrow to update everyone. This virus or whatever it is, they reckon it started in Longleat Safari Park. They got the whole place under quarantine.'

'And you were going there *alone*?' Rosie said, staring at John in mild astonishment. 'You must be crazy. Or very brave.' She held John's eyes for a moment longer than seemed polite.

'I have to find my wife,' John said, more abruptly than he'd intended. 'She works at the park. I think something might have happened to her.'

'And you only just found out?' Rosie asked. Her curious eyes shone. 'I mean, you didn't realise something was wrong when she didn't come home?'

'We're not— We're currently estranged,' John said. 'She was staying with a friend.'

'Who did you say you were again?' Bill asked.

'I don't think I introduced myself,' John replied. 'John. John Sharrock.'

'Sharrock…' Bill repeated. He stroked his moustache. 'I think I've heard that name. You're not a writer, are you? I remember an article in the *Wiltshire Times*. Something about a local author getting a big book deal.'

'That might have been me,' John admitted. He still had the newspaper article in a drawer somewhere back in the house.

'A famous writer, eh?' Rosie said. She smiled at him, bit her lower lip slightly. 'I should fetch our famous author a drink. What would you like? We have beers, ciders, wine. How about whisky? I've heard it's popular with you creative sorts.'

'I…' Memories of the night of the crash struck him like the bumper of an out-of-control car. 'Nothing alcoholic,' he said politely. 'Perhaps just a coffee. If that's okay,' he added, noting the flicker of disappointment on her pretty face.

'Coming right up,' said Rosie, pouting slightly. She walked slowly back to the kitchen, hips swaying.

John cleared his throat and focused his attention on Bill. 'Listen, I appreciate everything you've done for me,' he told the Welshman. 'But I can't stay. I need to reach Longleat. Do…do you drive? If you could give me a lift at least as far as the other side of Lake Shearwater—'

A scream from the kitchen cut off his words like a knife to the throat. John leapt up from the table and rushed behind the bar, Bill hobbling behind him.

Rosie was backed up against a fridge-freezer. Crouching opposite her, fur standing on end, tail swaying from side to side, was a large tabby cat. It hissed at the girl, swiped at her with razor-sharp claws.

'Charlie's gone mad!' Rosie screamed.

Charlie. Where had he heard that name recently? John suddenly remembered Mike's tearful story about a dog, also named Charlie, mauling to death the woman with whom he had been having an affair.

'Off with you!' roared Bill. He slapped his hands together, trying to startle the cat. The big tabby ignored him. The Welshman grabbed a wooden rolling pin from the worktop and brandished it.

'Don't hurt him,' Rosie pleaded with her father. 'He's sick!' Demonstrating no appreciation for his owner's entreaty, Charlie swiped at her again.

John took two swift steps forward. He bent down and wrapped his arms around the cat. It immediately went ballistic, hissing and scratching, a whirlwind of thwarted fury. Claws scratched at him, left bloody grooves down his arms and hands.

John paid it no mind. It was just pain. A welcome kind of pain—the kind that could be measured and treated and would eventually go away. Besides, it barely registered as a dull ache. More the ghost of pain than pain itself, the kind experienced in a dream or numbed by a local anaesthetic.

Must be the adrenaline, John thought.

'In here!' Bill barked, pulling open the door to a small storeroom currently filled with boxes of non-perishables and tins of Hermes' Gourmet cat food. John lobbed the furious cat into the room and quickly closed the door. Its outrage was audible. In another time and place, the scratching of its tiny paws on the wood might have been amusing.

'I'm so sorry,' Rosie said breathlessly. 'I forgot all about Charlie. His eyes…did you see his eyes? They were bloodshot. Like he was some sort of demon.'

'Keep him in there and do not open that door,' John said. 'Not until there's a cure for…whatever this is.'

'You're hurt,' Rosie said. She placed her hands gently around John's wrists. Her touch made him shiver. 'Let me see to those cuts. There's a first aid kit near the bar.'

Rosie spent the next hour cleaning and dressing his wounds. Despite the initial severity of their appearance, the scratches were not deep. John watched Rosie work, her auburn hair shiny and smelling vaguely of flowers as she bent before him, soft tongue poking gently between her lips in concentration. 'Do you have any pets?' she asked, not looking up.

'Yes. Alfie, a shih zu. He lost his mind recently as well. I locked him in the conservatory. I hope he's okay.'

'You never told me about your books. What are they about anyway?'

'They're…fantasy novels.'

'Like Harry Potter?' Rosie asked innocently.

'Something like that,' John replied wryly.

'You must be very proud,' Rosie said. 'I always wanted to write. Never had the knack for it. Dad has some stories to tell, though. You should speak with him. Maybe you can write his autobiography.' She nodded at Bill, who sat nearby, polishing off another pint.

John smiled despite himself. It felt good to have this attractive young woman fussing over him. Still, he knew it was time for him to leave. 'Some other time,' he promised. 'I'm having some trouble remembering my own life, to be honest. My memory recently has become one big blur.'

'Why?' asked Rosie. Concern spread across her heart-shaped face. 'Is something wrong with you?'

There's something wrong with you, John. Ever since you came home, it's like you've been replaced by someone else. Are you on drugs?

John blinked. Where had that come from? It was as though someone had just spoken a thought directly inside his head.

He turned to the proprietor of The George Inn.

'Bill, I really should get going. I've checked the windows. The snakes have left. The way should be clear now.'

'First thing tomorrow morning,' Bill promised. 'As soon as the sun's up and I can see what's on the roads, I'll drive you right up to the gates of Longleat.'

'I don't have time to wait,' John protested. 'Maria could be in danger.'

'It's already the middle of the night,' Bill replied. 'A few more hours won't make a difference. There's a bed made up for you. Get some rest.'

John yawned suddenly. He *was* extremely tired. 'Fine,' he said. 'The first light of dawn, we move. Deal?'

'Deal,' Bill replied, with a smile.

John allowed Rosie to show him to one of the guest rooms on the upper floor. It was an eerie feeling, having the entire inn to himself. The George dated back to the 14th century. How many generations had quenched their thirst within these walls? How many thousands of ghosts had navigated this crossroads during their life's journey?

A chance conversation in an internet chatroom had steered John to a life he could never have imagined. Had he been but a minute later turning on his computer, had he chosen to go for a walk at that moment instead of seeking connection online to assuage his loneliness…

Most people thought their lives the result of a handful of major decisions, made with open eyes and freedom of will. In reality, every path ever taken was prepared days, years, centuries in advance. *It's like looking at the stars,* John thought, only a few thousand visible to the human eye. Yet, billions of stars existed in the Milky Way alone. Each was potentially larger and brighter than anything the human eye could ever perceive.

John remembered the words of the volunteer catechist who had prepared him for his baptism. Taking a handful of lessons had been a necessary formality in order to marry in the same Catholic church as Maria's parents. The wisdom of that particular insight had become a truth he had reflected upon often of late.

Despite the vastness of existence, it is the gift of humanity to be able to cherish what we love. And in cherishing what we love, we find the meaning of God.

2007

'How do I look?' she asked.

She looked stunning. The most perfect thing he had ever seen.

'Beautiful,' he said simply.

The final haunting notes of "Ave Maria," her song, drifted away on the piano. The murmur of the assembled slowly quietened. Hundreds of family members, friends, and colleagues had turned out for their big day. He hadn't even realised they knew that many people.

'Out of ten?' she asked. Anticipation hung in her voice like the veil that hung over her hair.

'Ten,' he said. The answer she'd been waiting months to hear. It had become a game between them. She would ask him to rate her outfits, and he would try to answer honestly, with the condition that the perfect score would always be out of reach until the moment he saw her at their wedding. For how could anything ever compete with how she looked in this very moment?

The priest conducted the ceremony in Spanish, her native language. Remembering the lines had been difficult and saying them had proven even more tricky. He had stumbled over a word or two, but the priest had charitably allowed him to proceed. Until they reached the part where he had promised to cherish and respect her. He kept accidentally mispronouncing 'respectar,' *to respect, as* 'rascar,' *to scratch.*

Maria's family and friends chuckled, for they knew what he meant. The priest, however, did not smile. He insisted that he repeat the line, over and over, until he got it right, his face burning in embarrassment.

For respect was the foundation of any relationship, particularly one ordained by God, and no healthy love could flourish without it.

17

John's eyes shot open. He felt a moment of panic, unsure where or even who he was. He expected to see Maria on the bed opposite him, feel her warmth beside him. Then, he remembered he was in The George Inn, sleeping in one of the guest rooms. He checked his phone, which was charging on the bedside table.

3:50am. He'd been asleep a little over an hour.

He rolled out of the grand, king-size bed and went to the bathroom. The light buzzed slightly when he switched it on before settling into a faint hum. He checked the bandages on his arms, wincing at the burning sensation beneath, and examined his face in the mirror. The lump on his temple seemed to have gone down. He was halfway through relieving himself when he heard a faint rattling sound coming from the other side of the wall.

He dismissed it as inconsequential, reasoning that The George was an old building with any number of potential issues. He washed his hands and then downed the glass of water by his bed. He walked over to the curtains and peered through the window. The village was swollen by darkness, only faint outlines of houses visible beneath a sky that was once again pregnant with cloud. There was no sign of the strange red star.

He was about to close the curtains and return to bed when he noticed a bicycle leaning against the front of the inn, just beside the entrance. It hadn't been there when he arrived at The George, else he would surely have noticed it.

There was a sudden thudding sound from the neighbouring room.

John hesitated. Then he pulled on his jeans and T-shirt and moved quietly to the door of his room, opening it a crack. He peered out but saw only dark hallway beyond.

He heard the rattling again. It was coming from the same room as the thudding sound.

John opened the door and crept into the hallway. He noticed that the door to the room adjacent to his was open a fraction. The rattling was coming from within, as though one of the many ghosts that had passed between The George's walls was shaking the chains that bound it to this place.

Very slowly, John pushed open the door to the neighbouring room and stepped inside.

The room was unoccupied, the bed empty and the linen unruffled. However, the window was all the way open. Every so often a breeze would slither into the room and rattle the poorly fitted blinds that covered the window.

John crossed the room to the window and looked down. A bicycle was directly below. Was it possible someone had climbed up through the window? He supposed it could be done with a rope or grappling hook. But why would anyone want to sneak into The George?

John noticed the object on the floor then. It was lying on its side, right next to the bedside table, most likely blown over by a gust of wind. This must be what had caused the thud he had heard moments ago.

He picked it up and examined it in confusion. It was a statue of an angel, crudely built, as though made by the hands of a child. One of the wings had been broken off by the fall. He put the statue back on the table and placed the broken wing carefully beside it.

He was on his way back to his own room when he heard footsteps echoing down the darkness of the corridor ahead.

'Hello?' John said aloud. There was no answer. He fumbled around on the walls for a light switch but found nothing. Throwing caution to the wind, he followed the direction of the footsteps.

He passed through a door that seemed to open into the private living area of the owners. It has been left open and unlocked—a testament to how much Bill and Rosie trusted him, this man they had only just met.

One of the rooms just ahead seemed to demand his attention. The door stood half-ajar, the words 'ROSIE'S ROOM: KEEP OUT!' printed on a sign affixed to the top of the door. Prettily sketched flowers garlanded the letters, a young girl's affectation that had yet to be cast off by the room's inhabitant.

John heard soft footsteps coming from within the room. He thought he caught a glimpse of a shadowy figure through the crack in the door. There was a soft grunt, and it seemed too deep to be that of a woman.

John froze, unsure what to do next. This wasn't his house, and he had no right to intrude upon what anyone chose to do in their own home. But something felt wrong: the sudden appearance of the bike, the footsteps in the corridor, the dread knotting his stomach. He had to be sure Rosie was safe.

He crept up to the doorway and peeked within.

A man stood just inside the room. He was going through a chest of drawers, rifling through what appeared to be women's underwear. Something about the figure seemed familiar. It was the way he stood, the exhausted hunch of his thin shoulders, the fuzzy hair around the sides of his balding crown, shiny in the light of the moon that intruded through the naked window.

The pervert from the police station.

John flicked on the light switch. The pervert froze, a deer caught in the headlights as illumination flooded the bedroom, one greasy hand clutching a pair of Rosie's panties. He turned to stare back at John, eyes wide with shock.

John hit him before his brain could even register his anger. His knuckles cracked the deviant's jaw, dropped him to the carpet where he groaned and twitched, a pitiful sight in the harsh glare of the light above.

'You sick bastard,' John spat. 'What the hell do you think you're doing?'

Rosie shifted on the bed. 'What's going on?' she whimpered. Her pretty hair was a tangle, her thin nightclothes barely covering her modesty.

John felt a sudden surge of protectiveness towards this young woman. 'This arsehole broke into The George and let himself into your room,' he said. 'Did he hurt you?'

'*John?* Who was here? What…what are you talking about?' Rosie sat up and looked wildly around the room, confusion chasing the sleepiness from her eyes. John followed her gaze.

The pervert was gone.

'He was here a second ago,' John said, agitated. 'I followed him to your room.'

Rosie looked at him strangely. It took John a moment to realise she was afraid. *Of him?* That made no sense.

'I want my dad,' she said quietly.

More footsteps echoed down the corridor, the slow and unsteady footsteps of Bill. The Welshman rounded the doorway and stopped when he saw John. 'What's going on in here?' he demanded.

'Rosie's room was broken into by a pervert,' John said. 'I caught him going through her things while she slept. I hit him, and I think…he must have run off.'

Bill looked at the open drawer, at the black panties crumpled accusingly on the carpet. 'Rose?' he questioned.

His daughter looked at her father, then back at John. 'I didn't see a pervert,' she said. 'Only John.'

Bill's expression grew dark. His eyes met John's. 'You're bleeding,' the Welshman said. His voice was colder now, the warmth in his manner extinguished.

John reached up to his mouth, felt the wetness on his lips. His fingers came away slick with blood. 'I-I don't understand,' he said in confusion.

'I think you'd better leave,' Bill said. The Welshman visibly tensed, as though preparing for potential violence. This old man, unsteady on his feet, readying himself to protect his daughter from a stranger half his age.

Monster, said a voice in John's skull.

'There was a man here,' John said. He kept his voice cool and matter of fact. 'A pervert. I saw him yesterday in Warminster Police Station. He could still be here. Don't go back to bed until you've checked the entire building.'

Then, he left the room, went back through the hallway, and took the stairs down to the bar area. He unlocked the front door and let himself out. The bike was still there.

He could have used it as evidence his story was true. Could have argued his innocence. Could even have protested the injustice of it all and demanded the lift to the park he had been promised. Instead, he climbed on the bike and rode back the way he had come, heading up the A350, and from there, to Lake Shearwater.

18

Lilith Von Goth pulled her shawl tighter as she approached the dark woodland beside the lake. A chill wind blew across Lake Shearwater, causing goose pimples to rise on her pale skin. The trees up ahead would provide shelter from the cold, as would the warm bodies gathering within. The headlights of idling cars flickered among the trees like will 'o wisps, the purr of their engines a siren song drawing the lost to their embrace.

The surface of Shearwater was a black mirror, a window into the underworld. She might have been looking out over Cocytus, the grey river of lamentation which surrounded Hades in Greek mythology. In *Dante's Inferno*, Cocytus was the frozen lake in which those guilty of betrayal were imprisoned for eternity.

Lilith wasn't certain if she were the betrayer or the betrayed. It didn't matter now, she realised. Those were the sorts of trivial questions Kimberley would struggle with. Lilith was above such concerns. She was a daughter of the moon, a creature of blood and magic and whatever earthly satisfaction she desired was her due.

Her platform shoes crunched over stones and branches as she struggled up the shallow embankment to the edge of the forest. She could already hear the sounds of carnal pleasure taking place ahead. Excitement warred with anxiety. Her nerve faltered. She pulled out her phone, tried to call him one last time.

No reply.

Lilith Von Goth pushed through the trees and entered the clearing.

A couple looked up as they saw her, their bodies intertwined. He looked at her hungrily, while his partner smiled at Lilith from where she knelt on all fours in the dirt. 'Hi,' she said. 'First time?'

'Yes,' Lilith replied in a daze.

'Go ahead and join the others,' the woman said, nodding towards the centre of the clearing. 'We'll join you in a minute.'

The couple resumed their fucking as Lilith walked past them, the woman's moans following her like the cries of a dying murder victim. The night air smelled musty, of decomposing leaves and car exhausts and sex.

A small group had gathered besides a large white camper van. A young woman was on her knees pleasuring a heavy man twice her age, while several other men and women watched. Lilith felt a mixture of disgust and excitement at the scene.

A hand brushed her arm. She turned and stared into the face of a stubbly, balding fellow. He looked exhausted, and there was a fresh bruise on his cheek. He smiled at her, revealing crooked teeth. 'What's your name?' he whispered, his tired eyes glittering.

'Lilith,' she replied. She felt transfixed by his hungry gaze.

'*Lilith*,' he repeated. He seemed to taste the word, rolling it around his tongue. 'What brings you here tonight?' His voice was soft. Soft like a velvet glove, clutching something sharp and deadly.

'Curiosity,' she replied, uncertainly.

'Is that all?' he asked. His eyes went to her chest and remained there. 'You were just curious?'

'Hurt, too,' she said. 'I'm hurt. I always do this when I'm hurt.'

'Do what?' he asked. The corner of his mouth twitched upwards. His eyes still hadn't strayed from her chest.

'I seek out things that are bad for me. Bad men. Abuse. Sex.'

The man's smile turned into a beaming grin. Brighter than the lights of an onrushing car.

'What if I told you that you'd found them?'

Lilith ought to have excused herself then. This man disgusted her. It wasn't his age: he was only in his mid-30s, and she had always preferred more mature men. This fellow was repulsive in other ways. He was poorly dressed and tired-looking and he reeked of desperation. He was *weak*.

Her phone buzzed suddenly. She immediately reached for it, hope bursting within her chest. Could it be him? She looked at the screen.

It was only her mother. Probably phoning her to complain some more about Steve, or to admonish Lilith for the way she had spoken to her earlier. She cancelled the call.

She stared at the man opposite. His eyes were voracious. Desperate to devour her. He *wanted* her, she realised. It felt so good to be wanted.

'I would say that's exactly what I hoped for,' she ventured. She didn't react as his thin fingers moved from her arm to her shoulder, and then around to her breasts.

'How about I help you out that corset?' he said eagerly. The man's tone was repellent and promised dark things, but the part of her that was in control now hungered for it. Yearned for it like a secret being dragged into the light yearned for the darkness.

Lilith could smell the man's stale sweat as he positioned himself behind her and began unclipping her corset. She closed her eyes, unshed tears smearing the thick mascara she wore. 'Hurry up,' she said desperately, her voice sounding childish to her ears. Or perhaps it was the innocent girl she once was, projecting her pain into the future until it was finally vocalised here in the present.

Someone screamed nearby.

At first, Lilith wondered if it was her. All the hurt, all the anguish, involuntarily bursting out. But it wasn't her who had screamed. The cry had come from the woman on her knees opposite the large-bellied older man. She stared down at her naked thighs in horror. They were covered in something the colour of rust that clung to her pale and bruised legs. It took Lilith a moment to realise the rust was *moving*, propelled by thousands of tiny legs. The girl was being swarmed by an army of wood ants.

Lilith saw the vast carpet of insects swarming across the forest floor then. Her breath caught in her throat. It was as though every ant in the woods had attacked at once: millions upon millions of *Formica rufa*, the red wood ant, amassing to repel these foreign invaders.

The ants rose to the girl's face, an unstoppable torrent of the insects. They swarmed her mouth, her nose, her ears, and even her eyes. She screamed again and again, scratched wildly at the biting insects, heedless of the damage her nails were doing to her skin.

The overweight fellow she had been fellating moments before reeled away, beating ineffectually at his wilting cock, which was now covered in ants.

More screams and shouts pierced the forest night. A man who had been watching the carnal display threw himself to the ground and rolled around and around, bellowing in animal terror. His features were invisible beneath the army of six-legged horrors eating him alive.

Lilith heard a muttered curse behind her and glanced back to see the pervert who had been undressing her flee back to the lake, running with a pronounced limp. She looked back at the forest floor. The carpet of ants was only a few inches from her platform shoes.

The sight of her own doom but moments away finally stirred her into action.

She stomped down, crushing hundreds of the insects beneath her five-inch heels. This time she did scream. Like a banshee heralding the deaths of all those closest to her, she unleashed her fury upon the hostile army in miniature. Ants died, but others replaced them, an inexhaustible legion spewed forth from the very depths of Hell.

Lilith turned and ran. She almost tripped in her unwieldy shoes on more than one occasion, and though her thick black stockings and corset protected her from many of the bites, she felt the painful nip of mandibles on every inch of her exposed flesh. Some of the night's guests tried to take shelter in their cars. The tiny soldiers found their way into each and every vehicle, trapping their unfortunate victims in a ton of steel and subjecting them to death by countless bites.

Lilith was almost at the edge of the forest. She saw the couple who had initially greeted her, both buried beneath millions of ants, their bodies still entwined in death. How were there so many insects?

2.5 million ants for every human being. Even in the midst of terrified flight, Lilith's brilliant scientific mind spat facts at her. This woodland could potentially contain billions of the insects. Depending on the individual, a human being's surface area contained room for around 50,000 ants. If every ant in the forest were to attack a target in unison until it was entirely covered by insects, they could strip a human being of skin in…what? A few days? A few hours?

Slapping biting insects away from her face, Lilith Von Goth burst from the trees and threw herself into the lake.

19

Colour was slowly bleeding back into the world as John veered off the main road and on to Clay Street, though sunrise was still a way off. The expression on Bill's face buzzed around John's thoughts like a fly he couldn't swat, poking at the guilt and grief that always lurked just beneath the surface. It only took a small misunderstanding like the one which had occurred in Rosie's bedroom to dredge up bitter memories and drag him down into a pit of self-loathing.

John tried to focus on the road ahead. Clay Street was eerily silent. The handful of houses lining the route to Lake Shearwater were dark and unwelcoming. When John had last passed this way, he and Maria were celebrating becoming first-time homeowners. They had come to Shearwater to enjoy an ice cream in the late summer sun. The road down which he now cycled had been packed with cars and pedestrians eagerly making their way towards the lake. John had lowered the roof of his convertible and basked in the afternoon heat while Maria fiddled with the radio, sunlight glimmering in her chestnut brown hair.

That had been less than a year ago. Now, the gold and the warmth had been replaced by the cold monochrome of a twilight purgatory. He might have been cycling through the astral plane, surrounded by nothing but the spirits of the dead and the memories of flame now turned to ash.

What had happened to him and Maria? How could a love that was once as impregnable as a fortress have fallen so swifty and catastrophically to ruin?

A dark shape appeared on the road just ahead, interrupting his thoughts. John manoeuvred the stolen bicycle around it, glanced down as he passed by. It was a dead badger, blood leaking from its mouth, entrails exposed by whichever vehicle it had collided with.

Roadkill was not uncommon in this part of Wiltshire. Perhaps the badger had mistakenly attacked a passing car and gotten the worse of the exchange. It was a sad sight, to witness a creature so fierce and tenacious reduced to mere carrion. In its own domain, the badger was a proud creature that could see off any predator. A ton of steel roaring down the road like an angry lion was a threat it could never hope to understand, and it had paid the price.

John was cycling hard now, droplets of sweat forming on his brow despite the chill. He raced over a pedestrian crossing. Another memory of his last visit to Shearwater dislodged from the recesses of his brain like a stone from the tyre of a bike. He had stopped his car to allow a young couple to cross the road on their way to the lake. Their daughter's toddling footsteps had caused a small queue to form behind him. John remembered his jaw had been clenched. Why?

He had been angry. Annoyed at this trifling delay. Maria had worn sunglasses. To shield her eyes from the sun, or to hide her sadness? What had she been sad about?

They had argued earlier that day, he now remembered. The two of them had spent the morning moving belongings from their old rental to their new house. John's red convertible was fun to drive around Wiltshire's twisting country roads but had proven sorely impractical for moving home. With the car lacking rear seats and boot space, they had been forced to stack furniture on the passenger seat and transport it across town over at least a dozen journeys.

Maria had accidentally scratched the soft plastic of the car's interior, and John had lost his temper. Could he really be blamed? The car had been his pride and joy, a symbol that John Sharrock had finally achieved something.

The book deal had changed everything. It had seemed like a minor miracle, a poke in the eye to those who had told him he would never amount to anything. To the English teacher who declared to the entire class that none of them had the talent to write professionally; to the school itself, which seemed to revel in stripping pupils of their ambition, ensuring they emerged from its dreary halls to take their rightful place in society's forgotten strata of working-class subsistence, too poorly educated to know how to go about changing their circumstances and too poorly motivated to force themselves to try.

Two of John's childhood friends had recently taken their own lives. He couldn't put the blame directly on the school, of course, but he had little doubt it had injected its insidious poison in them during their formative years.

John Sharrock had proved everyone wrong. In doing so, he had secured his and Maria's future. At least, so it had initially seemed.

While his first novel had been the outpouring of a decade's worth of ideas, a frenzy of self-realisation of his latent talent, the second had been much more an obligation; one for which he had never planned but was now contractually bound to deliver. He had worked on the novel day and night. He gave up going to bed alongside Maria in order to write until the early hours, when the combination of guilt and tiredness would somehow unlock his inner muse and enable him to put some words on the page.

Maria never complained. Instead, she was the dutiful wife and partner. She went to work and came home and prepared his dinner and made him tea and coffee and kissed him goodnight.

Shortly after John began writing his second novel, Maria developed an anxiety disorder. She would struggle with intrusive thoughts and joint pain and fatigue. There were times she couldn't walk without a stick. John had panicked then, for he desired nothing more than to protect her. But there was no one to protect her from, no external adversary he could fight.

Instead, he had gone with her to therapy and spent countless hours researching how to improve her physical and mental health. He would often take Maria away to the Canary Islands, where the climate and relaxed atmosphere seemed to improve her well-being. It had become their special place. He could immerse himself in his work while she rested.

John finished his second book, and it was successful despite the difficulty he had writing it. The third and final book was an altogether more torturous undertaking.

The pressure of delivering the perfect ending seemed to hang over him like the Sword of Damocles. He spent entire days reading negative reviews online. When Maria got home from work, he would be sullen and irritable, jealously guarding the tiniest morsel of his time like a dying man clinging to his last breath.

When had she begun to withdraw from him? When had the love turned to resentment, the adoration in her eyes replaced by anger? Couldn't she see he was doing this for her?

If he failed to deliver this final book by the agreed deadline, he would lose his book deal. He would have to repay the large advance he had been given. They both would lose the house they had just bought.

Maria was desperate for a baby, but she didn't seem to see that the book was the key to everything. The house, the fertility treatment, the future, it all rested on this. He couldn't go back to having nothing. To *being* nothing. He had to finish it.

Whatever it took.

He once more struggled to recall the last handful of months. His head was suddenly throbbing again.

He had finished the book. He knew that much. But what about the rest? Maria had left—he recalled that moment vividly. Everything else seemed like a blur.

Why couldn't he remember?

Confused by his thoughts, John lost track of his surroundings. Before he knew it, Lake Shearwater emerged on his right. The ground near the lake was rocky and uneven, and so he dismounted the bike and wheeled it along the shore. He was still struggling to piece together the last few months when he spotted a figure huddled on the grassy slope leading down to the water.

It was a woman. She was dressed all in black and purple, a chest-hugging corset undone halfway down her back. Her dark hair was a sodden mess. In fact, she was soaked all over. She was shivering uncontrollably in the cold.

John dropped the bike and rushed over to the woman. She looked up as he hurried over, alerted by the metallic clang of the bike hitting the ground. Her grey eyes were wide with terror. She appeared to be in her early twenties, perhaps a decade younger than him. Make-up had run all over her cheeks, only partially hiding the hundreds of tiny red marks that covered her face.

'Jesus!' John exclaimed. 'You're covered in bites. You poor thing. Here, let me help you up.' He extended a hand. After's a moment's hesitation, she took it. He hauled her gently to her feet. John was surprised to find her eyes were level with his own. A moment later, he noticed she was wearing huge platform shoes which boosted her height by at least five inches. They were covered in metal spikes, as though she were a barbarian princess going to battle, like in one of his novels. 'I'm John,' he said gently. 'Do you mind if I ask your name?'

'Lilith,' the woman replied nervously. She closed her eyes and seemed to shrink in on herself. 'Actually…it's Kimberley. Lilith is…*the other me.*'

'The other you?' John echoed, confused.

'Lilith is who I become when I'm hurt or afraid,' Kimberley explained. 'She's not like me. She's strong and capable and fears nothing. When I feel like I'm losing myself to the darkness, when I feel myself spinning out of control…Lilith takes over. You must think I'm crazy.'

'Not at all,' John said hurriedly. Something about the young woman's words resonated with him in a way he couldn't explain. 'What happened here, Kimberley?'

The woman pointed at the woods beyond the lake. Her hand trembled slightly. As she gestured, her sleeve fell back from her arm and John saw the scars covering her pale skin. He pretended not to notice. 'I was…with some friends, in the forest. The next thing I knew, ants began pouring out of the earth. Millions of them. They swarmed everyone. Everyone except me and…one other. We ran, and I threw myself in the lake. *Formica rufa* don't like water.'

'*Formica rufa?*' John asked, puzzled.

'Red wood ants,' Kimberley explained. 'I wrote an essay about them as part of my Master's. Studying biology, you learn the Latin names of hundreds of animals. I even took additional classes in Latin.'

Let me teach you.

The words seemed to appear from nowhere inside John's skull. It was as though Kimberley had spoken them aloud. He stared at her, feeling a dull throb in his temples. 'We should check for survivors,' he managed. 'These attacks have been happening all over the Warminster area. Not just ants: dogs, cats, rats, even a mother duck, if you can believe that.'

'Male ducks can sometimes be aggressive towards people,' Kimberley said. Her voice was soft and very earnest. She spoke with exaggerated care, like a young girl eager to explain some hidden knowledge to her parents but afraid they might tell her to shut up. 'Mother ducks are usually too focused on their young to pose a threat.'

'Not this one,' John said grimly. 'Wait here. I'll be right back.'

'Aren't you afraid?' Kimberley asked. Her voice was curious now.

Jon shrugged. 'A year or two ago, I would have been terrified. Sometime during the last few months, I seem to have gained a great deal more confidence.'

He walked over to the edge of the trees, noting the sound of a car engine running just ahead. John cautiously entered the clearing but stopped in horror when he saw the slaughter that had taken place.

Naked and partially clothed bodies were strewn over the forest floor. John was unable to tell the men apart from the women as each corpses' face had been eaten away to the point of unrecognizability. Only bone and sinew remained and, in one case, a puffy mass of red tissue weeping crimson droplets. Despite what he had just told Kimberley, John felt nauseated by the gruesome sight and had to look away.

There were half a dozen vehicles parked around the clearing. Two of them held bodies within, their faces eaten away, limbs contorted into agonised shapes. One of the cars was still running, the warm engine sending wraithlike exhaust fumes into the damp forest air. There was no sign of the ants.

John hurried back to Kimberley. She was staring at her phone. She gave it a shake and sighed in frustration. 'Ruined,' she said. 'I should have thought to put it somewhere safe before jumping in the lake.'

'I wouldn't be too hard on yourself,' John replied. 'Your quick thinking saved your life. Listen, there's no easy way to say this: everyone is dead. It's like something from a nightmare in those woods. At least the ants are gone.'

'Do you have a phone?' Kimberley asked. 'We should call the police.'

John pulled out his phone and dialled 999. He waited a moment for the call tone to kick in. Instead, the phone's speaker spewed out a bunch of static. He tried calling three more times, each with the same result.

'I think my phone's dead, too,' he said in annoyance. He closed his eyes, trying to ignore the throbbing in his skull. 'There's a car idling in the woods. You can get warm. Dry yourself with the radiator.'

'What then?' Kimberley asked, eyes wide as she looked around. 'Could…could you take me home? I don't know how to drive.'

John shook his head. 'I need to reach Longleat. It's best I go on foot. The army is trying to keep everyone away. If they see a vehicle on the road, they'll turn us back around.'

Kimberley stared at him, confused. 'Longleat? Didn't you say animal attacks have been happening across the area? There are dozens of dangerous animals in Longleat. What could possibly make you go there?'

'My wife,' John replied simply. 'My wife is there, and she might be in trouble.'

'You're married?' Kimberley asked. She watched him carefully now.

'Yes. Things are strained right now, but I love her, and I need to find her. I'm worried about her.'

The young woman said nothing for a time. Her grey eyes seemed to stare into his very soul. 'Let me come with you,' she said eventually. At the dubious look on his face, she quickly added, 'Just until we reach Longleat. I don't want to stay here in case the ants return.'

John stared at the woman in surprise. 'You said it yourself, it'll be extremely dangerous.'

She shrugged. 'You seem kind, and strong. I think you would protect me.'

John took a moment to compose his thoughts. He couldn't risk her slowing him down, especially with Maria being in danger. He'd need to be able to focus all his strength and attention on getting his wife to safety. On the other hand, Kimberley wasn't a child and was clearly capable of making her own decisions.

If he left her here, he would be leaving her at the mercy of whoever or whatever might happen upon her. She was vulnerable, yes, that was evident by the fresh marks he saw under her sleeves, but she was also smart. She could at least give him useful tips on different animal species that could help him through the safari park.

'Okay, then,' he said finally. 'I guess you're stuck with me until we reach Longleat, Kimberley.'

'Just "Kim," if you don't mind,' she replied, the shadow of a satisfied smile at the corner of her mouth. 'Let's go.'

As they walked back to the woods' entrance, something buzzed. Kim pulled out her phone and appeared to check it. She smiled suddenly, the unknowable depths of the lake opposite reflected in her unusual grey eyes.

John took a few more steps before an uncomfortable thought occurred to him.

I thought she said her phone was ruined?

20

By the time Kim had dried herself in the cabin of a worn-out Ford Escort, dawn had broken over Lake Shearwater and the surrounding forest. Knives of sunlight stabbed down through the branches overhead, painting the trees in such brilliant gold it was hard to conceive of the horrors that had so recently taken place.

The bodies, however, told no lies.

Flies had begun to pitch on the dead exhibitionists. Organs that had mere ago hours ago been powering life itself within temples of flesh and blood, would soon putrefy and be eaten by migrating bacteria. Everything was food for something else.

The universe is a hostile place, John thought, somewhat sullenly. His mood had taken a downturn with each minute he had put off heading towards his destination. He couldn't stop his musings as his eyes took in the death surrounding him. *Any peace we find is a fleeting miracle we should thank God for while we have the grace to acknowledge our good fortune.*

'Do you ever think about death?' asked Kim unexpectedly. She walked beside him as they traversed the woodlands, the top of her head barely reaching his chin now that she had removed her shoes to navigate the treacherous footing. According to Kim, ants could feel vibrations in the earth. The last thing either of them wanted was to disturb a colony by tripping over a stray root and tumbling to the dirt.

John glanced at his new companion. 'Sometimes, I guess. I never used to. Not even when I was younger and got hit by a motorbike. More recently, I've become aware of losing the things I love.'

'I noticed you have a slight limp,' Kim replied. She said it apologetically, as though worried she might offend him. 'From the motorbike accident?'

'Yes,' John said.

'And you weren't afraid? Why not?'

'I suppose I didn't care enough back then to worry about it. When I was your age, or maybe a little younger, I wasn't very happy.'

Kim went quiet for a time. 'Why is that?' she eventually asked, fingers fiddling with her slightly damp sleeve.

'I didn't really have many friends. I never knew how to talk to people. It was much easier to lose myself in fictional characters and worlds than to be a part of the real one.'

'I love to read,' Kim replied enthusiastically. 'My room at my mum's house is full of books. She says I should get rid of some to make space.'

John smiled. He remembered having similar conversations with his own mother on countless occasions. 'What kinds of books?'

Kimberley shrugged. 'Science books. Astrology. Fantasy. I loved fantasy when I was in secondary school. I used to write. I don't have many friends either,' she added conspiratorially.

'I write fantasy,' John said. 'I mean, I'm an author.'

Kim stared him, her eyes wide. 'Seriously? What fantasy do you write? High fantasy? Epic fantasy? I like dark fantasy. The good guys winning all the time gets boring. I like it when the hero is the monster.' She looked at him out of the corner of her eye.

John reeled slightly like he had been punched. It was like Kim had just read his mind. A vision of Maria suddenly pushed itself into his mind's eye, face twisted in grief, dark brown eyes glistening with tears. He cleared his throat and tried to focus on the present. 'You might like my books. The characters are many shades of grey. No, not like *that* book,' he added, seeing her mischievous smile. 'Don't tell me you've read it.'

'I have,' she replied. 'I enjoyed it, too. At least parts of it.' Her sudden laughter was like the tinkling of tiny bells.

John and Kim passed the next while talking about books they'd read. She was a charming conversationalist, interested in many of the things he enjoyed. Like him, she was an introvert. Maria was always the opposite, much more an extrovert, a lover of people and music and places. She had taken his hand and guided him into a world he had until then only glimpsed from the outside.

Kim must have read his thoughts again or least seen something in his expression. 'You mentioned you've become more conscious of losing the things you love,' she said carefully. 'What did you mean?'

John hesitated, searching for the right words. 'I lost my father when I was four. He died in a car accident. Sometimes, I think of him. He died suddenly. I never got to say goodbye.'

'I'm sorry,' Kim said. 'My dad left when I was very young. I haven't seen him in years. Not having a father around sucks. My stepfather, Steve, tries his best but hates his job. He and mum argue constantly.'

John made a sympathetic noise, and the two walked in companionable silence for a time. 'What do you enjoy about writing?' Kim asked him.

John thought about this. 'I think it's the sense of control,' he replied. 'Writing is my escapism. In the worlds I create, everything makes sense. I can't be hurt there, and if something bad happens, I can fix it. The characters all get what they deserve. I'm not good at much, but writing is the one thing I do well. If I fail at that—' He suddenly remembered he and Maria arguing, his obsession with finishing his book driving his marriage towards the rocks. He winced. 'Then, I've failed at everything. I'm worthless.'

The trees thinned until they could see the road up ahead. It appeared to be shrouded in a thick, grey fog.

'You mentioned things are complicated with your marriage,' Kim said, glancing at him. How did she keep doing this? Plucking his thoughts from his skull and giving voice to his fears as though she could peer inside his head! 'Tell me about your wife.'

John closed his eyes for a moment. 'I told you that, when I was younger, I was very unhappy. Well, then I met Maria—and suddenly I wasn't unhappy anymore. She taught me how to laugh. How to love. She taught me how to be a real person. No longer a ghost, hiding from the world.'

'You sound like you loved her very much,' Kim said. There was a strange edge to her voice.

'I still do,' John said quickly.

'Why did you separate?' Kim asked. 'If you don't want to talk about it, I understand.'

'It's…a long story,' John said hesitantly. 'The short answer is that I-I screwed up.'

'I'm no one to judge,' Kim said. The edge in her voice was gone, replaced by an earnestness that immediately put John at ease. She gave him a warm smile. 'Are you religious?'

'Technically, I'm a Catholic,' John said. He felt a little stab of shame. Maria was a devout Catholic, and John had always admired her for her faith. A part of him wanted to be like her, to put aside the cold, logical part of his mind that questioned everything and just accept a truth greater than himself. Did he truly want to believe, or had he just wanted to please Maria? 'I suppose it would be more honest to say I'm agnostic. Who knows what's out there? I like to think I'll see my father and other loved ones when I'm gone. How about you? You mentioned you had a Master's in science? I guess that means you're an atheist.'

'Why would you think that?' Kim asked. Her mysterious eyes glittered with amusement.

'Well…isn't science all about dealing with the reproducible, that which is demonstrably real? Not gods or miracles or…magic.'

Kim's smile was as wide as a crescent moon. 'Here's a secret for you, John. Science *is* magic.'

****

They emerged from the woods to a scene like something from a waking dream. In both directions, the road was quickly swallowed by thick fog. It hung in the air like the breath of some primordial titan, enshrouding the immediate area in a ghostly curtain that reduced visibility to less than a hundred metres. John couldn't see beyond the broken wooden fencing that marked the edge of the field on the opposite side of the road.

'Which way?' Kim asked.

John nodded at the worn asphalt leading into the fog. 'This road should take us to the outskirts of Longleat. From there, we can observe the army presence at the park.'

'What are you planning to do once we get there?'

'I'll figure it out,' John replied, hoping he sounded more confident than he felt. 'Come on.'

They clambered down the embankment, trying not to slip on the dew-slick grass. Their slow descent to that isolated road felt like climbing into some ethereal otherworld, a place that was both part and not part of the land of the living. John felt a deep sense of foreboding take root in his chest. Next to him, Kim seemed unmoved by the strange shift in the air. He felt something tickling the back of his hand and glanced down.

It was a death's-head hawkmoth. The insect's wings quivered and the skull pattern on its thorax twitched, seeming to laugh at him. An instant later, it flew off. He watched it go, tracking its fluttering movements through the air. It dwindled until it was a tiny speck. A moment later, it was swallowed by the fog.

'Did you see that?' he asked Kim. His new friend wasn't looking in his direction, however. She was staring at the ruined fencing surrounding the fields at the side of the road.

'See what?' she said distractedly.

'Never mind. What's wrong?'

'Something broke through that fence,' Kim replied. 'Not just in one spot either. There are holes in it all the way down the road.' She pointed. Her sleeve fell back from her arm again, revealing her scarred flesh. She caught John staring, and her eyes narrowed slightly.

'What could do that?' John asked, pretending again that he hadn't noticed her cuts. 'Cows? Don't tell me there's a herd of killer cows on the loose.'

His attempt at a joke floundered between them like a dying fish. Kim carefully rolled her sleeve back down. 'Cattle kill more people every year in the UK than any other animal. A cow weighs over half a ton and can run at speeds of 25 miles per hour. If you're Usain Bolt, you might be able to outrun one over a very short distance. Everyone else is fucked.'

Hearing Kim curse surprised him slightly. 'Are you okay?' he asked. 'You seem angry.'

'You saw the scars,' Kim stated.

‘Yes,’ John admitted.

‘You aren’t going to ask about them?’

‘I didn’t…’ John began, unsure what to say. ‘I assume… I mean, did you cut yourself?’

‘Yes,’ Kim replied.

‘Why?’

‘The sight of blood calms me.’

John said nothing. He tasted copper all of a sudden. Sharp, metallic.

‘Sometimes,’ Kim explained, ‘when I feel disconnected, like I’m spiralling out of control…cutting brings me back to myself.’

‘Oh,’ John replied, unable to think of anything to say to that. A shiver ran down his spine. He thought he could hear a faint beeping noise. It was coming from the fog up ahead.

‘How does that make you feel?’ Kim asked. She watched him now, eyes as dark as sin.

‘It makes me feel sad,’ he said. ‘I understand why you do it, but I wish you wouldn’t hurt yourself.’

‘Why?’ Kim asked. The puzzlement in her voice, the confusion on her face, touched something deep within him. ‘Why does it matter?’

‘Because…because it’s self-destructive. The world hurts everyone eventually. You shouldn’t make its job any easier.’ He stopped in the middle of the road. Kim stopped with him. She stood there, looking up at him, shivering in the cold, her corset still half-open down her back. The mask of self-confidence fell away. She suddenly looked like a child. A lost and confused child, her pain spilling out of her for all the world to see.

'Hold still a moment,' John said softly. He moved behind her and fastened up her corset. 'There. That's better.'

'Thanks,' said Kim, numbly.

John hesitated. Then, he embraced her, holding her tightly against him. Willing his warmth into her cool, shivering body. She froze like prey caught in the path of a predator.

'It's okay,' he said gently.

A second or two passed—and then her head rested against his shoulder, and she relaxed into his arms.

They stood like that for what felt like a long time. Somewhere on her person, Kim's phone buzzed again. She ignored it. John thought about mentioning the phone, pointing out that she had evidently lied to him. He decided against it. Everyone was entitled to their secrets.

Eventually, they parted. Kimberley smoothed out her long, black hair, a small smile on her face. 'What about you?' she asked softly.

'What about me?' John repeated, confused.

'Do you ever feel like you're losing control?'

You've totally lost it.

John jolted. Where had those words just come from? Someone had said them to him, not so long ago. Who? Why?

'John? Are you okay?'

Kim's question jolted him back to the present. 'I remember a night,' he said slowly, once he had recovered himself, 'some years after my dad died. Something had happened, some argument with my family. Or perhaps an incident at school. I awoke in the middle of the night feeling like something was trying to force its way into my body.'

Kim watched him carefully. '*Something?*' she echoed.

'It's hard to describe. It felt…*furious*. Full of hate. Like some kind of demon.'

'What did you do? I know about demons. I know the spells to keep them at bay.'

John felt his fists clenching. He forced his hands to relax. 'Nothing.'

'Nothing?' Kim raised an eyebrow. 'You didn't speak to anyone about what you experienced?'

'No.'

'Have you ever felt like that since? Like something was trying to take control of you? Some kind of…stranger?' Kim's grey eyes seemed to glitter.

John hesitated. There was something lurking at the edge of his consciousness. A memory, wispy and ephemeral. He tried to reach for it, but it was already gone.

'I'm not sure,' he answered. 'Sometimes, when I've been afraid or stressed, I've sensed…a darkness, in the back of my skull. I know it is capable of very bad things, but I've never let it out. Though…I think I haven't been myself of late.'

'How would you know?' Kim said softly. 'How would you know if you were yourself or if something else had taken over? Would you even ask for help?'

'I don't think I would. I don't like to ask for help.'

'Why not?'

'I….' John began uncertainly. He heard Maria's voice, repeating something once said by family that had long since abandoned him. 'Because I'm strong,' he said. 'I've always had to be strong, for me and for everyone I love.'

'And what about you?' Kim asked. The smile she gave him was knowing, as though she was aware of some important fact he had missed. 'Who will be strong for you? Who will help you when you need it?'

John stared into the fog for a time, saying nothing. He heard the beeping sound again. 'We'd better get going,' he mumbled, nodding at the curtain of mist ahead.

His trainers crunched down the worn asphalt road, the beeping growing louder with every step. Having earlier removed her huge boots, Kim moved as silently as a mouse on her stockinged feet. Soon, they passed the broken remains of a deer. The animal had been hit by something moving at great speed, and its once-sleek hide was now nothing more than a skin bag for shattered bone and burst organs. Dark skid marks on the road careened into the thick fog, a stage screen that hid whatever horrors awaited from a curious audience.

John and Kim plunged into the fog, following the source of the beeping noise. They passed another deer, and then another. The last wasn't yet dead. It struggled pathetically, broken legs twitching as it made an eerie bawling sound. One eye was a ruptured mess, the other the bloodshot red of a creature infected with the virus, or whatever it was that was causing animals to act crazy. The two travellers on the road looked at it sadly, but there was nothing they could do to help.

When they finally reached the heart of the horror in the mist, John wished he had followed Kim's earlier suggestion to stick to the woods.

An ambulance van was lying on its side. The front half of the vehicle was wrapped around the trunk of a mighty tree. The front bumper was folded back on itself, the driver's compartment a mass of warped steel. Most shocking of all, a pair of legs emerged from the profane mess. The upper half of the body was trapped within. The green ambulance trousers worn by the corpse were somehow still spotless despite the devastation, though one of the victim's shoes had fallen off to rest on the dirt by the side of the road. A lanyard with a name badge was nearby. It read: "Esteban Calavera."

The rear doors of the ambulance had been forced wide open by the impact. The right side hung loosely from broken hinges. Groaning on the asphalt, spat out of the vehicle like a fallen angel ejected from Heaven, was someone John recognised. In fact, he had last seen him only a couple of days ago, waving at John from across Warminster High Street.

'Adam?' John said, astonished. He hurried over to the fallen man. Adam's right arm was badly broken, bone poking out just below his elbow.

'*Justin*,' Adam said urgently. His face was a tapestry of cuts and bruises. 'In the back of ambulance. Don't worry about me. Check on Justin!'

John's eyes went to the ruined patient compartment. The medical apparatus within was almost wholly destroyed, the impact of the crash having torn it from the sides of the vehicle. The beeping sound he had first heard on the road was coming from somewhere within.

Kim fearlessly climbed up into the back of the van and began pulling away fallen equipment. 'Help me,' she yelled at John, who clambered up beside her. He heard the faint moans from beneath the pile of fallen gear and sprang into action, tearing away monitors and defibrillators, lifting a fallen shelf and tossing it from the van. He cut his fingers on something, ignored the stinging and the blood and redoubled his efforts.

Finally, after what felt like an age but must have been only a few minutes, they reached the stricken Justin. He was still strapped into his stretcher. The man's face was a puffy mess, his features resembling those of the Elephant Man, the titular character from the classic David Lynch film. Despite his hideous appearance, he sucked in ragged breaths, his chest rising and falling.

'*Justin*?' called Adam again from outside the van. His voice cracked with pain or grief or perhaps both.

'He's alive,' shouted John. Adam gave an answering sob of relief. 'Can you help him?' John asked Kim. She bit her lip and examined Justin. Tubes ran from his arm to somewhere in the wreckage, but it was impossible to ascertain which metal box was keeping him alive.

'I'm a biologist, not a doctor,' she said. 'But he seems stable, at least for now. You should check on the man outside. You know him?'

'We go to the same gym,' John confirmed. 'Wait here.' He slid back out of the ambulance and approached Adam, who had managed to climb to his feet. 'What happened?' John asked, once the man looked to be in no immediate danger of collapsing.

Adam grimaced. Several of his teeth were missing, bloody holes punched into his smile during the moment of impact. 'Our bees…swarmed Justin without warning. I pulled him to safety. Called an ambulance. We were on our way to the hospital when a herd of deer appeared on the road. They charged at the van. I remember the driver yelling. Then, nothing. What…what happened to the paramedics?'

John gazed at the catastrophe of crushed metal wrapped around the tree. At the obscene sight of the disembodied legs hanging from the wreck. They looked like they belonged to a children's doll; the innocent daydream of an infant's fancy, transposed into the nightmare of a violence and twisted steel and lives brutally taken.

'They didn't make it,' he said. 'I'm sorry.'

Adam closed his eyes and leaned on the van, supporting himself with his uninjured arm. They stood there in silence for a time. A soft wind gusted down the road, scattering leaves around them.

At least, John assumed they were leaves. They fluttered around, and John saw that they were in fact moths. A sudden terror filled him, a primal fear he had not felt in a very long time. He stared at Adam and the ruined van, torn between a fierce desire to protect the two injured men and the irresistible urge to flee this place before it was too late.

'I'm very sorry, Adam,' he said, trying not to let his panic show. 'But I must go. My wife needs me. Do you have a phone?'

Adam shook his head. He hacked up blood from somewhere deep in his chest. More blood than any healthy man ought to cough up.

John pulled out his phone, but the battery had died. A blank display stared back at him. 'Shit,' he said.

Kim poked her head out of the back of the van. 'He's asking for you,' she told Adam. She flicked hair out of her eyes. 'John? Are you okay? You're shaking.'

'We need to go,' John said urgently. He shoved his hands in his pockets. They were trembling. The feeling of impending disaster intensified. 'Adam, come with us to Longleat. There will be medics there. Your husband has to remain here, it's too dangerous to move him. We can send someone for Justin—'

'No,' Adam growled. He stood in the back of the van, barring the path to his husband. An implacable guardian, allowing nothing to harm that which he held dearest to his heart. 'I'm not going anywhere. I won't leave Justin.' He spat out blood again.

'You're hurt,' John tried again. 'Internal injuries can be fatal if they don't receive urgent medical attention—'

'No,' Adam said again, more fiercely this time. 'I'm staying. Do you understand? I will not abandon him. I have to stay.'

Stay. The word seemed to echo around this world-within-a-world, this fog-enshrouded demiplane of grey walls and hidden horrors. Moths circled the broken ambulance. No one else present appeared to notice the insects.

'We'll fetch help,' John promised, staring at the moths with rising dread. 'As soon as we reach Longleat, we'll demand they send immediate assistance. Wait inside the vehicle and close the door. Help will arrive before you know it.'

Adam watched in silence as they made their way around the mangled van and hurried up the road in the direction of the park. Just before he disappeared, Adam seemed to mouth a single word at John, a word that once again poked at forgotten memories and sent waves of anxiety though his chest.

Stay.

2013

'Why do you love me?' he asked.

She shifted slightly on the sand. 'Why do you ask?' she smiled. The sun was a shining golden coin overhead; an infinite treasure, a restorative battery whose energy never ran dry. After several weeks on the island, Maria was nearly the woman he remembered before she became unwell. Her dark eyes were once again bright and joyous, her olive skin seeming to sparkle in the light of their glorious benefactor.

'Well, I know why I love you,*' he replied teasingly. 'You're beautiful and kind and smart. I mean, I can barely speak a few words of Spanish. Your English is better than mine, and I'm supposed to be a writer.'*

'It's not,' she said, laughing. 'And you're a bloody talented writer.'

'So why do you love me?' he asked again.

'You're an extremely good person,' she said. 'And you always see the best in people.'

'I do?' he asked in amazement.

'Yes,' she said. 'You get angry sometimes. But you're very fair.'

'I do get angry a lot,' he admitted. 'Too often lately. It's the book. I'm sorry.'

'It's okay.'

They both were silent for a while. 'Why else do you love me?' he eventually asked.

'John!' she exclaimed in mock annoyance.

'Last time, I promise,' he said with a grin.

She went quiet for a time and stared down the beach at the sea. She appeared to listen to the whisper of the waves before replying.

'You're very strong,' she said at last. 'And you never give up on anything.'

John thought about this. 'I can be stubborn,' he agreed. 'And I try to be strong. But what about you? You left your family and friends and moved across Europe to be with me.'

She shook her head softly. 'I'm not strong.'

'You are,' he argued. 'You're the bubbliest person I know. You're always so positive. You make time for your friends and family even when you're feeling unwell. You've been there for me even when things have been hard this last year. I would call that strength.'

'I'm happy you think so,' Maria said. 'But I know I'm not strong.' Her eyes met his. Despite the sacrifices he had made for the sake of his book, the love he saw there burned as fiercely as ever. 'You're *my strength, John.'*

21

'John.'

He blinked. Old memories had swallowed him again without warning, like the whale from the famous story, rising from the abyss of his mind to engulf him until everything outside it ceased to exist.

'We're here,' said Kim. 'Are you with me?'

'Yes,' said John. 'Sorry, I was distracted.'

Kim's grey eyes narrowed slightly. 'Were you thinking about *her* again?'

'You mean Maria?' He didn't like the other woman's tone. 'She's my wife, and she's in danger. Of course I was thinking of her.'

He swallowed his annoyance and examined their surroundings. The fog had cleared, leaving only a few wispy tendrils to obscure his view of their destination. They were standing on the side of the road leading to Longleat Park. Ahead and to the right, Longleat House was a glorious monument to Elizabethan extravagance.

He and Maria had taken part in a tour of the building the year previous. The décor was certainly impressive, but the contrast between the opulence and inherited wealth of the estate, and the modest three-bedroom house he and

Maria had just bought, was galling. No one needed a house with 128 rooms and an art collection worth more than that of most national galleries.

A gigantic tent had been erected opposite the fountains in the house gardens. Military personnel in Multi-Terrain Pattern camouflage uniform swarmed the area, their faces covered in respiratory masks that from a distance made them look alien. A military blockade had been erected at the end of the road. Steel barriers and armoured trucks blocked access to anyone approaching the park from the surrounding area.

John felt his heart sink. There was no way he was going to be able to sneak past the soldiers without being spotted. Why had he been so sure he could overcome this obvious problem? Of late, he seemed to veer between overwhelming confidence and quiet despair. While he was silently berating himself and wondering what to do, Kim gave him a gentle nudge. 'Look,' she said excitedly, her mood shifting with the speed of a hummingbird in flight. 'They're packing up to leave.'

It was true, he realised. The masked soldiers were in the process of taking down the tent and loading their equipment into the vans parked nearby. John noticed dozens of white zip bags arranged on the garden lawn. The bags varied in size, from only a metre in length, to one big enough to contain a school bus, or something similarly proportioned.

'Should we wait until they've left?' John whispered to Kim.

Before she could reply, a camo-clad figure stepped out from the cover of a bush thirty feet ahead.

Kim took an involuntary step back, her grey eyes wide with panic. John tensed and thought about trying to make a break for it, but the soldier held up a hand. The guard carried an assault rifle under his arm, and though the barrel was not strictly aimed at the two of them, it was angled so that it left little to no doubt as to the potential consequences should they fail to obey.

'Halt,' the soldier commanded. His voice was a deep Northern growl that resonated authority. 'This is a restricted area. What are you doing here?'

'I'm looking for my wife,' John said, deciding honesty was the best approach. 'She works at the park. She didn't come home yesterday, and no one has been able to contact her.'

The soldier approached and halted a short distance from John. He tilted his masked head slightly, like a bird of prey trying to perceive the severity of a threat. 'You said she works at the park?' he asked. His voice had softened slightly.

'Yes,' John said uncertainly. Dread knotted his stomach.

'And who are you?' the soldier asked, turning to Kim.

'I'm a friend of John's,' she replied. She straightened her back and thrust out her chest, and her voice was suddenly steely, as authoritative as that of a college professor.

'Has either one of you set foot in the park in the last week?'

'No,' John said.

'No,' echoed Kim.

The soldier said nothing for a time. 'How can I be sure?' he said at last. 'We have no idea how contagious this is. If you've been inside the park—'

'We haven't,' John said, as firmly as he dared. 'I'm a writer. She's a student. I've barely been outside my own home in the last week.'

The soldier was silent again. He appeared to be weighing up his next words. 'I think you had both better come with me,' he said finally. 'Stick close.' He turned and made his way up the road, angling towards the huge tent in the gardens. John and Kim looked at each other and then hurried after him.

Other soldiers looked up as the two made their way into the military camp. Each wore one of the strange respiratory masks that reminded John of a Stormtrooper, or perhaps the Predator from his favourite childhood films. They concealed the faces of the soldiers so utterly that even their eyes were invisible behind the visors.

It must be an airborne virus, he realised. *The thing that's driving all the local wildlife crazy. That's why they're all wearing masks.*

As they neared the tent, two soldiers dragged what appeared to be a black rug across the grass towards a third soldier waiting beside a white zip bag. John stared at the dusky thing. With a rising foreboding, he realised that what he had taken to be a rug was in actuality a dead chimpanzee. Dark red streaked the ape's head from where a soldier had put a bullet in its skull.

Within the bag, the two soldiers positioned the dead chimp. Once a wonder of nature, now a bundle of soiled fur and decomposing meat. The third soldier reached down and slowly pulled on the zip until the body disappeared from sight.

'Go in,' ordered the guard who had guided them through camp. He thrust aside the large flap that served as the tent entrance and gestured at them to enter.

John stepped inside, Kim just behind him.

The interior of the tent had been converted into a full working office. Rows of desks were filled with laptops, printers, trays loaded with folders and papers, scientific journals, and other paraphernalia. A whiteboard had been positioned halfway down the tent so that it was visible from any given desk. Diagrams had been sketched in blue marker pen, cross-sections of the craniums of various mammalian species. Complex-looking formulae had been scribbled beside the diagrams. A large question mark had been hastily added beneath in red marker, next to which had been written the words: "No hope?"

No hope? For a second, John could've sworn he heard the words spoken aloud.

A tall man in an officer's uniform stood opposite the whiteboard. He, too, wore an alien-looking respiratory device over his face. As John and Kim entered the tent and hovered uncertainly just within, he turned and appeared to notice them. His hands went straight to his hips.

'What are you doing in here?' he demanded. His voice was the cut glass accent of the English upper-middle class. 'Where are your masks?'

John struggled for the words with which to respond when their guide entered the tent and threw a salute. 'Sir.

I found these civvies wandering around the area outskirts. Neither has been in proximity of the park in the last seven days. This gentleman claims that his wife works at the park. She has not been heard from since the attacks began.'

The officer's masked face turned from John to the soldier, and then back to John. He gave a slow shake of his head and released a heavy sigh. 'In the circumstances, I suppose I can't very well begrudge your presence here. I am Lieutenant Colonel Andrew McCormack, Warminster Garrison Commander. Please—join me in my office at the back.'

John and Kim made their way to the rear of the tent. Masked faces turned surreptitiously to regard them as they passed. John felt like a curiosity, some lesser life form being brought among advanced beings to be gawked at. The sense of being examined was overpowering.

In contrast, Kim seemed to revel in the attention. Somewhere on their trek up the country roads, she had put on her platform shoes again. She strode down the centre of the tent like some Gothic dame, the embodiment of feminine confidence and mystique.

John felt terribly out of place in his jeans and T-shirt and trainers. He wasn't a soldier or a scientist or an enchantress in black and purple. He was just a struggling writer desperate for some word of his estranged wife. What had the lieutenant colonel said?

In the circumstances.

The sense of dread he had felt since arriving at Longleat seemed to suck the strength from John's legs. He stumbled, and Kim reached out a steadying hand. 'Careful, John,' she said.

They joined Lieutenant Colonel McCormack at his desk. The officer sat arrow-straight on his chair, hands crossed on his desk as though preparing to deliver sombre news. John noticed that his fingers were long and slender—like those of a surgeon rather than a soldier.

'Before I begin, may I ask your name?' said the lieutenant colonel.

'John. John Sharrock,' John replied.

The officer's head turned to Kim. 'And you are, madam?'

'Lilith Von Goth,' she answered softly. Her voice had changed. The uncertainty and girlishness were gone, replaced by an assuredness of iron.

John glanced at the woman next to him in surprise. It was as if she had become a different person entirely.

You've become a different person entirely.

Alien words again, forming unbidden inside his head. Though, hadn't Maria said those words to him, once?

Lieutenant Colonel McCormack clapped his hand together suddenly, snapping John's attention back to the tent. The officer's expression was unknowable behind his mask. 'Mr Sharrock,' he began, 'what I am about to tell you may prove deeply upsetting. Would you prefer to discuss this in private?' The lieutenant colonel nodded meaningfully at Kim, or Lilith, or whatever his new acquaintance currently called herself.

'I…' John began. He glanced at the woman beside him. 'It's okay, she's a friend. What's going on?'

'Late yesterday afternoon,' began McCormack, 'my garrison was alerted to an emergency developing in Longleat park. The animals had begun to attack visitors to the park, as well as the keepers themselves. The attacks were unprovoked. Initially, we believed the attacks were a few isolated incidents. However, it quickly became clear that something more insidious was afoot. The attacks were not limited to predators, nor to species with a predisposition towards aggression. It was as though some sickness had infected the minds of every animal within the park. Lives were lost, some in the most tragic of circumstances.'

Maria, John thought in rising horror. Beneath the desk, he felt his legs begin to tremble.

'I wish that were the extent of the madness,' the lieutenant colonel continued. There was a deep weariness in his voice, as though he hadn't slept in some time. 'As you are likely by now aware, whatever sickness possessed the animals in Longleat appears to have already spread beyond the park, despite our best efforts to quarantine the threat. Animal attacks are increasing throughout Wiltshire at an alarming rate. At this point, our best guess as to the cause of the sickness is some kind of virus. It has yet to manifest in humans, but we can take no chances.' He tapped the front of his visor.

'What about the workers at the park?' John demanded. 'You said lives were lost. I need to find my wife! Do you understand?'

McCormack nodded. He spread his palms in placating fashion. 'Forgive me, Mr Sharrock. I thought it best to start at the beginning. Once it became apparent the situation in the park could not be salvaged, I was forced to order my men to destroy the animals within. We rescued those workers and visitors that survived. There were some casualties. I know this is difficult for you, but could you please tell me your wife's name?'

'M-Maria Sharrock,' John stammered. His voice shook, the trembling in his body so fierce he thought it might tear him apart. He felt a hand on his and saw Kim's fingers squeeze his own. Her fingernails were as black as his despair, but her strength nonetheless flowed into him, as though channelled from some bottomless well of eldritch power.

McCormack typed something on the laptop on his desk. His alien visor stared at the screen for a long moment.

'There's nothing on record,' he said at last, his voice heavy with relief. 'If she were among the deceased, it would show here.'

'Then, where is she?' John growled.

'We escorted everyone still within Longleat to safety. The survivors were taken to Warminster garrison. We recorded their details and have provided medical attention if necessary. Bear with me while I check the database.'

The officer tapped away at the keyboard. He stared at the screen. Then, he tapped some more. Another pause.

'Strange,' he said. 'There's nothing here about a "Maria Sharrock." You're certain she was present at the park during the attacks?'

'Where else would she be?' John demanded. 'Could your soldiers have somehow missed her?'

McCormack shook his head, but his voice contained the slightest hint of doubt. 'It is highly unlikely. The park itself is in rather a sorry state, however, so I suppose it is not completely outside the realms of possibility.'

'You need to go back and search for her,' John exclaimed. 'She's still inside the park. Don't ask me how I know, I just do.'

'I am sorry, Mr Sharrock,' said McCormack. 'We must evacuate the area immediately. My regiment has been ordered back to Warminster garrison. This…*phenomenon*, whatever it is, has become a regional emergency. Everyone within a fifty-mile radius of Longleat is to be relocated to another part of the country until the government has a handle on the situation.'

'No,' cried John angrily. 'You can't do this! I'm not going anywhere until Maria is found!'

'Mr Sharrock—' McCormack began, but John cut him off.

'Let me look for her,' he demanded. 'I'll wear a mask. I know my way around the park. Please,' he continued, gesturing at the band around the lieutenant colonel's finger. 'I see you're married. You understand. I can't leave without finding my wife. I can't.'

McCormack appeared to hesitate.

'*Please*,' John begged. He had never begged before in his life.

A long silence followed.

'As you wish,' McCormack said eventually. He sighed and sat back in his chair. 'You understand the danger, yes? Most of the animals were neutralised, but a few evaded my soldiers. These predators may still be in the area. I assume this young woman won't be going with you?'

It took John a moment to realise his hand was stinging. Kim's fingernails were digging into his flesh, hard enough to draw blood. 'I'll go alone,' he said.

'Very well. Once you have concluded your search, make your way to Warminster garrison with all haste. I wish you godspeed. Now, if there is nothing else—'

'There are two men stranded on the road back to Shearwater,' John cut in, remembering Adam and Justin. He couldn't shake the feeing he had abandoned them and left them to their fate. He'd had no choice but to leave. Hadn't he?

At least the shaking in his legs had subsided. He had a task on which to focus. Something he could control. 'They were being transported to hospital in an ambulance van when it hit a tree. They're in a serious condition and require urgent help.'

'I will send a medic immediately,' McCormack promised.

'Thank you.' Something suddenly occurred to John. 'You know…I thought I saw a red star in the sky last night. Do you know anything about it?'

McCormack froze as though he'd just been slapped. 'It's best you don't speak of that,' he said angrily, his sonorous voice now an urgent hiss. 'Forget all about it. Do you understand me? You could destroy everything.'

'Yes. Sorry,' John said, shocked. He backed slowly away from the desk. He had no idea what had upset the man.

'Good,' said the lieutenant colonel. He appeared to relax, his agitation forgotten as quickly as it had occurred. 'I wish you luck finding your wife, Mr Sharrock.'

****

Once they had been escorted back out of the tent, John stood next to Kim and watched the camp in silence for a while. Something troubled him. He stared down at the mask McCormack had handed him.

'Did anything about that strike you as odd?' he asked Kim. 'It all seemed…too easy. Too convenient. The soldier just letting us pass. The lieutenant colonel's explanation about the local animal life going crazy. Did you see the way he reacted when I mentioned the red star in the sky? I don't trust him.'

'What are you saying, John?' Kim watched him curiously. There was a strange look in her eyes. She seemed almost amused.

'I don't know. This just all feels wrong. Even the ant swarm back in the forest. There must be billions of insects all around us. Why aren't they attacking at this very moment? There's something McCormack isn't telling us, Kim. I need to get to the bottom of this. But first, I need to find Maria.'

Quite unexpectedly, Kim tutted. John glanced at her, puzzled. 'What's wrong?'

'What's wrong? You know what's wrong, John. You keep talking about her.'

‘*Her?* You mean Maria? She’s my wife.’

Kim’s lips twisted. ‘So you keep saying.’

John shrugged helplessly. What had gotten into Kim? He lifted the respiratory mask and placed it on his face, preparing to head into the park.

‘So, this is it? You’re leaving?’

Kim was glaring at him. John stared back through the glass visor. Her grey eyes were narrowed, and her pale cheeks were flushed. John adjusted the mask once. With the apparatus over his face, his breathing felt laboured, the respiratory tube seeming to steal the air from his lungs and spit it back only with great reluctance.

‘I have to do this alone,’ he said. ‘It’s dangerous. Go with the soldiers, Kim. You’ll be safe in the army garrison.’

‘She doesn’t love you anymore,’ Kim said abruptly.

John reeled in surprise. ‘What did you just say?’ he growled.

‘She’s moved on, John. You’re not together. Why do you care what happens to her?’

Now, it was John’s turn to feel himself go hot with anger. ‘What sort of question is that? We’ve been married nine years. What kind of man abandons his wife?’

‘You did,’ she said nastily. ‘You know you did.’

John reeled as though he’d been struck. ‘What…what are you talking about?’

‘It doesn’t matter,’ Kim said. ‘You should focus on the future and not the past. I’m sorry, John, but she’s probably dead. It would be easier for you to give up now.’

‘I never give up,’ John snarled.

They stood there facing each other in the grey morning light, faceless soldiers milling around them. The scientist and the writer, a word and an equation, written in the firmament upon the scars of creation.

‘I’d better go,’ John said, breaking the silence.

Kim sneered. ‘Leave, then. *Leave*, like you always do.’

‘Like I always do? We’ve only just met, Kim. You don’t know anything about me.’

Kim crossed her arms. Suddenly, she was a young girl again, the hurt on her face disarming John’s anger and making his heart ache. She backed up a few steps, then spun around, hurling her phone at the ground so hard it broke apart. She hurried away without a backward glance.

John watched her go, then picked up the pieces of her phone and put them in his backpack. Confusion warred with a deep sense of sadness. He forced himself to calm, took as deep a breath as he could manage with the respiratory mask covering his face.

He made his way to the blockade opposite the entrance to the park. The guard on duty put his hand out, ordering John to stop. The soldier’s radio crackled. He appeared to listen to someone relaying orders on the other end.

A moment later, the guard waved John through.

John Sharrock approached Longleat Safari and Adventure Park. The entrance opened before him like the maw of some great beast. It was only when he was very near the threshold that he noticed the dark stains on the ground. The large hole in the wall, as though something had smashed its way out.

'*What happened here?*' John whispered.

22

Twenty Hours Earlier

Bob Davis winced and rubbed his back. It had been a tough few days. First, poor young Savannah had been savaged by the animal she adored, Charlie the chimpanzee. Then, this very morning, Nico the gorilla had taken unexpectedly ill.

Bob himself had helped the park staff carry the magnificent animal to the boat. Even heavily tranquillised, the proud king of Gorilla Island had been a fearsome sight to behold up close. Yet, there had been a strange look in the silverback's eyes: confusion and perhaps even a little fear. It was hard to imagine such a mighty creature being afraid of anything. It was easy to believe he would live forever, that he was as immortal as time itself. But Nico was old. Perhaps now, at last, he was nearing the end.

Bob hoped he was wrong. The sentinel of Half Mile Pond had been his silent companion on the lake for years. A familiar, albeit leathery, face that had greeted him morning and night. A four-hundred-pound anchor to keep him from drifting into troubled waters when times got tough. Bob prayed that Nico received whatever care he needed from the park veterinarians and pulled through.

The younger visitors to the park absolutely adored the big silverback gorilla.

The thought of smiling youngsters instantly made him think of his own grandchildren. His daughter was bringing them over later that evening. He was so proud of her his heart could burst. The chemo had been incredibly hard on the entire family. Advanced ovarian cancer had a poor outlook, but she'd remained positive and made it against the odds.

She's a Valleys girl, he reminded himself. *Hard as the rock my pa once worked.*

Bob had come to southwest England in the late 80s after the government had closed most of the UK's surviving coal mines. He had been young then and had never personally set foot in a working mine himself—the water was more to his liking—but he remained proud of his roots.

He still harboured some vague hope that a successful Brexit would lead to a rebirth of the mining industry, a return to the storied days of his father and his father before him. His daughter told him he was being silly, that the pits were a thing of the past.

He conceded she probably had a point, but it wasn't always easy to let go and accept change, accept that something you grew up knowing in your bones to be true was now as obsolete as the telegram.

'Here you go, Bob,' said the fellow behind the counter, a new caterer whose name Bob had yet to remember. The Welshman gratefully accepted the proffered sausage-in-a-bun with one hand and took his small handful of change in the other. He stared at it in consternation, one bushy eyebrow raised. 'Blimey. Food prices have shot up and no mistake.'

'You're lucky I have anything left,' the food vendor replied busily. 'The park's been heaving this morning. Half-term, I guess.'

Bob took a bite of his sausage and wiped sticky ketchup from his moustache with the back of his hand. He looked out over the food court, took in the bustling crowds. There were many children milling around, eyes wide with excitement. A few young brows were furrowed as irritable children dragged their parents to one of the confectionary stalls or overpriced restaurants.

A hungry child was as dangerous as any of the wild species in the park, Bob thought wryly. Longleat would make a killing this week if visitor numbers kept up. It was just a shame the weather wasn't playing ball. The sky was covered in dark black clouds that looked likely to shed their burden at any moment.

He was about to make his way back to the boat when he spotted a familiar face over by the churro stand. He shuffled over and waved in greeting. 'All right, Maria, love?'

She turned, a churro raised halfway to her mouth. She lowered it guiltily and smiled at him. Maria was often smiling or laughing. Though maybe not quite so often of late. Despite her warm expression, her eyes were tinged with sadness. 'Hey, Bob. I'm just getting lunch.'

'One of your five a day, eh?' he joked, gesturing at the churro.

'Just a quick snack before I go back to the Village,' replied Maria. The African Village was the first stop on the Drive Thru Safari on the other side of Half Mile Pond. Maria had been working there for the past few weeks. One of the zebras was very close to giving birth, and Maria was excited about witnessing the event in person. She spoke often about having children of her own. Or at least she had up until recently.

Something had happened between her and her husband. Bob didn't like to pry. He was just there to offer her support and a kind word when she needed it. She reminded him of his own daughter, the same lust for life, the way she could brighten the place just by walking into a room.

'You're eating right, though, aren't you?' he asked, unable to resist the fatherly impulse to check she was looking after herself. She looked tired, though that might be because of all the extra shifts since the incident with Savannah.

'Yes,' she replied. 'Well…I'm trying! It's difficult, living with my friend and…with everything else happening.' She looked at the ground.

'Aye, I can imagine,' Bob said sympathetically. 'Besides, who am I to say what's healthy and what's not?' He winked at her and waved his sausage-in-a-bun around to demonstrate his point. Someone walked past and jostled him, and the sausage slipped from his grasp. 'Ah, bollocks,' he said, staring mournfully down at his spoiled lunch.

'Oh no, Bob!' Maria exclaimed. 'Wait, let me get you another.' She immediately set off towards the sausage-in-a-bun van, one hand digging through her bag for her purse.

‘Hey, now don’t be silly!’ Bob exclaimed. ‘It was my own bloody fault. Besides, I need to lose a few pounds.’ He patted his stomach ruefully.

‘You don’t,’ she said, laughing

‘I do. I look ruddy pregnant.’ Pain flashed on Maria’s face, and Bob immediately regretted his jest. ‘Sorry, lass,’ he said. ‘Did I say the wrong thing?’

‘No, no, it’s fine,’ Maria replied. She smiled to reassure him, but there was a moistness in her soft brown eyes now. ‘I need to use the bathroom before I head back to work.’

‘Aye, lunch time’s over,’ Bob replied, pretending to check his watch, feeling guilty.

But to his surprise, Maria embraced him. Her voice was filled with warmth as she said, ‘Thanks for stopping to say hello. Have a lovely day, Bob.’

‘You, too, lass,’ he replied, returning her hug with a fierceness that surprised him. ‘Chin up.’

He watched Maria hurry off towards the public toilets. Just as he was turning away to head back to his boat, he noticed a strange fellow lurking nearby. A cap concealed the man’s face, and there was something peculiar about him, a sense of wrongness he couldn’t quite put his finger on.

A century ago, Welsh miners exploring new sections of cave would bring along canaries to detect the presence of dangerous gases before it could poison them. If this man were an undiscovered cave, Bob reckoned a canary would drop dead within seconds of exposure to him.

Making a mental note to mention the fellow to security, Bob made his way back to the boat. The Welshman spent the next couple of hours ferrying visitors back and forth across the lake. Some of the guests were disappointed not to see Nico, the park's famous gorilla. Not wanting to upset the young ones, Bob told them the silverback was resting in his private house on the island. He explained that the gorilla got very grumpy if he missed his favourite cartoons in the afternoon, which amused the children to no end.

Just before four in the afternoon, rain came down, and the stranger with the cap got on the boat.

Bob noticed him straight away. He was of average height, lean and muscular, but beyond that, it was hard to make out his features. His hat seemed to cast his face in shadow, left Bob guessing if what he was seeing was facial hair or a trick of the light, if the stranger's eyes were brown or amber or something else, some colour that defied description. His very presence made Bob uncomfortable.

The ageing Welshman was desperate for him to disembark the boat along with the other guests as soon as they reached shore. But as Bob finished delivering his speech about Gorilla Island—a canned explanation he had given a thousand times—and guided the boat towards the docking platform, a chill enveloped him.

He turned his head to see the stranger standing right behind him.

'Tell me,' said the man, his eyes seeming to glitter from the shadows that covered his face, 'where is the tiger?'

Bob wasn't a man for complicated words, but one came unbidden to him then, a word that summed up the stranger's voice as completely as a snake swallowed a newborn chick.

Insidious.

'The tiger?' Bob repeated dumbly. He was transfixed by the stranger's smile. It seemed wrong, his teeth slightly too large for his mouth… 'It— That is, you can't get to it unless you're in a vehicle,' he mumbled. 'It's part of the safari trail.'

'Which part?' the stranger asked patiently. His expression didn't alter a fraction.

'You…you turn right just before the African Village,' Bob said. 'As I said, you need a car—'

He blinked. The stranger was gone. Bob docked the boat and let the passengers off. He didn't spot the stranger among the disembarking guests.

He spent the next hour questioning what he had witnessed, wondering if he was going mad.

He had just finished ferrying across the final lot of passengers before his shift ended, listening to the patter of the rain on the lake, when he heard the screams.

23

She knelt beside the expectant mare. The animal snorted in protest, and she placed a hand on the zebra's head sympathetically. 'It's okay,' she said softly. 'I know, it's hard. Not long now.'

It had been a very long time already. Zebras had a gestation period of thirteen months, the longest of any member of the horse family. The expectant mother met her eyes and, as if reading her thoughts, gave an exasperated whinny.

The rain continued to pour down. It had been raining since early afternoon, and her clothes were drenched. She didn't mind. The rain helped disguise her tears.

'Good girl. Let me get you a treat,' she said, giving the animal another stroke. She squelched across the soaked grass towards the feed shed, pausing to wave at a safari van as it splashed down the road. The looks of delight on the faces of the passengers always made her smile, even in times such as these.

As she opened the shed door, the honk of a car horn sounded from deeper in the safari park.

She shook her head in disapproval, wet brown hair dancing wildly over her shoulders. Car horns were discouraged—loud noises could startle the animals.

Was someone shouting? What was going on today?

She peered out of the shed, a basket of apples under one arm. A giraffe skittered into view. It looked spooked.

She exited the shed, froze when she heard another shout followed by a scream. A car horn honked again, and this time it kept on going, an endless whine that made her nerves rattle. What was going on?

The zebra herd melted out of the rain. Something was terribly wrong with them. The eyes of the animals were wide with terror, their ears pressed against their heads in fear. One of the animals bolted, almost knocking her over in its panic.

Shaken, she collected the apples that had spilled out the basket in the near collision and wiped rainwater out of her eyes. That was when she saw the expectant mare.

The zebra was on its side, breathing wetly. Blood soaked the grass where its throat had been torn open. Its eyes met hers one last time, terrified, uncomprehending.

The growl of a tiger split the air. The basket fell from her suddenly nerveless fingers, apples spilling everywhere. It sounded like a demon escaping from the gates of Hell. Like innocence lost.

Like the dying of a dream.

****

Denise Robinson stared glumly out of the windscreen of her Toyota Corolla. It wasn't the park or the weather that were responsible for her present gloom. It was the stacks of accounts waiting for her back at the office, a mountain of paperwork that would take her months to get through.

The new tax year was underway, and her clients were all desperate to reduce their liabilities for the coming year. There was also the looming issue of a potential Brexit. No one quite knew how much extra administrative and bookkeeping overhead a vote to exit the European Union would create for British industry.

She supposed all the extra business would be good for her accountancy firm, but what was the point in spending every waking hour staring at spreadsheets and tax return forms if she had no time to spend with her nearest and dearest?

The problem was, she couldn't say no. The clients kept on queuing for her accounting services, attracted by the excellent reputation she had established. She made a point of going that extra mile wherever possible. She had spent the best part of yesterday afternoon researching the finer points of Hungarian double taxation law for one of her clients, the author. She supposed she ought to charge him extra for her time but, in truth, she hadn't even charged him for the last two years of her services.

The car's windscreen wipers scraped the scratched and pitted glass. The rain was falling heavier now, beating at the roof of the Corolla like a thousand tiny feet stamping in unison. She was lucky the old rust bucket hadn't yet sprung a leak.

Her husband had told her to take the Corolla and leave the expensive new BMW at home. The monkeys at the park were notorious for clambering over shiny vehicles and pulling off anything they could detach with their mischievous paws. In all probability, the Toyota was worth less than the expensive rosewood dresser taking up both the boot and the rear seats. Denise had picked it up earlier that morning from an antique dealer in Longbridge Deverill.

Antiques were her guilty pleasure. Two large rooms of her office space were already packed to bursting with vintage furniture. Real estate rarely lost money and a good pension plan could reap dividends, but a carefully chosen antique, now *that* was the ultimate investment.

Denise Robinson stared out through the rain-swept safari park, trying to glimpse one of the animal residents and dreaming of where to put her new rosewood desk, when she spotted a figure over by the wire mesh fence. The barrier separated the safari trail into zones for each of the animal groups. The larger predators were each kept in their own highly secure area. The stranger seemed to sense her watching him and turned.

He wore jeans and a T-shirt, making no concessions to the weather. Rainwater poured off the lid of the cap he wore. She couldn't see his face but somehow knew he was smiling at her. He raised his arms, and she saw that he was holding a pair of wire cutters. He turned back to the fence.

Denise felt a deep chill pass through her. Something about the man seemed terribly *wrong*, like an accounting error that went undiscovered until it was too late. She thought about stopping the car and getting out to ask him what he was up to, but the sudden honk of a car horn jerked her attention back to the road.

A car raced towards her, fog lights glaring like the tractor beam of some alien starship. The driver didn't appear to see her, or else didn't care.

'You're going the wrong way!' she shrieked. She pulled the steering wheel hard to the left, saw the onrushing vehicle screech around her at the last possible moment. It roared on down the road, the driver heedless of the fact he or she had almost caused a terrible accident.

Denise Robinson collapsed back in the driving seat. Her heart raced. She'd been moments from a serious collision. She almost wanted to laugh. The car would have been no great loss, but she rather enjoyed being alive. She turned to examine her rosewood desk, worried that it had taken a knock when she had been forced to steer wildly away from the onrushing vehicle. She breathed another sigh of relief. It was unharmed.

A thought occurred to her. What was she even doing in the safari park? She had driven to Longbridge Deverill to pick up the desk, clearly, but afterwards…

Another car horn trumpeted. This one was far louder than the last, and it took her a moment to realise it was not a car horn at all. It sounded…*like an elephant?*

A massive shape lumbered out of the rain. Denise watched in stunned horror as it thumped down the road towards her, tree trunk legs shaking the earth with every stride. It paused just before it reached her. Its trunk seemed to probe the windscreen, searching for a weakness. Two shining orbs of crimson malice stared down at her, leaving no doubt as to the monster's intent.

'Please, not the desk,' Denise said softly, transfixed. She placed a protective hand on the antique. The elephant bellowed in fury and reared up on its hind legs.

Like the fist of an angry god, eight tons of raging elephant smashed down.

****

The Bat Cave was every bit as terrifying as he'd feared.

Gary Pike wasn't a fan of dark places or small, furry bloodsuckers. His daughter had assured him the Egyptian Fruit variety fed only on fruit and leaves. The same couldn't be said of the eight-legged monstrosity staring at him just then with its multitude of eyes.

'Rosie,' read his daughter. 'It says she's a…Chilling Rose Tarantula.'

'*Chilean,*' corrected Gary. He placed a hand on his daughter's shoulder. 'Come away from the glass, sweetie.'

'But, Dad…she's just a spider. Spiders don't hurt people. Do they?'

'Not usually,' Gary allowed. There was something about the way the tarantula was twitching that unsettled him. Though it would be fair to say he'd been unsettled ever since his daughter had convinced him to visit the Bat Cave with her. How could he say no? She was fearless, an intrepid adventurer. Her mother had been much the same. Both quite unlike him, Gary Pike, Warminster's third-best real estate agent.

'Can we check out the bats now? Please?'

'Okay. But stick close to me,' he said, as much for his benefit as hers.

The bat enclosure was packed with visitors to the park. He saw the same nervous smiles on the faces of other parents that he was certain was plastered across his own. As he stepped into the near lightless section of the man-made cave, the colony of bats suddenly detached from the slimy ceiling and swooped to the opposite end in a flurry of fluttering wings and high-pitched squeaks. The effect was incredibly eerie.

Laughter and delighted shrieks echoed through the cave. His daughter squeezed his hand and squealed. Gary squeezed his daughter's hand in return and tried to calm his racing heart.

'Did it scare you?' he asked as the bats settled down.

'Yes,' she replied.

'Me, too.'

She looked at him and scrunched up her face. 'Don't be silly,' she said assuredly. 'Nothing scares you.'

He chuckled and ruffled her hair. 'Let's get some ice cream,' he said.

The crowd dispersed, though one figure at the back of the cave remained. He leaned against the wall, arms folded, features hidden in the shadow of his hat. Gary immediately had a bad feeling about the fellow.

He put his arm around his daughter's shoulder and guided their path away from him. The sinister figure smiled suddenly, teeth seeming to glow from the shadows of his face, and brought two fingers to his mouth, as though whistling for someone, or something. No sound emerged, but Gary felt a sudden stab of pain in his skull. He shook his head and hurried towards the exit.

Even the muted light of a rainy day was bright compared with the dimness of the cave. Gary blinked a few times, waiting for his sight to adjust. The man in the cave had unsettled him. Luckily, the little miracle beside him chased away the anxiety like the sun chased away the clouds.

'Ice cream or crepes?' he asked her.

'Both,' his daughter said, her eyes shining.

'Hey, I'm not made of money,' he said, grinning. In truth, he'd received a decent bonus this month after a solid year of house sales. It had started off strong with the pretty Spanish lady and her writer husband purchasing their first property from him. One could never predict the future, Gary reasoned. Best to enjoy the present while you could. 'How about we begin with ice cream and maybe we can think about crepes before we leave tonight? A special treat for the birthday girl.'

Her delighted grin was the best reward a father could ask for. He looked around for an ice cream vendor.

'Look, Dad,' she said suddenly. 'Wolves.'

'What?' he said distractedly, unsure if he'd heard her right.

'Wolves,' she repeated. He felt her fingers tighten around his.

He finally looked at where she pointed.

He froze.

Two large wolves padded towards them, their fur dark wet. Their muzzles were bloody, pink drool hanging from mouths bristling with teeth. Other visitors noticed the wolves, and then the screams began. One of the wolves growled and leapt at an older woman, knocking her to the ground. Its jaws closed around her neck.

Panic seized hold of Gary with an iron grip. It was all he could do to scoop his daughter up and stare wildly around for some place safe. He ran back towards the Bat Cave, plunging into the darkness, heart racing like it was about to burst. He slipped on something, bat guano maybe, and fell hard, though he managed to shield his daughter from the fall.

'Daddy?' she said, terror in her voice now. 'Daddy, get up!'

He struggled to rise, his knees feeling like someone had taken a hammer to them. Maybe the wolves would go in search of other prey, maybe the park security would stop them before—

A howl echoed through the cave, and Gary Pike knew that all his worst fears had come true.

****

Bob Davis spun the boat around as quickly as he could manage, powering the vehicle back towards the docking platform. The light was beginning to fade with the onset of evening, but he saw the same crowd he had only just dropped off waving their arms around desperately. They were screaming and shouting in panic.

One of them looked around wildly, then leapt into the lake. Bob watched the rippling water, transfixed, waiting for their head to re-emerge, prepared to dash over to the emergency life vest and toss it to them in case they couldn't swim. But no one resurfaced.

A blood-curdling roar tore through the dusk air. Bob's mouth dropped open in shock as several large, feline shapes appeared and pounced on the guests, mauling them without a shred of mercy. It was the lions, he realised. Somehow, they had escaped their enclosure. But even in the wilds, a lion would steer clear of people unless the predators were old or sick or starving. The young pride that Longleat had housed the last few years was none of those things. What the hell was going on?

Bob Davis didn't have the foggiest, but he'd be damned if he would hide out on the water while innocents were being slaughtered. 'Come on, you heap of junk,' he bellowed at the boat as it ate up the final stretch of lake. Some of the guests were trying to fight back against the pride. It was a losing battle, Bob knew. Nonetheless, he ploughed on towards shore.

A colossal shape suddenly barrelled into the water. It struck Half Mile Pond with an impact that felt to Bob like the meteor that had wiped out the dinosaurs. Water exploded into the sky, pouring furiously over the side of the boat, which rocked and tilted drunkenly. The Welshman stared at the struggling titan in utter disbelief.

Is that a ruddy elephant?

Two lithe, lupine shapes splashed down into the water to either side of the boat and joined the elephant as it swam south towards the opposite shore. Towards the main park and thousands of unsuspecting guests all packed closely together…

Bob thrust his fears aside as he finally reached the wooden docking platform. He grabbed the anchor from his tiny office. In truth the anchor was mostly decorative, since the boat never left the lake, but the heavy iron object was something he could use to attempt to fend off the lions.

As he stepped off the boat, however, he saw that he was too late. The last of the victims was being dragged over the blood-soaked grass by her head, which was caught in the jaws of the largest lion. The dying woman thrashed wildly, but even as Bob hobbled over the platform and raised the metal anchor threateningly, she went as limp as a child's doll.

A moment later, she slid out of the beast's mouth. The animal fixed its gaze on Bob, who saw that the lion's eyes were wrong somehow. They appeared to be flecked with blood, as though something had detonated in the animal's brain. The rest of the lions turned to Bob, who was now surrounded.

The Welshman felt terror threaten to unman him. Then, he thought of his daughter. How she'd fought back against the cancer killing her. She hadn't surrendered, and neither would her father.

Let the proud die fighting the pride.

He bellowed at the top of his lungs, took a step forward and swung the anchor. The lions seemed to hesitate. He took another step forward. 'Come on, you bastards,' he shouted.

The lions turned and ran.

Bob stared after the fleeing pride, too stunned to move. He looked around. The ground was littered with the dead—at least a dozen men and women slaughtered in less time than it took to dispose of a trapped mouse. The carnage was overwhelming, and Bob had to stop himself from bringing up what little lunch he had eaten earlier that afternoon. He stared helplessly at the bodies, not knowing what to do. Nothing had ever prepared him for this kind of disaster.

He was still wondering whether to go look for help or take the boat back to the opposite shore and warn the park staff when a familiar face burst through the bushes lining the side of the lake.

'Maria?' he called in astonishment.

She was soaked with rainwater or sweat or both, her thick brown hair a sodden mess. Her makeup had run everywhere. She panted for breath, her clothes a muddy ruin.

'Tiger,' she said, her voice shaking. She pointed behind her with a trembling finger. She noticed the bodies then and released a strangled gasp.

Bob immediately understood. 'Forget them for now,' he said urgently. 'Get to the boat.'

Together, they raced down the platform and hurled themselves on the boat. *Come on, come on,* Bob urged, silently begging the boat engine to kick into gear. They eased away from the dock just as the tiger melted into view.

It was majestic, dwarfing the lions. A male Amur tiger in the prime of its years, the world's most perfect killing machine. Bob understood then that the pride hadn't run away from him, they had fled the coming of this unstoppable predator, the deadliest thing in Longleat.

The great cat watched the boat with huge, luminous eyes. Its striped body slunk down to the wooden platform with appalling grace.

‘Can tigers swim?’ Bob asked, dreading the answer.

‘They are excellent swimmers,’ replied Maria shakily, confirming his worst fears. They watched the killer approach the water and prod at it with claws that could dismember a man in a single swipe.

‘We gotta get to the other side,’ Bob growled. ‘We gotta call security. Call the police. Call the ruddy *army*. What’s happening, Maria?’

‘I-I don’t know,’ she replied haltingly. She sounded broken. Confused. Like everything she had thought to be true had proven horribly wrong. Bob felt the sudden urge to put his arm around her, to let her know everything would be all right. But then he saw the tiger had disappeared and knew that would be another lie.

They were almost at the opposite shore when he saw the shape closing on them in the water. He glimpsed the tiger’s eyes glittering in the darkness, the implacable stare of the predator fixed upon them, and he knew what that meant.

The side of the boat finally pulled level with the wooden platform. ‘Off,’ Bob ordered Maria. ‘Get yourself to safety.’

She obeyed, and he stepped off the platform beside her before stopping and turning to face the lake. When she saw he wasn’t following, she turned back. ‘What are you doing?’ she asked.

‘There’s something I need to do,’ he growled. He raised the anchor. ‘Go! Run, and don’t stop running until you’ve found safety. I said, RUN!’

She gave another strangled gasp. Something golden slipped from her neck as she turned and finally did as he demanded, running from the lake and back towards the adventure park, towards the safety of numbers. Bob stared at the glittering object on the ground and turned back to Half Mile Pond. He watched the dark shape arrowing towards him with a surprising sense of calm. It was only a few seconds from reaching him.

Hopefully, he could delay the tiger long enough for Maria to reach safety. He thought of his own daughter again then, and his granddaughter. He wished he could tell them how much he adored them one final time. But that was the way life went, sometimes. He reckoned they already knew.

He glanced at the water again, expecting to see the striped killing machine emerge at any moment. There was nothing. Bob Davis narrowed his eyes, wondering where the beast had gone.

He was still wondering when hippos burst from the lake to either side of him, their cavernous jaws gaping wide, and bit him apart.

****

She ran. Terror filled her, lent strength to her tired limbs, but the grief in her heart was unbearable. She wanted to lie down and die. She wanted to claw her eyes out. She wanted to scream until her voice shattered and her chest collapsed.

She wasn't the only one screaming. The madness on the safari trail had reached this part of Longleat, too. She caught glimpses of senseless chaos as she sought safety. Fragments of isolated horror reflected incompletely, as though from shards of a broken mirror. An elephant smashing through the walls surrounding the park, striking them with such force that it broke off a tusk and collapsed to its knees. A woman rolling on the ground as a huge constrictor snake squeezed the life from her chest, her family trying futilely to pull the serpent off, hitting it with handbags and water bottles. A troop of monkeys mauling a middle-aged man, biting at his fingers, plucking greedily at his eyes while they howled in savage glee.

She tried every place she could find to hide, tried to escape the danger, but it was all around her, suffocating her, hungry to pull her apart. Her family was a thousand miles away. She was all alone.

John had always been there to protect her. Her strength. Now, he was gone.

She closed her eyes and ears to the horror going on around her and hid in the last place she hoped the madness couldn't find her. She curled up into a ball, hugged herself, and prayed to God. She didn't move when the gunshots sounded. Nor when she heard the shouts of angry men calling back and forth outside her hiding place.

Darkness fell, and still she remained in her safe place. The relentless rain sought to drown her. The merciless stars gazed down cruelly upon her, laughing at her. This guileless, too-trusting child, a lamb in a pitiless world.

Still, she prayed.

2011

'Do you ever pray?'

He looked up from the laptop screen. Maria watched him with a worried expression. She placed a steaming cup down on the tiny IKEA kitchen table that doubled as his desk and hovered by him uncertainly.

'Thanks,' he murmured. He blew on the hot tea. 'Why do you ask?'

'I...was just curious, that's all.'

He sat back in the dining chair. His back hurt, his butt hurt, and his neck was beginning to ache. The writing setup wasn't ideal, but it was the best they could manage in their tiny, one-bedroom flat. The place had recently become infested with spiders, and they were both finding hard it to sleep without imagining tiny black shapes scuttling over them at night. 'Not often,' he admitted. 'I think prayer serves a purpose...but I prefer to place my belief in myself. At least when it comes to things I can affect.'

She thought about this for a moment and nodded. 'You know I like to pray.'

'Of course.' He smiled at her. 'Maybe I should join you at church sometime. Maybe around Christmas time?'

'That would be nice.' She looked past him.

'Maria…are you okay?' he asked, concerned by the shadow he saw in her expression.

'I found a letter from the credit card company,' she blurted out. 'Two letters, actually. John, we owe almost fifteen thousand pounds!'

For moment, he was too surprised to speak. 'What were you doing looking through my things?' he asked, anger warring with shame. He hadn't wanted to worry her. This was his mess to deal with.

'I was just tidying,' she replied. 'I didn't mean to. How do we owe so much?'

John took a deep breath, trying to quash his rising annoyance. 'Weddings are expensive,' he said reasonably. 'Plus, the flights, moving to Warminster…all these things cost money.'

'Still…' she began, not quite willing to give voice to the rest of the sentence.

'What is it?' he insisted.

'I've been talking to my family,' she said, the words leaving her mouth in a hurry now she had decided to open the gates. 'They're worried, John. You haven't worked for over a year now.'

'I got laid off,' he said angrily. 'And I have been working. Contract work, here and there. It's not much, I know, but at least I'm contributing something while I write my book.'

'I'm happy you're writing a book,' Maria assured him. 'But all the money I earn is going on bills, and we're still fifteen thousand pounds in debt.'

'I *am fifteen thousand pounds in debt,' John insisted heatedly. 'Not you.' He saw the hurt in her eyes and got up out of the chair to place his hands comfortingly on her shoulders. 'Look,' he said, 'I've just signed with an agent. He thinks this book could be huge. I have it in me to do something great. Just wait and see.'*

'I hope you're right,' she replied. She didn't quite meet his eyes.

'Trust me, Maria,' he implored her. 'I love you.'

'I trust you.' This time, she met his gaze, and the adoration in her smile doused the embers of his anger like cold water over hot coals. 'And I love you, too.'

24

The Present

The park was a ruined, twisted mockery of the place he remembered.

John Sharrock padded silently through the wreckage of Longleat Safari and Adventure Park. The café to his left, an overpriced but colourful diner he and Maria had taken shelter in during one memorably stormy visit, was a nightmare of broken glass with bullet holes punched into its lurid façade.

To his right, the mirror maze was similarly shattered by gunfire. The jagged hole in the wall John had noticed upon entering the park was surrounded by collapsed masonry. Upon further examination, he saw a huge, ivory tusk resting forlornly on the rubble. John walked over and bent down to pick up the strange object. It had been snapped off near the base. He suddenly remembered the gigantic white zip bag in the estate gardens and knew then what had befallen the park's prized African elephant.

If this virus could drive even a bull elephant crazy, what hope did anything else have of resisting the sickness? He remembered what Lieutenant Colonel McCormack had told him back at the command tent.

Most of the animals were neutralised, but a few evaded my soldiers.

John thought that perhaps he should have asked the military officer for a weapon.

The food court was in an even worse state than the entrance to the park. John stared at the carnage with a deep sense of sadness. Everything was destroyed. The places he and Maria had eaten at, the spots where they had sat and laughed and talked about their dreams for the future. All ruined. How had it come to this?

He walked slowly between overturned tables and broken chairs, stepped around a sign advertising fresh churros that was covered in dried blood. The sweet pastry was one of Maria's favourite treats. The sight of the wooden board so despoiled felt like sacrilege.

The ground was littered with bullet casings, a violent rain that had stripped all life from the park in the military's effort to contain the sickness. Discarded food and drink containers spilled their contents over the damp tiles. As John stepped over a half-eaten sausage-in-a-bun, a memory suddenly popped into his mind.

Maria's father had stopped his battered old SEAT to grab a *chorizo*-in-a-bun from a roadside food stall during one of John's early visits to Spain. It was something his own father might have done, 20 years and thousands of miles removed, before his accident. A small but powerful reminder that despite the language and cultural differences, people were largely the same the world over.

John had grown to love Maria's father. He was an intimidating figure, at least at first. A broad-shouldered, serious-looking man, he was for many years the sole breadwinner for his family, a provider who would leave for work at 6am and not return until evening to ensure his daughters had food on the table and the best schooling he could afford for them.

Though the communication barrier had been tricky at first—the two men had spoken very little of each other's languages—John had since come to learn that Maria's father was a passionate, loving patriarch who possessed the same essential goodness that John so cherished about Maria.

The fog on the road to Longleat had sprung up again without warning. It enveloped the park in a ghostly miasma, hiding potential threats behind a wall of grey. John saw something gargantuan emerge from the mist, and his heart leapt in his chest.

For a moment, he thought it was another elephant, a raging titan that would trample all before it until the army returned with their artillery and put it down. But it wasn't. It was something far more ancient, a primordial king that had inherited and then lost the world in a devastating catastrophe even it could not have survived.

Tyrannosaurus Rex. The mighty theropod would likely still rule the land had it been alive today. But the twenty-foot lizard glaring down at him was merely a life-sized replica, part of the park's new Jurassic-era display.

Like most young boys, John had loved dinosaurs. They were the tireless champions of his youthful imagination, chasing away his childhood fears—and John had been afraid of a great many things. Even as a thirty-something, he had been secretly delighted when Longleat had brought a dinosaur model exhibit to the park.

Despite everything, John realised he had a smile on his face. He approached the model Tyrannosaur and placed a hand on its great taloned foot. A roar emerged from a speaker somewhere above, and John grinned. He wished he could summon his loyal dinosaur army from his imagination to fight for him now, to seek out Maria and make sure they both were safe from whatever dangers might emerge from the fog to threaten them.

More reptilian grunts, growls, and hisses emerged from hidden speakers cunningly hidden in the foliage. There was another sound, too. John listened and thought he could make out the sound of whimpering.

He moved from dinosaur to dinosaur, navigating carefully through the fog, trying to find the source of the sound. The prodigious neck of a Diplodocus, a huge sauropod, reached towards the heavens. The spiked and plated tail of a Stegosaurus, an armoured herbivore the size of a van, almost tripped him up. John gave it a rueful glare and touched one of the spikes. It was incredibly sharp. He pulled his hand away and stared in surprise. A bead of blood blossomed on his fingertip.

A whimper drew his gaze to the base of a horned Triceratops opposite the Stegosaurus.

It was the pervert. The deviant he had last seen pleasuring himself in Rosie's room at The George.

The balding, scruffy-looking fellow was sitting with his back against the model dinosaur, his narrow shoulders hunched. He noticed John watching him and flinched away.

'*You*,' John said, feeling his fists clench in anger. 'What are you doing here? How did you make it inside the park with all the soldiers outside? Who the fuck are you?'

The pervert stared at him, uncomprehending. The man's eyes were wide with terror. 'The w-wolves…' he stuttered. 'The wolves are coming.'

'Wolves?' John repeated. An echo of the other man's fear seemed to settle into his bones, and he felt his heart race.

'The b-brothers,' the pervert stammered. 'I don't know their n-names, but I know what they are. F-fear and loathing. The d-doom of mankind.'

John stared at the pervert. There was something oddly familiar about the wretched fellow, but he couldn't put his finger on exactly what. 'You followed me into The George Inn,' he said angrily. 'You let yourself into Rosie's room. What the hell were you doing?'

Tears sprung up in the other man's eyes. 'I'm s-sorry,' he said. 'I can't control myself. *I'm a piece of shit.*'

John blinked. The man's words poked at something deep within him. He wanted to be furious with the miserable-looking fellow, but there was something terribly sad about him, pathetic as he was.

'What's wrong with you?' he asked tightly. 'No, I don't mean the wolves! You mock me in the police station, then you follow me to the George Inn and, somehow, you're here in Longleat despite the danger everywhere around us. Let me ask again. *Who* are you?'

'You already know,' said the pervert. His voice sounded strangely familiar somehow. 'I am *weakness. Failure.* The man no one wants to be. When the wolves come, we are the first to succumb to their fangs.'

John shook his head in frustration. 'This is hopeless. I can see I won't get any sense out of you. Look, the park is dangerous. Whatever's happened to you, whatever you've done, we can deal with it later. The important thing right now is that you go somewhere safe.'

The pitiful fellow stared at him. 'You're not going to hurt me?'

'I'm not going to hurt you,' John replied. He exhaled a deep breath. 'I have more important things than you to deal with right now. The army has ordered everyone to Warminster garrison. Take yourself there now. Go on.'

The balding, poorly dressed man pushed himself up off the ground and lingered uncertainly before scurrying off.

'One more thing,' John called after him. 'Have you seen a woman with brown hair? She's about my height. A few years younger than me.'

The man paused for a moment and shook his head. He limped off, disappearing into the fog while John watched.

25

The thick grey mist was settling in thicker than soup. John could barely see his own hands in front of his face as he wandered around the dinosaur exhibit. Once, he thought he heard a howl from somewhere to the north, across the lake. The weird fellow had said the wolves were coming. What had he called them?

Fear and loathing. The doom of mankind.

The man had seemed half-crazy, spouting nonsense, but John nonetheless felt a sudden burst of anxiety for Maria's safety. She was the light that brought meaning to his life. She was the heart of the sun.

He remembered the promise he had made to her father. He would protect her at all costs.

Lost in the fog, he felt the old, familiar feeling of loneliness begin to prickle his skin. It was the worst feeling a person could experience, John thought. If someone had to experience loneliness, let it be without first knowing the warmth of companionship.

Physical pain could be a horrible thing, but it was at least a sensation rooted in flesh and blood, of being alive. Nothing was as hellish as being trapped in a conscience disconnected from everything and everyone, a crushing straitjacket of despair that carried the weight of an uncaring universe.

John remembered the first time he had visited Maria and stayed with her family. They were exploring the streets near her house when an old man on crutches had hobbled into a coffee shop, a look of despair on his face. He had no money and no family or friends left, and he had a haunted look in his eyes that spoke of a life in which no hope remained.

Maria had gone to him. She had taken him by the arm and guided him to a seat and then bought him a coffee.

John knew then that he was going to marry her.

Lost in his thoughts, he wasn't paying attention to his surroundings until he stumbled across the entrance to the Bat Cave. It was Maria's least favourite part of the park, but John had found the darkness within eerily peaceful.

There was an information board on the wall outside, a few surprising facts wrapped into a narrative about the potential dangers that lurked in a world over which humanity assumed it held dominion.

There are over 8 million animal species on Earth. For every one human, there are seven birds, 500 fish, and 2.5 million ants. Fortunately for mankind, they have no natural predators. For thousands of years, they have ruled the Earth unchallenged. But what if that changed?

Something about the text struck John as familiar. He wondered if he'd read it before, perhaps on one of his previous visits to Longleat. Whomever had written it had apparently possessed an impressive gift of foresight.

After a moment's hesitation, John ducked into the cave, thinking to check for any sign of Maria before moving on to the west side of the park. He stopped in horror when he saw the bodies.

A man of around forty and a young girl who must have been his daughter lay savaged on the floor of the artificial cave. The father looked familiar, and it took John a few seconds to realise it was the estate agent who had sold him and Maria their house the previous year.

John's heart felt like a lump in his chest. He never cried, not even when he was a boy, but he felt moisture in his eyes then and blinked it away. The girl had her arms wrapped around her father, as though she sought the safety of his protection even as death approached. The dimness of the cave hid her features, yet the sight of her small body moved him to a great sadness.

He closed his eyes and tried to compose himself. On the ceiling above, the excited squeaking of dozens of bats sounded suspiciously like laughter.

John's eyes snapped open. He glared up at the miniature imps and their raucous mockery and saw the red balloon hugging the ceiling.

'**Happy Birthday!**' was printed in big letters on the front.

2015

He finished hanging the bunting and took a step back to examine his handiwork. It was slightly crooked. It would have to do. He didn't have time to stand around putting up decorations.

He went back to his desk in the conservatory of their new home. Sat down and stared at his laptop, looking without seeing. On the wall, the clock ticked its merciless metronome rhythm. It seemed to taunt him. Another day almost over, and no words written.

His deadline was breathing down his neck like one of the great fire-spewing dragons from his novels. He rubbed his face, massaged the tired hollows beneath his eyes. He hadn't slept well in weeks, maybe months. Maria was out shopping with Elsie. His wife had wanted to spend the afternoon of her birthday with him, but John had told her he needed to focus on his manuscript, and so she had made other plans. Besides, they had a small party planned for that evening.

He had taken Maria to the shops to buy party food and drinks for their friends. Her friends, really, people she had met through Facebook or worked with since they had moved to Warminster. He liked them well enough, but this was a bad time for interruptions.

Still, it was Maria's birthday. She and her family had always treated birthdays as something to be celebrated. He remembered the party they had thrown for his twenty-fourth. The music, the laughter, the endless smiling photos that usually made him a touch irritable but, on that day, made him feel very special. Maria's mum had even baked him not one but two cakes.

He looked at the bag of balloons sitting accusingly on the new sofa. He'd tossed them there after getting home from the shops and had forgotten about them. He hesitated, wrestling with the voice that kept asking why bother?

Then, he got up and inflated the balloons. He fetched some sticky tape and fixed them to the ceiling. He returned to the conservatory and stared at his computer some more. He checked his e-mails. He scrolled social media. He twiddled his fingers. The devil made work for idle hands.

Maria returned home a short time later. She greeted him with a kiss and immediately ran upstairs with her carrier bags. She came back down and made them both some mate, *the bitter herbal tea he had grown to like if never quite love.*

'Did you have a nice time with Elsie?' John asked. He took a sip.

'It was really nice,' Maria said. 'How did the writing go?'

'It went okay,' John lied.

'Do you think you will finish your book in time?'

'I hope so.'

They sat in silence for a while. Then:

'Lizzie is getting a tortoise,' Maria said. She grinned. 'A new friend for her rabbit.'

'That's nice,' John said.

'Remember we have our first appointment at Salisbury Hospital next week.'

John blinked. He'd forgotten it was the initial consultation for their fertility treatment. 'What time was it again?' he asked.

'Two-thirty,' she replied. 'Are you excited? Our first step towards getting a little Lizzie of our own!'

'Or a Clint,' John replied mischievously. The happiness on Maria's face expelled the darkness from his skull like torchlight chasing away an unwelcome guest. 'Clint Sharrock. It has a nice ring to it.'

'We're not calling our son Clint!' Maria, laughing.

'Hey! My dad wanted to call me Clint,' John said. 'Oh, and look, I put the balloons up.'

'Thank you!' Maria said. She leaned over and gave him a quick kiss. 'I'd better get ready. The guests will arrive soon.'

Their friends arrived, and they spent the evening making merry and listening to the world's most eclectic mix of British and Spanish hits. They sang "Happy Birthday" to Maria in English, and then in Spanish:

Qué los cumplas feliz

que los cumplas feliz

que los cumplas, Maria!

que los cumplas feliz.

Maria blew out the candles on her cake and smiled like she was the happiest woman in the world.

As the night wore on, John found himself growing restless. The guilt from his unproductive day of writing was like a parasite in his brain, twisting the words of his guests to better feed his frustration. One of the Spanish partygoers, Esteban, swallowed the last of the San Miguel John had purchased at the supermarket earlier that day and grinned drunkenly. 'More beer?' he asked.

John tried to keep his irritation from his face. He'd been waiting for the alcohol to run out as an excuse for bringing the evening's festivities to a close. 'We're all out,' he said. 'I guess it's time to call it a night.'

Their guest tapped his nose, as though he knew some great secret that he wasn't supposed to be privy to. 'Ah, but I saw the Bacardi in the cabinet. You were keeping that from us, eh?'

The rest of the group laughed. John felt a flash of anger, tried to keep a smile fixed to his face. 'We're saving that for when I finish my book.'

Esteban laughed and looked around conspiratorially. 'Surely the great writer can afford another bottle? Look at this beautiful house. The fancy new car outside.'

The words tumbled out before he could stop them. 'We won't have a beautiful house unless I can get back to writing my goddamn book. When are you leaving again?'

Maria stared at him in horror. John looked away, rubbed his face to hide his shame behind his hands. 'I'm sorry,' he said eventually. 'I'm just really stressed at the moment.'

'No hay nada,*' Esteban said. 'Don't worry about it, amigo. We understand.'*

The guests left shortly after. Maria tidied while John sat back down with his laptop. Once she had she finished washing the dishes, she came and stood beside John. 'Are you okay?' she asked. 'I'm sorry if the party bothered you.'

'It didn't bother me,' he said. 'I hope you had a nice day.'

'I did,' she replied. A thought seemed to occur to her. 'Wait here,' she said. She ran upstairs.

She reappeared a few minutes later. Her arms were wrapped around her body. 'I bought something for you,' she said flirtatiously. 'Well, for us.' She spread her arms to reveal a black satin nightie.

'You look amazing,' John said, and he meant it.

'I thought we could go to bed early,' Maria said. 'I kept a bottle of wine in the back of the fridge for us.' She smiled impishly.

John looked at his wife. 'I was going to work late this evening,' he said guiltily.

The hurt in her eyes made him hate himself. 'Again?' she exclaimed. 'John...it's been over a month. You never come to bed with me anymore. Do...do you still love me?'

'What kind of question is that?' he said angrily. 'Of course I love you.'

'You seem to care more about your book,' she said, her temper rising in response to his own.

'I have four months to finish this fucking book,' John yelled suddenly. He slammed the lid of his laptop down hard enough to crack the screen. 'You weren't complaining when my books cleared our debt.'

Maria flinched. 'But you've had all year,' she said quietly. 'You sit in here all day, all night. I don't know what you're doing. Messing around on the internet and watching porn probably.'

His rage threatened to overwhelm him. 'Leave me the fuck alone,' he rasped.

She looked at him for a long moment, her expression unreadable. Then, she went to the living room and began taking down the birthday decorations. He listened to her, wanting to say something, not knowing what to say. She went upstairs.

He opened his laptop again. Stared at it. He put his head in his hands.

Finally, he got up and went to the hallway. He was at the foot of the stairs, wondering what to say to Maria, how to apologise, when he heard the muffled sobs from their bedroom.

26

John left the Bat Cave in a daze. He couldn't understand why the army hadn't taken away the bodies of the little girl and her father, or why they hadn't disposed of the bats.

He tasted blood in his mouth again and spat a mouthful of crimson. His head throbbed. What was happening to him? Nothing seemed to make any sense. Surely animals that could fly would be top of the list of those the military would want culled, if this was an airborne virus as McCormack claimed?

He wandered through the fog like a lost spirit. Despair slowly settled over him, and he called out Maria's name again and again, not caring what might hear him. If there were hostile predators nearby, he imagined they would find him regardless of the noise he made. Humans were used to paying attention only to what they could see but, in the animal kingdom, every sense was vital for survival.

He ghosted through the Jungle Kingdom and its various enclosures. It had once housed porcupines, anteaters, aardvarks and other strange creatures that had delighted Maria on their last visit together. The meerkat enclosure had been the crown jewel of the Jungle Kingdom.

Now, it was a wasteland in miniature, a rocky diorama like a scene from an old western film. It was riddled with holes leading to a network of tunnels that had been burrowed by the small mammals in order to move around the enclosure out of sight.

There were no meerkats peering out at him from subterranean hiding places as John hunted desperately for some sign of Maria. No laughter or whimsy. Only silver bullet casings and sad, rust-coloured stains on the ground to tell the story of the great silencing of the Jungle Kingdom's wondrous menagerie.

A dark shape soared overhead. A raven suddenly landed in the meerkat enclosure. It hopped over to a tunnel and stuck its head in. Black wings flapped powerfully for a couple of seconds as the bird struggled to secure its prize.

Finally, it popped back out of the hole, dragging the body of a meerkat in its beak. The animal was dead, perhaps gassed by the military while it sought refuge in a place it thought safe. The raven noticed John then, its beady eyes taking in this unexpected visitor.

John froze, readying himself for a possible attack. But the raven merely examined him. If anything, the bird appeared puzzled, as though it couldn't quite decide what it was seeing. It released the body of the meerkat and gave a throaty croak. Then it fed, tearing off chunks of fur, stripping away the stringy flesh beneath.

A howl sounded from somewhere, louder than the last time. The raven looked around and took to the wing, disappearing into the fog, leaving its dinner behind and John alone once more.

He quickened his pace. If the wolves found him here, he would be completely exposed. He needed to find Maria, and he needed to get his hands on a weapon.

Soon, he arrived at the shore of Half Mile Pond. A cruise boat bobbed listlessly on the water. There was something about the island in the middle of the lake, John recalled. It was important. He gazed out, trying to penetrate the mist that hung over the water, trying to force himself to remember. All that came to him was a cavernous sense of sorrow—as deep and impenetrable as the lake before him.

He spotted something on the wooden docking platform. He stared at it, hardly believing his eyes. The necklace was tarnished by dirt, yet the small, heart-shaped ruby was unmistakable. It was Maria's pendant.

It was the first gift John had ever bought her. The first gift he had ever bought any girl. He had taken it to the post office, popped it in an envelope and scribbled down Maria's address with a confidence that had seemed entirely alien.

John had been forced to wait to discover if Maria had received his surprise. The motorcycle accident had occurred a few days after, leaving him hospital-bound and without any means to contact her. It was the early 2000s and mobile phones were only just entering the mainstream. Mobile internet access was virtually non-existent. When he was finally released from hospital, the first thing John had done was e-mail Maria and ask if she had received the heart.

Maria had been stunned by the gift. Her mother had demanded to know who had sent it and why. Her sister had cautioned her not to expect anything to come from this, especially after the mysterious Englishman had gone silent without warning for weeks. He had probably forgotten her already, they assured her; abandoned her for a prize closer to home, a prize within easier reach.

But John did not abandon people. Neither did he choose an option simply because it was easier.

He placed the pendant in a jean pocket. He had no idea how it had ended up here, but the presence of the pendant hinted that Maria was still on this side of Half Mile Pond. Some sixth sense told him that whatever lurked on the opposite side was ruinous, and he was keen to avoid crossing the lake.

He followed the shore, skirting the Monkey Temple, a stone enclosure housing a colony of marmosets with a faux-Aztec façade, and then Stingray Bay and Penguin Island. The grimy water tanks that had housed the stingrays were empty now. Penguin Island, too, was as desolate and empty as the frozen tundra from whence the flightless birds originally came.

With the exception of the bats and the wolves, it seemed the soldiers had spared nothing in their mission to stop the spread of the virus. John thought of Alfie's sudden madness, as well as the other animal attacks in town. It had been a hopeless cause. Everything was dead or infected. The sickness had spread like wildfire and there was no stopping it.

He continued his circuit of the lake's southern shore until he reached the western wall. He was running out of park to explore. A deep anxiety took hold. What if she wasn't here? The alternative didn't bear thinking about.

He circled back the way he had come, crying Maria's name over and over. A howl answered him, and his despair turned to fear. Fear, and a deep feeling of self-hatred. Why couldn't he ever find what he was looking for? Too stupid to see what was right in front of his face.

Disgusted with himself, he tore off the mask and tossed it on the ground. He knew he was acting irrationally, but it was hard to know the right thing to do. Hard to focus when it felt like his thoughts were being pulled in so many different directions.

As he hurried back through the main square, he became aware of a squeaking sound. Not one an animal might make, but rather a rhythmic, high-pitched metallic sound, a cadence of squeals. It was coming from a small park just off the square.

John plunged through the fog until he reached the waist-high gate in the park's wooden fence. It was halfway open. Colourful farm animals on thick springs simpered up at him. The seats on their backs, designed for young children, were empty. However, one of the swings in the centre of the park was not empty. Sitting on the swing, swaying back and forth, was a familiar figure.

'Kim?' John said, confused. 'What are you doing here?'

She looked up. Her grey eyes met his dispassionately. 'I'm waiting for someone.'

'Why didn't you go with the soldiers?' John demanded. 'It's not safe! There are wolves prowling around.'

'I'm a daughter of the moon,' she said coldly. 'The wolves won't harm me.'

'Where is your mask?'

Kim looked at him curiously, as though trying to peer inside his head. 'Where is *yours*?' she asked softly.

'I took it off,' he admitted, though he had the weirdest feeling she was referring to something else entirely. 'I wasn't able to see properly.'

Kim made a *tsk* noise, as though that much had long been obvious. John saw something glittering in her hand. He noticed one of her sleeves was rolled back.

'What were you doing?' he said urgently. 'Before I got here? What's that in your hand?'

'Does it matter?' she said dully. Her voice was dead, devoid of emotion. 'Tell me something, John. Why did you do all this? All these weeks of messaging. Why, when you were still in love with your wife?

'I have no idea what you're talking about, Kim,' John said helplessly. 'We've only known each other since last night.'

'Check your phone, John.'

He pulled his phone out of his pocket. Somehow, the screen was lit up. The battery hadn't died after all. He navigated to the messages, eager to prove to Kim that she was mistaken. He was about to hold up the phone to show her when he saw the texts between himself and—

Kimberley Grimes?

There were binders' worth of texts. Hundreds of messages, spread over several months. Endless back-and-forth exchanges of 'good mornings,' 'goodnights,' ideas, opinions, jokes. Photos, none of which he remembered taking. A solid week of Kim messaging him about her latest essay, the two of them discussing Latin, and Kim taking great delight in teaching him scientific names of various animal and insects native to Britain.

'How?' he whispered. 'I-I don't understand.'

'Now you know how I feel,' Kim said. She raised her hand, repositioned the glittering object against her arm.

'Wait!' John shouted. 'Don't. Stop it. I told you, I don't want you to hurt yourself. I want to help you, Kim.'

Kim's lips twisted. 'Help me? You can't even help yourself, John.'

He tasted blood again. His hand suddenly hurt. Had…had he hit himself? He suddenly remembered the thud of knuckles striking his head. The dull headaches. The hot throbbing inside his skull. Rushing to the bathroom to spew vomit into the toilet bowl, staggering back to bed to sleep off the grogginess, a tiny voice warning him not to, that he could cause himself serious harm.

The howls of wolves pierced the fog, closer now. Always closer.

'I have to go,' John said. 'The wolves are coming.'

'This is how it is always going to be, isn't it, John? Despite claiming you care about me, you run off as soon as your beloved wife demands your attention.'

Kim lowered her hand, placed the glittering object on the swing chair beside her and stood. Against the grey fog, her black and purple garb rendered her something otherworldly. A dark angel, sent to impart wisdom to the deserving and punish the unworthy. 'You know the story about the two wolves? Inside us are two conflicting wolves: one good, representing light and hope, the other evil, symbolizing darkness and despair. The one that prevails is the one you feed.'

'I know the story,' John said quietly.

Kim stared at him. Her grey eyes seemed to see beyond the present, seemed to encompass the past and the future and someplace else, somewhere outside of what he could see. 'The wolves were not the ones you needed to be concerned about, John.'

She turned and walked into the fog.

'Wait,' John called. 'I'm sorry. I'm sorry if I hurt you, Kim. I must find her. I must find Maria.'

Kim paused. She cocked her head slightly, as though in communion with something from somewhere up above, or perhaps down below. 'Your wife is in the same place she's been trapped for months,' she said eventually. 'A trap you made, John. A place with no obvious way out." She drew in a deep breath, letting it out slowly. "Take the blade. You might need it.'

A place with no obvious way out.

There was a place he and Maria had visited on several occasions. One of the park's oldest and most famous features, a place they had spent hours wandering in search of an exit, laughing and arguing and enjoying every minute of it.

At last, John knew where to find Maria.

2015

'I think I'm sick.'

The car was already covered in a sprinkling of white dust. They'd only been in the supermarket for ten minutes, but the early winter snowfall was unrelenting. Maria's breath misted in the frigid air. There was a strained expression on her face, and she struggled to keep up, even with him carrying several bags of groceries.

Her health had begun to falter again of late. The near miraculous recovery she had experienced during their time on the island was unravelling. She tried to hide her fear from John, but he knew it was there.

'What do you mean?' she asked.

'I haven't been feeling right,' he said slowly. He felt wretched, bringing up his own problems when Maria was suffering. He wondered if he should have said anything to her at all. But he had no one else to talk to. His mum was dealing with struggles of her own.

'You've been very bad-tempered,' Maria said. It wasn't an accusation, just a statement they both knew to be true.

'I know,' he said. 'I'm sorry. It's not just that. I can't sleep. I've been having constant stomach trouble.' He

didn't mention the hitting or the strange thoughts. He didn't want to worry her. Instead, he said, 'I think I'm having some mental health issues.'

'You should see a doctor,' Maria said. 'I'm not good at dealing with these things.'

Something about what Maria had just said hurt John deeply. 'It's not that easy to make an appointment,' he said hotly. 'Besides, what's a doctor going to do? It's all in my head.'

'Perhaps they can give you some medication to help,' she replied, refusing to rise to his anger. She looked tired.

John frowned. 'I just need to finish this bloody book. Then, we can go away somewhere and rest and get better.'

The book dominated his thoughts. He had less than three months to deliver a first draft of a novel. He had barely written a handful of pages. The countless hours he had spent hunched over his laptop should have been sufficient to pen War and Peace.

'We won't be able to go away when we have a baby,' Maria said abruptly.

John winced. The subject was a touchy one, for several reasons. Their sex life had dwindled to next to nothing, and resentment seemed to have fizzled to a dull acceptance. It was the proverbial elephant in the room, a looming problem they couldn't deny but chose instead to ignore.

The tests from the fertility clinic had also come back, and the news wasn't great. It was likely they'd require more than the three cycles provided by the National Health Service. The news had left John feeling even more inadequate than before, and the looming possibility of having to pay for private treatment gnawed away at him like a rat. It was even more pressure to finish the book and avert a looming financial disaster.

Why the hell hadn't he been able to write the book in good time, like every other author seemed to manage? Perhaps that was why people like him didn't land big book deals. It was tacitly understood by everyone in the publishing world that he was doomed to failure, that whatever necessary qualities were instilled by university and a good middle-class upbringing were lacking in someone of his background.

Maria had believed in him. Did she still? He looked at her then, staring out of the car window at the snow, dressed up more warmly than even the late winter day necessitated. She was a creature of light, of sun, of joy.

A thought occurred to him then. What if he *was the one making her unwell? What if his darkness were somehow extinguishing her very essence? He recalled the story of Hades and Persephone from Greek myth. The King of the Underworld, Hades, had kidnapped Persephone from the world above while she was gathering flowers. Though she grew to love him, no sunlight penetrated the Underworld and, without Persephone, the plants in the world above withered and died. Not wishing to see Persephone unhappy, Hades allowed his wife to return to the world above for six months of the year, thus beginning the cycle of the seasons.*

John and Maria had spoken in the past about moving to her homeland, but he didn't want to abandon his own family. That, and he wasn't good at change. Maria adapted to new situations with a smile and an open heart. He clutched to what he knew like a monkey clung to a tree in a tropical flood. He ought to have made more of an effort to find friends here in Warminster. He ought to have—

'John, look out!' screamed Maria. He managed to slam his foot on the brakes a moment before he hit a silver Vauxhall that had just driven past the turning. He hadn't spotted it. The car swerved madly on the road for a second or two before pulling over.

A man and a woman got out. They were of similar age to John. She looked extremely angry, and as he turned onto the road, she flagged him down. Beside her, the woman's partner looked flustered and apprehensive. John hesitated, then slowed his red convertible and pulled in just before the silver Vauxhall. He rolled down his electric window as the couple walked over.

'What the hell was that?' the woman shouted. Snow flecked her freckled cheeks, red with anger and the cold. 'You almost killed us. Haven't you noticed the weather?'

John felt his blood turn hot. 'I didn't see you,' he said, trying to keep his voice level. 'It was a mistake.' Every muscle in his body wanted to explode with rage.

'We're sorry,' Maria said. 'At least no harm was done.'

'Come on, Nikki,' said the man beside the woman. He took a gentle hold of her elbow. 'Charlie's waiting in the car.' John looked past the man to the brown rottweiler watching them through the rear passenger window of the Vauxhall.

'Don't, Kev,' the woman said angrily, shaking her partner off. She glared at John, eyes narrowed in fury.

'Fucking boy racers in their fancy cars. Watch where you're going.'

'Boy racer?' *John said aloud. Rage drove his next words with the inexorability of a charging rhino. 'I'm the same age as you, you stupid cunt.'*

'John!' gasped Maria beside him.

The woman went even redder. She turned and stormed back to her car, but as she left, she punched the bonnet of his car in anger. The metallic thud *hung in the air like a call to arms.*

Before he knew it, John was revving the accelerator until his car roared like some demon unleashed. All he need do was release the clutch, and he would wipe this stupid bitch off the road...

The woman turned and stared at him in horror. She jolted as if she'd been physically hit and quickly got in her car. Her partner scurried in beside her, his face as white as a ghost, and looked at John as though a monster had just emerged out of the winter snow.

'What are you staring at?' John snarled. His furious gaze went to the rottweiler, who watched the exchange in confusion. His big eyes looked at his owners questioningly, like a child seeking reassurance.

John took his foot off the accelerator. He sagged in the seat. His hands shook. He risked a glance at Maria. She looked terrified.

'I'll get help,' he managed to say, not sure if he was talking to Maria or to himself. 'Tomorrow morning, I'll call the doctor.'

Maria said nothing. She stared at her feet the entire journey back home and didn't speak.

Later that evening, John wrote more words than he had managed in months.

27

He stumbled through the hedge maze. Green walls higher than his head surrounded him in every direction he turned. Tendrils of mist snaked around corners, taunting him, beckoning him onwards, only to lead him to another wall of shrubbery that barred his every effort to find his way.

Memories seemed to haunt his every step, fragments of everything he had forgotten stabbing at his consciousness with the sharp edges of a long-suppressed truth.

She was somewhere in this maze. He had to find her. He had to save her from this madness and guard her from whatever was happening. The wolves howled again, ever closer. Had they found her already? He prayed that somehow, God had protected her. Strange, that he should discover his faith now of all times.

He wandered for what felt like hours. Just as he thought he had found the path, another wall rose to block him. Perhaps it was the fog tripping him up. He recalled navigating the maze with Maria in happier times, when the sun was shining and the sky was blue overhead. It had seemed simple then, effortless. Everything had just made sense.

He turned a corner and almost walked into another wall. Panic welled up. What if they were lost in the maze forever? What if, someday a million years from now, future archaeologists found his bones in the maze and marvelled at the stupidity of this hapless writer who had become hopelessly lost. And what of Maria?

Despite his terror, his mind railed at the thought of anything happening to his wife. There was nothing he wouldn't do to protect her. No road he wouldn't walk. No monster he wouldn't slay.

It was as though the fog was teasing him, purposely leading him astray. He reached for the heart pendant in his pocket. It was strangely warm in his hand. A suspicion took hold.

John held the heart up before him as he delved into the hedge maze. Every time a branching path opened before him, he stopped and concentrated on the ruby in his palm, feeling it grow hotter when he chose the correct direction. He let the pendant guide him. Deeper and deeper into the maze, the howls of wolves on the hunt haunting him every step of the way, until finally he turned a corner and saw that he had reached the very centre.

The heart of the maze is where he found her.

She was huddled on the ground, her hands clasped together, her eyes closed as if in prayer. John gasped when he saw her. Her eyes fluttered open.

'*John?*' she said slowly, as though awakening from a dream, uncertain if her eyes were playing tricks on her.

'Maria!' he cried. He rushed over to her. 'Are you hurt?'

'I…don't think so,' she said numbly, staring up at him as if he might disappear back into the fog.

'Let me help you up,' John said hurriedly. He could hardly contain the relief that flooded through him. He reached down a hand. Maria flinched back from it. 'What's wrong?' he asked, face creasing in confusion. 'I came to find you, Maria. I've come to rescue you.'

Maria's large brown eyes were haunted. 'You've come to rescue me?' she echoed, anxiety in her voice.

'Of course,' he said. 'Elsie said you hadn't come home. I couldn't leave you in danger. There was this duck in the garden, and Alfie attacked me, and…it's like the whole world has gone mad, Maria.'

'I don't understand, John,' she replied. Her words were slow, halting. She seemed to be fighting with herself, waging some internal struggle. 'You put me here. Now you want to pull me back out?'

You put me here. What did she mean? Was she referring to the emotional distance between them? Or something else?

John swallowed, uncertain what to do. He wanted to go to her, to lift her up from the ground and wrap her in his arms. But the fear in her eyes made him hesitate. Was she…was she *afraid* of him?

'At least let me help you up,' he said uncertainly.

She nodded after a moment's thought, and he took her hand, pulling her gently to her feet. He noticed she no longer wore her wedding band.

'I found this,' he said, showing her the heart pendant. 'It's yours.'

Maria shook her head. 'It's not mine anymore,' she replied. She gave him a haunted look, as though afraid that would somehow provoke him.

'Maria…' John began. He put the heart back in his pocket. 'I don't know what's happened. With us, or with all these animal attacks. With *anything*. But we need to get to Warminster garrison, where it is safe. I'm going to get you there in one piece if it's the last thing I do. Do you understand?'

She stared at him for a long moment, as though trying to understand what, or who, was standing before her. *Like the raven in the meerkat enclosure*, John thought.

Finally, Maria nodded, though the apprehension in her eyes remained.

'Can you remember the way out of here?' John asked, gesturing at the maze.

'I think so.'

'We'll leave the park by the entrance and head east,' John said. 'There were soldiers outside, but they're probably gone now. The holiday village might still be occupied. There's safety in numbers. You…you've heard the wolves?'

Maria nodded again. Her long, chocolate brown hair was a wild mess, and her Longleat uniform was covered in dirt and grime, but she was nonetheless the most beautiful sight John had ever set eyes upon.

The heart of the sun.

'They're on the hunt,' John said. 'If they catch us, I don't know if I can fight them. We need to hurry.' He looked up at the sky. The day was already fading. How long had he been at the park? Could it really be almost evening?

Let the night come, John thought. He carried the light with him now.

28

They left the park without running into any potential predators and made their way east. The military camp had vanished so completely it was as though it had never been there at all. Longleat House hunched in the fog like some dying colossus, a fading wonder that belonged to a bygone era.

John thought about hurrying to the grand old building and checking if anyone yet remained. Perhaps he could request shelter or some form of transport back to Warminster. But the ornate windows were unlit, and the water fountains in the stately garden had been turned off. No one remained within Longleat House. He and Maria were alone in a world of ghosts.

He tried to make conversation with his estranged wife as they walked, but it was as though Maria were a ghost herself. She looked at him only rarely, and her replies were short and guarded. He wished there were some way to reach across the chasm that separated them, to find common ground and bask in the warmth of shared familiarity again. But she was a closed book.

He took out the heart pendant again and stared at it, wondering what to do. The jewel had lost some of its lustre. The red ruby of their love had become a pale grey stone. It broke his heart to see the dying of their fire, knowing it should never have come to this. His task now was to be hard like a tempered blade, to be the weapon that protected her until they were free of this madness.

They moved through the outskirts of Longleat Forest under a twilight sky. Even now, the fog was thick enough to swallow the surrounding trees. It wasn't uncommon for mist or fog to cover the western edge of Salisbury Plain and the surrounding areas late in spring, but the grey pall had been a permanent fixture ever since John had reached the outskirts of Longleat.

He thought of the alien respiratory masks the soldiers had worn, the unidentified flying object—had it *truly* been a helicopter?—hovering over Cley Hill a few nights ago. He recalled the strange red star in the night sky. He wasn't one for conspiracy theories, but they couldn't all be coincidence. The unexplained phenomenon turning animals crazy was connected, somehow.

He thought of his mum. He hadn't spoken with her since their brief conversation in the sandwich shop. He hoped she and Alfie were okay. A lot of strange things had happened in the last few days, but they were his tether to reality. As was the woman silently trudging along beside him.

'Do you remember the first conversation we had?' he asked. His voice was quiet, hesitant. Whatever was going on between them, he didn't want to upset her.

'I remember,' she said. She didn't look at him.

'We were in an internet group chat,' he continued. 'I think…I remember you were practising your English. And someone said something rude about someone else's mum.'

'Yes,' Maria said.

'And I said something like, "Don't be rude about mums. They're awesome." And then I think I added, "I love my mum."'

'Yes, you did,' she said.

He glanced at her. Her eyes were unfocused, seeing another time and place. 'And you said…' He closed his eyes, trying to remember. 'You said, "That's very sweet. I love my mum, too." And I thought, she seems like a nice girl. So, I messaged you. I'd never done that before. Messaged a girl, I mean. And we talked for over an hour before you had to go. Just before you left, I asked for your e-mail address. I remember. You seemed happy I asked. I almost didn't, but something told me that if I didn't be brave that *one time*, I would regret it for the rest of my life.'

Maria finally looked at him. Her brown eyes were racked with pain. 'John…why are you saying all of this?' Her voice cracked slightly.

'I just— I wanted you to know that day changed my life,' he said. 'It was the day the old me died, and I became something better.'

Maria blinked rapidly, turned her face away. 'Please, don't,' she said, in a strangled voice.

'Sorry,' John mumbled. Guilt and confusion spread its wings over him like the shadow of some huge predatory bird. He stared into the fog. Dark shapes towered just beyond the misty curtain, vertical shadows that seemed to pierce the very heavens. He knew immediately what they were. Giant redwoods, trees so tall one could easily believe their boughs contained mysteries known only to the gods and their servants.

Beyond the redwoods, John knew, the holiday village spread out, filling the cradle of the forest like a happy infant. It had opened just over 20 years ago and was a popular resort for holidaymakers keen to reconnect with nature whilst enjoying the luxury of its vacation lodges, restaurants, spas, swimming pools, and even a tram train.

John and Maria had never stayed in the resort. Partly because of the cost, and more recently because a holiday abroad offered a more reliable prospect of sunshine for Maria.

As the estranged pair descended the shallow hill towards the holiday village, and the ghosts of buildings melted out of the fog, it became clear that John's hopes of finding other people were in vain. The place was deserted.

Wispy patches of fog curled around the scattered possessions of holidaymakers who had upped and left in a hurry. Tables and chairs had been overturned. Suitcases lay open on the ground, spilling their contents over the grass. Train tracks wound around the edge of the holiday park, and someone had left a pair of children's shoes in between the rails. There was no sign of the tram or the child. John hoped the latter had managed to escape this colourless purgatory.

His eyes followed the tracks into the fog. He and Maria were perhaps a couple of miles from Warminster. Not much farther to go now. He had made it to Longleat park, managed to locate Maria amongst the chaos. The hardest part was almost over. They hadn't heard the wolves in almost an hour.

As if on cue, a familiar howl emerged from the woods behind them. It was answered by another howl. They sounded close. Much too close.

Maria jumped. Her eyes widened in terror. Perhaps out of habit, she looked to John.

'We need to get to cover,' he said urgently. 'Look, just ahead of us. You see that?'

'The spa,' Maria replied. Her voice trembled.

'Come on,' he shouted. They ran towards the sprawling building on the western edge of the village. The baying of the wolves followed them, growing louder every second.

John risked a glance behind him. Two pairs of sinister eyes shone from lupine shapes that moved like wraiths in the fog. The wolves' maddened eyes were fixed on their prey, narrowed in hunger, shining with the thrill of the hunt. Pants of savage desire rolled wetly from throats that had already tasted the blood of man.

John remembered the bodies of the girl and her father in the bat cave. The gaping wounds in their throats. The glistening pools of their lifeblood, from which these two demons had drunk so deep.

Fear seized him. Fear for what would happen to Maria when the wolves caught up with them. Fear as well as self-hatred, for it seemed he would fail to protect her.

Ahead of them, a figure emerged from the fog. It was the pervert. The balding fellow limped down the train track, his arms wrapped around his thin body as though ashamed the world might see his weakness. He looked up when he heard the wolves howl and stared around in wild terror.

'Run!' John yelled at the man. The hapless figure's gaze shot towards John and Maria, and he hurried towards them. As he drew closer, however, he slowed, then stumbled to a halt. The man stared at John as though unexpectedly faced with something even more terrifying than the predators pursuing them.

'You…' he gasped, putting his palms up as though desperately seeking to protect himself. He backed away from John.

'What's wrong?' John exclaimed. 'Hurry! We need to get to the spa.'

The pervert moaned something unintelligible. He brought his hands up to his face and clawed at his eyes. John took a step towards him, thinking to calm the fellow, but the man suddenly turned and ran in the opposite direction.

'No!' John yelled. But it was too late.

The wolves appeared and howled with renewed anticipation. They raced towards the cowering fellow, who froze, paralysed by fear.

John and Maria reached the main spa building just as the first agonised cries and delighted growls and snapping jaws formed a cacophony of horror.

John frantically tried the main entrance door, only to find it locked. He slammed into it with his shoulder. It didn't give an inch.

'Here!' Maria screamed at him. She'd found a fire escape door on the side.

He hurried through after her and slammed it shut. There was no lock on the door that he could see, so he grabbed a couple of chairs from the table just inside the reception area and wedged them against the door.

Through the glass panel and the fog beyond, he could just about make out the silhouettes of the two wolves savaging the pervert. The noises they made were profane, the tearing and the snarls and screams going on and on. The wolves howled in triumph.

John turned to Maria. 'We need to find somewhere more secure—' he began. He stopped when he saw the expression on her face.

His wife had her eyes squeezed shut. She was crying, tears running down her cheeks. 'They killed him,' she sobbed. 'He didn't even try to fight.'

'He was afraid,' John said. 'I think…I think he hated himself. He gave up. Listen, we need to get away from here. Those wolves are infected by the virus, or whatever this is. I don't think they'll stop hunting us. We need to find some place safe until we can figure out what to do.'

Maria nodded and wiped away her tears. John took a quick look around. They appeared to be in a small waiting area. Cream-coloured tables piled with folded towels were positioned around the room. Pots and tubes of various moisturisers, creams, and other beauty products were arranged artfully on shelves. Ceramic cups still filled with dark liquid rested beside a coffee machine on the central desk. It looked as though everyone had fled.

The two of them left the waiting area and wandered down a wooden corridor lined with small treatment rooms. Massage tables had been abandoned halfway through sessions. Expensive massage oils on side tables leaked their fragrances from open bottles. John smelled grapefruit oil and lavender and other scents that evoked memories from what seemed like a previous life.

Strangely, everywhere he looked, women's underwear was scattered over the tables and the wooden flooring. Some of it was decidedly racy. John saw black lace bras, narrow strips of silk that he recognised as thongs. Even a purple corset.

Some instinct compelled him to glance at Maria. Her mouth was set in a thin line. He was suddenly overwhelmed by guilt. They said nothing as they continued to explore the spa. They wandered in silence through abandoned apartments, saunas dripping with steam, a large dining hall set with plates of expensive food, abandoned mid-meal.

He and Maria had dined at some pricey restaurants since he had got his book deal. None had ever provided the joy he had experienced at his absolute favourite place to eat in the world.

'Are you hungry?' he asked Maria. 'I don't know if we'll have the chance to eat when we get to the military garrison.'

Maria shook her head. But a moment later, she grabbed a slice of bread from a table. John took a couple of bottles of water and stowed them in his backpack. They left the restaurant and continued through the spa. John poked his head into a small gym and took a quick look around. 'Think we have time for a quick workout?' he joked.

Maria gave him a strange look. For the first time since he had found her in the maze, there was the faintest hint of a smile on her face. He remembered how proud he had been when she had gotten fit and ran a 10k with him.

Maria hadn't been much into running but was a fantastic dancer, whereas he couldn't dance to save his life. She had tried to teach him once or twice. Perhaps he had improved the tiniest fraction, he grudgingly admitted.

Finally, they reached a large spa area that opened though large glass doors to an outside pool surrounded by hanging plants. The fog had finally cleared. Night had arrived, and moonlight bathed the dark water in shimmering silver. John stared out at the scattered clouds and the twinkling stars above. For the first time in he didn't know how long, he felt some small measure of peace. Maria hesitated, then came to stand beside him.

'It's lovely here,' she said, seeming to offer him a small olive branch.

'We should have come sooner,' he said, dreamily. She looked at him, and then away again. She seemed like she was about to say something, only to stop herself. She stared at some dirt on her clothes. They really were filthy, John saw.

'If you want,' he said slowly, 'you can shower here. I'm sure the guests wouldn't mind you borrowing their clothes. I'll keep watch.'

'Thank you,' she said. 'I would appreciate that.' She turned away, only to hesitate again.

'Are you okay?' he asked, concerned.

'It's…it's just that since you found me earlier, I thought maybe I'd seen glimpses of the old John. My John. I don't…I don't know what to think. I'm sorry. I'll be back soon.'

She departed to find some clothes and a towel, leaving him staring after her in confusion. The old John? Her John? He'd always been hers. Hadn't he?

He turned back to the glass doors dividing the interior and exterior halves of the circular pool and stared out at the evening sky. He squinted, searching for the red star. The soft pitter-patter of a running shower sounded from somewhere nearby. Maria had clearly located a fresh set of clothes and was finally cleansing herself of the day's horrors.

There. He saw it. The red star, hanging ominously in the night like a beacon to the gates of Hell. When Maria was finished showering, he would show it to her. Whatever it was, he was now sure it was related to the virus. If he could just put the pieces together—

His train of thought crashed and died when he saw four other red stars appear, two on either side of the pool.

Not stars. Eyes.

Lupine forms tensed, the stuff of primordial nightmares preparing to invade the waking world. John stood transfixed as the wolves pounced. Time seemed to stand still. The glass doors shattered. The brothers of destruction hurled themselves into the spa.

John staggered back, half frozen with shock. He shouted Maria's name, but he knew she couldn't hear him from the shower. The two wolves shook shards of broken glass from their dark fur coats. Their muzzles were soaked with blood. Lips like dark worms peeled back to reveal fangs defiled with the flesh of man.

As one, the wolves darted towards him. John's heart hammered. When he was a young boy, and even a teenager, when something caused him great stress, his legs would shake uncontrollably. They trembled now, a trauma response that threatened to paralyse him. He tried to back away, to put some space between his vulnerable body and those snapping jaws. He had to protect Maria.

He retreated until his back pressed up against something. The brothers snarled and barked, saliva dripping from their stinking maws, excitement shining from eyes that glowed with a diabolical fervour.

He was against the wall now. Nowhere to run. One of the brothers darted in, so fast he didn't even register the movement. Pain exploded in his right thigh. The wolf latched on to him, fangs piercing flesh and muscle with outrageous ease.

The wolves had come for him. *Fear and loathing. The doom of mankind.*

Agony shot down his left arm. The other wolf had caught it in its jaws. They were crushing it, tearing flesh, splintering bone. The brothers had him pinned. He was trapped, held down as though by medical straps, paralysed as though caught in a nightmare.

The distant roar of the shower abruptly ceased. Somewhere, he heard a beeping noise.

He felt warmth on his leg. Numbly, he looked down.

He saw blood. It ran down the inside of his jeans, dripping over his trainer in a slow trickle. The wolf that had torn open his leg released its hold and howled triumphantly.

'John?' echoed Maria's voice. She sounded suddenly afraid.

Somewhere, something stirred.

2015

He stared at the shattered remains of the glass. He saw blood.

Maria wandered into the kitchen and froze in shock. 'John!' she exclaimed. 'What happened? Are you hurt?'

'It's just a cut,' he said hollowly. He grabbed some kitchen towel and wrapped it around his hand.

'That was your favourite glass,' she said sadly. 'The one I bought you for your birthday.' Her eyes took in the remains of the pint glass. 'His Lordship's Beer' had been printed in bright letters on the side. The words were indecipherable now, the proclamation as broken as the glass they adorned.

He shrugged.

'Was it an accident?'

'No. I broke it.'

'Why did you do that, John?' Her voice was quiet.

'I was angry,' he said.

'You're always angry! Sometimes...sometimes, I don't recognise you anymore.'

He sneered at her. 'I'm not the one who's changed. I'm the same as I've always been.'

'What do you mean?'

'You spend most of your time around Elsie's now. Elsie, or some other friend.'

Maria was quiet for a moment. 'When I'm here,' she said, 'you make me feel like I'm bothering you. I wanted to give you space to work on your book.'

'Okay,' he said curtly.

She grabbed a brush, began sweeping up the glass. 'You should tell the therapist about this tomorrow.'

'I don't have an appointment tomorrow,' he mumbled. 'It was cancelled. The therapist is ill.'

'Again?' She closed her eyes, seemed to compose herself. 'Why don't you sit down? I'll make you a cup of tea.'

'Okay,' he said. He went to the lounge and sat on the sofa. In the conservatory beyond, his laptop stared at him like a judge about to utter a verdict. He already knew what it would be.

Guilty. Two and a half months to write a book the length of Lord of the Rings*—and he was no Tolkien. He had fucked up. Royally fucked up.*

Maria brought him his tea. He took it from her with a grunt and stared into its golden depths. He knew what he had to do. It was the only chance he had left.

'I've been thinking,' he said. 'What if I go away by myself for a while? I can focus on my book with no distractions.'

Maria looked at him in confusion. 'Go away? What do you mean?'

'I want to go to the island. I felt happy there. I'll be able to write.'

'But what about me? What about the hospital?'

He winced. They had their first round of IVF treatment in the next few weeks.

'We'll cancel it,' he said. 'I'm sorry, Maria. This is too important. If I don't finish this manuscript, we could lose everything. The treatment can wait till later.'

'I don't want you to go,' she said. She had tears in her eyes now.

'I'm sorry,' he said again.

'You promised we wouldn't be apart after we got married. I don't understand, John. You have a beautiful house here. Your own office in the conservatory. I do everything I can to make you feel comfortable.'

'It's not you,' he said. The helplessness in her voice was like a knife through his heart. 'You haven't done anything wrong. It's my problem. I need to deal with it. I think...I think I need to do this.'

She looked at him with those trusting eyes. She looked away. Then, she nodded.

He drank the tea in silence. Maria disappeared upstairs to the nursery to work on her own small project. He had broken his promise to her. He felt wretched, but there was another sensation, too, gnawing away at his subconscious. The feeling as if a weight had been lifted. Was he feeling...relief? Anticipation?

Later that evening, there came a knock at the door. John got up to answer it.

It was his mum.

He hadn't been expecting a visitor. 'Mum?' he said with surprise. 'What's wrong?' Her face was pale, and there was fear in her eyes. The taxi that had dropped her off flashed its headlights and drove off.

'I've had a call from the hospital. You remember I had an appointment last week? I didn't want to worry you, but they called me back this morning for some more tests. It's not good news.'

'Yes? Mum, what is it? What did they say?' A cold dread wormed its way into his chest.

'It's cancer.'

Inside him, something broke. It might have been a cage.

Something slithered out.

29

He saw blood. It trickled down the inside of his jeans, running over his trainer. The wolf that had torn open his leg released its hold and howled triumphantly.

He brought his hand down and drove the knife through the face of the wolf. Kim's knife, which he had taken from the swing back at the park. He forced it as deep as it would go, feeling it puncture soft membrane, slide through the soft jelly within. The wolf jerked its head away, the handle sticking out of its punctured eye. It howled again but, this time, it was a howl of agony.

Its pain was like the first notes of a love song.

He drew his uninjured leg back, kicked it as hard as he could, felt ribs break, felt his own foot crack. It didn't hurt, didn't cause him any concern. It was just another note in a rising symphony. The impact lifted the wolf into the air, sent the animal flying across the floor.

The other wolf redoubled its attack, snarling in fury, biting savagely. It tugged his arm down, tried to wrench his shoulder out of its socket.

He watched it curiously, as though in a trance, as though he was detached from his body and something else was now in control of his limbs. He leaned down, took one of the wolf's ears in his own mouth, and bit down so hard he felt his teeth break. Dreamlike, almost lazily, he tore away a chunk of the wolf's ear. He tasted fur and gristle and blood and pain. He swallowed it.

The wolf went ballistic, snapping at his neck, some instinct compelling it to try to end the fight as quickly as possible. He caught it by the muzzle, fended off the snapping teeth, feeling its hot breath, thrilled by the sudden desire to reach in and steal the air from the creature's lungs. He wrapped an arm around the wolf's neck, pulled its head close to him. Then, he jumped into the pool.

The water surrounded him like a mother's hug. He rose to the surface, the thrashing animal kicking desperately to escape his grasp, scratching and biting, leaving him bruised and bleeding. It was a wild thing, a harbinger of terror, unbelievably strong.

He was stronger still.

He held its head under the water for what seemed like an eternity. He watched its struggles slow, observed as the life slowly faded from the beast. Once he felt it go limp, he released his grip and let the body drift away. He looked across the spa. Saw the other wolf. It shook its head madly, trying to dislodge the knife, trying to save itself from a fate that was sealed the moment it had forced him against a wall.

He slowly climbed the steps out of the pool. The water was red in his wake. It was a birthing pool, a stygian pit from which arose something unspeakable. Something raised in the darkness.

He stalked the wounded animal. The wolf's one remaining eye watched his approach. Even through the madness of its infected brain, it tried to scrabble away, to escape. It whimpered pitifully.

He found himself smiling. A smile so wide it could swallow the world.

He kicked the wolf. Again and again. He revelled in every thudding impact. Grinned at every crack of fracturing bone. When it was pliable enough, when it had ceased thrashing, he grabbed the animal by the scruff of the neck. He dragged it over to the sharp edge of the raised stone that ran along the edge of the pool. He traced a loving finger down its trembling head, then positioned it just so.

The first time he stomped down, he felt its jaw break. The third time, its other eye popped out. The fifth time, it finally stopped moving.

He lost count after that. Lost track of everything except the joy of release. The loosening of shackles, the removal of the switch. An open savannah, a vast playground in which the predator could hunt without—

'John?'

He looked up from his grisly prize. An angel had appeared, a maiden in white. She stared at him as though she had just been told Heaven was a lie.

Maria brought her hands to her mouth. Then, she turned and fled.

30

'Maria, wait!' he shouted, feeling himself snap back into his body. The beeping had stopped, leaving only an accusing silence by way of reply. He made to go after her but almost slipped on the gore oozing over the stone tiles. His entire body felt like it was on fire. Searing pain assailed him like the heat of a dying star.

He staggered after his wife, leaving a trail of blood in his wake. Down wooden corridors he limped, his broken foot dragging behind him like a guilty secret.

He reached the fire escape. The chairs had been tossed aside, and he dragged the door open with arms that were suddenly hideously weak. He caught a glimpse of white disappearing into the fog and followed it.

He reached the train tracks and the body of the pervert, the hapless fool who had succumbed to the wolves. His throat had been torn open, his crotch eaten away until all that remained was a glistening, seeping mass of dark red meat.

'Maria,' he called again. There was no answer.

He followed the rail tracks, moving as fast as his ravaged body would allow him. He squinted, trying to pierce the fog, desperate for any glimpse of the woman he loved. The woman he had sworn to cherish and respect.

Why had she fled him? He had only been trying to protect her!

He had the sudden feeling something watched him. Watching, and waiting. He looked around, thought he saw a pair of giant cat's eyes glittering amongst the fog. He blinked, and they were gone.

He searched around desperately. There was no sign of Maria. Had she gone towards the military garrison? He wavered, torn between following the train tracks and heading north back into the forest.

A fluttering moth emerged from the mist and wove circular patterns in the air before disappearing back into the grey, and John knew then that it had been sent to guide him, to lead him back to Maria. He left the tracks and headed back towards the tree line.

The agony was almost unbearable. The fight with the wolves had wounded him terribly. With rising alarm, he took stock of his injuries. His arm was in tatters, white bone poking out from beneath flesh that looked like sausage meat. Blood ran freely down his leg from the bite on his thigh, soaking his jeans, making his trainers squelch with every step. His T-shirt was shredded, furrows gouged in the flesh beneath. Dully, he knew that if he didn't receive help soon, he would bleed out.

Getting his wounds seen to would have to wait, though. First, he had to find Maria. Whatever she had witnessed back at the spa, it had been a necessary act, a desperate last resort to prevent certain ruin.

As John plunged deeper into the forest, he saw bodies: dead animals, their throats torn open. At first, it was only a smattering of rabbits, ferrets, and other small mammals. Soon, however, animals littered the ground like autumn leaves: badgers, foxes, deer, otters, and everything else that lived within the woodlands. It was as though a tsunami of death had swept through, killing everything in its path.

John again had the unsettling feeling he was being watched. He caught a glimpse of movement in his peripheral vision. He spun, wincing at the agony that exploded in his savaged leg. Was something stalking him?

He tried desperately to increase his pace, now terrified for Maria, but it was all he could do to remain on his feet. He heard noises up ahead: the *thud* of iron striking earth.

He reached a shallow depression in the forest floor. A stand of yew trees surrounded the hollow, their branches twined together like the arms of funeral mourners. Between a gap in two of the trees, John saw a visage he recognised from what seemed a lifetime ago.

It was Tom, the retired undertaker. The tall, silver-haired man whom John had last seen at the gym a few nights past was dressed in a dark suit. He gripped a shovel in his gnarled hands.

'Tom?' John called in disbelief. He made his halting way between the yew trees towards the older man. He saw then that there were fresh graves dug in the earth, rows upon rows of them. The carcasses of dead animals were stacked nearby, a lurid heap of bloody fur and limp tails and sad, flopping ears.

'Hello, laddie,' said Tom in his thick Geordie accent. He gave John a kindly smile. 'I've been expecting you.'

‘You have?’ John asked, confused and tired. So very tired.

Tom appraised John with his piercing blue eyes. ‘Aye,’ he said. ‘I was just getting things ready.’ He stuck his shovel in the earth and leaned on it. ‘I reckon you’re almost done.’

John sagged. Strength leaked out of him like air from a burst tyre, and he almost fell. He glanced up at the sky, expecting to see the red star looking down at him, mocking his weakness, but dark clouds blotted out the heavens. A storm had rolled in. Somewhere in the forest, Maria was alone. Alone and defenceless.

A deep rumble came from somewhere in the night. It might have been thunder.

‘I’m never fucking done,’ John hissed, through broken teeth. Bloody spittle sprayed from his mouth. He straightened. ‘I’m looking for my wife. Have you seen her?’

Tom blinked and cocked his head slightly, as though he’d made a misjudgement and was trying to decide how to course correct. ‘Why do you ask?’ he said carefully.

‘I have to protect her.’

Tom’s brow furrowed. He picked up his shovel again and resumed digging. A long time passed before he spoke again. ‘Some things,’ he said slowly, ‘can’t exist in the same moment in time. Light and darkness. Truth and lies. Life and death.’

‘I don’t understand,’ John said impatiently. ‘I don’t have time for riddles, Tom. If you know where Maria is, tell me.’

Tom's glacier gaze met his. 'Wisdom is the first and greatest of God's gifts, laddie. The power to know right from wrong. The ability to make or break a heart. You can't love a thing and seek to destroy it.' The old undertaker raised a finger and pointed into the forest. 'She went that way.'

A flying insect landed on Tom's outstretched finger. A death's-head hawkmoth. Somewhere in the forest, something beeped.

Feeling a sudden pressure on his chest, John turned and set off in the direction in which the old man pointed. As he stumbled away, the undertaker's parting words settled into the wounded writer like embalming fluid preparing a body for burial.

'I'll see you soon, son.'

31

He blundered wildly through the forest, branches scratching at his mangled arm and exposed wounds, so much pain that it all blurred into one endless stream of fire. The fog finally thinned, and the wind picked up. Rain fell. The storm had arrived.

John's breath rasped in his throat. He was fighting to get air into his lungs now. Every step was a struggle. The military garrison couldn't be much farther ahead. Had Maria reached safety already? He dared hope she had. It wouldn't matter if he didn't make it. So long as she was somewhere safe. Somewhere her light couldn't be extinguished.

Above the soft roar of liquid bullets striking the canopy above, slightly muffled by the rainwater filling his ears, he heard the low rumble of thunder. Except it wasn't thunder. It was something much, much worse. No mere warning, this was the storm's savagery unleashed.

The sound triggered something in John's fevered brain. A panic took hold. It was the same sensation he had felt when he had come across the crashed ambulance. An urgent awareness he was suddenly in great danger.

He saw a flash of white ahead. Twigs stabbed at him as he crashed through bushes towards the figure seated on the ground.

Maria hugged her knees. She was crying. All around his wife, covering the forest floor, were carcasses. Thousands and thousands of them, an unimaginable number of dead animals forming a macabre carpet, a sacrificial pit to some great and terrible deity. In the distance, the trees thinned, and the glow of lights glistened beyond. They were within sight of Warminster.

Maria suddenly looked up at him. Her brown eyes were pink with grief. '*It's killing everything,*' she sobbed. Her voice was hysterical, raw with anguish. '*It's killing everything. It's killing everything.*' She kept repeating the words, over and over, as though in a trance.

John knelt before his stricken wife. She stared through him, uncomprehending. It was as though he wasn't there at all.

'What is it?' he demanded. He withdrew the stained knife from his pocket. 'Whatever it is, I'll fight it. I'll kill it. Tell me. Tell me, Maria!'

Something landed on his hand. He blinked rain out of his eyes to get a better look, but he already knew what it was. A death's-head hawkmoth.

He looked up. A vast number of the insects flew in a huge circle above them, surrounding the pair like one of Saturn's rings. Legions of wings beating a lazy rhythm in the pouring rain.

It had rained on their wedding day. From the morning until the evening, a constant, steady pitter-patter that had done nothing to dampen the mood. John had stared at the grey skies and smiled, for they were as nothing before the radiance of the woman beside him.

The rain had been another baptism of sorts, washing away the remains of one life to prepare him for another. A life with the person who had made him a person.

The winged insect on John's hand shifted. The skull on the moth's thorax seemed to move, the mouth opening wide, a silent scream escaping its fleshless lips. The moth fluttered up to join its companions.

A roar seemed to shake the very earth beneath John's feet. Maria released a strangled sob.

The trees behind John rustled. With rising dismay, he turned…and terror stole his resolve like the first sin had stolen immortality from mankind.

The tiger emerged from the night.

It was magnificent and horrifying. A god of destruction in the flesh. The apex predator.

The beast took a few steps towards John and Maria. Muscles rippled appallingly beneath its sleek, striped coat. The rain seemed to part around the monster as it padded forwards, nature itself making way before this emperor in brown and gold. This foreign conqueror. This slayer of untold thousands. The scourge of the forest, this creature that had killed everything that moved or drew breath.

The tiger's amber gaze fixed on John. In those luminous eyes, he saw the insatiable hunger to devour. He saw the death of all things considered sacrosanct.

As the tiger drew closer, John saw himself reflected in the beast's lambent irises. Wounded. Exhausted. Small. Weak.

Utter despair washed over him. '*I-I can't fight this,*' he stammered, his voice cracking. The knife fell out of his nerveless fingers. He dropped to his knees, clawed at his face. Death had come for them at last.

Opposite him, Maria prayed.

The tiger continued its languid approach. It knew the hunt was over. It would savour its victory.

Then, the predator stopped in its tracks. Its glittering eyes narrowed, black pupils shrinking to focus on a new threat. Something even it hadn't anticipated.

A huge shadow fell across John, whose hands fell from his bloodied cheeks. He looked up.

Ancient eyes stared back at him from a leathery face. A massive simian form stepped around Maria, propelled on tree trunk arms. Rainwater ran down the silvery-black hair that bristled on its monstrously powerful back. It snorted at her, perhaps a greeting, perhaps a farewell to someone it recognised.

The one thing left alive in the forest, the one thing the tiger hadn't yet slain, faced the beast and roared its challenge.

The king had come to defend his domain.

'*Nico?*' Maria whispered. The silverback gorilla glanced at her. The look in his eyes was proud and sad. The great ape knew he was going to die here, that the final chapter of his long life was finally coming to an end. He looked at John, and then at the thinning trees and the lights of civilisation beyond. The meaning was clear.

Go.

John clambered to his feet, dragging Maria up beside him. The garrison was only a few minutes away. Behind him, the tiger snarled in anger. Nico's answering bellow shook the trees.

The gorilla leapt at the tiger. John took Maria's hand and ran.

2016

'What are you doing?'

He quickly turned off his phone screen and thrust the device in his pocket. He turned to glare at her. Tried to suppress the flash of rage, dampen the fire dancing through his veins.

'I'm trying to work,' he said coldly.

'Who were you talking to?' Maria's voice was quiet.

'Just an author friend.' Why did she keep insist on bothering him? He stared at her, willing her to disappear. This nuisance. This pain in his ass. His head throbbed. 'Are you going to accuse me of anything else or can I focus on getting this book done?'

Maria's eyes were filled with anger and hurt. 'You told me this would stop after you got back from the island. You said your book was finished.'

'I'm editing!' He snarled. 'A book isn't finished just because the story is written. Not that you'd understand.'

'I'm your wife,' she said. 'I'm worried about you, John. I'm worried about us. My friends couldn't believe you just went away for two months. They say—'

'Fuck your friends!' John roared. 'In fact, fuck Warminster and the people here.' He surged to his feet. 'How dare they judge me? What have they achieved? Everyone's the same in these small towns. Small-minded cretins jealous of their neighbours and gossiping about everyone else's problems while pretending their own shit doesn't stink.'

The fire inside him was all-consuming. The headache had turned into a raging inferno.

'Was it Esteban? What else did he say? Has that fucking Spaniard been talking more about shit about me? If I see him around here again, I'll let him have his bottle of Bacardi. Right between the eyes.'

Maria stared right back at him. Her brown eyes were wet with tears. 'There's something wrong with you, John. Ever since you came home, it's like you've been replaced by someone else. Are you on drugs?'

'Don't be ridiculous. You're the one who takes a cocktail of drugs every day.'

'You need help, John.'

'Help? No one has ever helped me in my life! I don't need help. I don't need therapy. I'm strong, and I'm successful, and I can do whatever the fuck I want. I always win. Tell me, when do I ever lose?'

'You're losing me, John,' Maria said quietly.

He laughed at her.

An hour later, she packed her bags and went to stay with Elsie.

32

The final stretch of countryside between the forest and Warminster garrison passed in a blur of rain and pain and relentless dread. Had Maria not been beside him the entire way, helping keep him upright, John would have fallen and not gotten back up.

At any moment, he expected to feel claws down his back or the weight of five hundred pounds of big cat knocking him to the ground, inescapable jaws crushing his neck like paper. But the tiger did not come for them.

They stumbled towards the flashing lights of what turned out to a military truck parked before a barricade. The harsh beam of a flashlight bathed them in an accusatory glow, and a soldier wearing one of the alien-looking respiratory masks ran out from a small office in which he was taking shelter from the storm. The soldier quickly examined them before radioing for help.

'…man in his mid-30s, badly wounded. Looks to have been attacked by a large predator. He's bleeding profusely. Immediate aid requested, over.'

They stood there in the downpour. Even terribly fatigued and woozy from loss of blood, John had the sense something was wrong. The garrison appeared to be deserted.

‘Where…where is everyone?’ he managed. His voice was little more than a rasp. ‘I thought…I thought the entire town would be here.’

The soldier was silent a moment before answering. ‘There has been an unfortunate development,’ he said regretfully. ‘The virus has already spread to humans. The masks are not as effective as we hoped.’

‘What do you mean?’ John asked, aghast. ‘We were told this place was safe!’ After all they had been through to get here, to learn that they were still in danger, that Maria still wasn’t safe, was almost too much to take. She had a strange look on her face. The whites of her eyes were pink, almost red, and she looked unfocused, as though unsure where she was or what was happening.

‘We need to get you both examined,’ the soldier said. ‘Questions can come later. Is this woman your wife?’

‘Yes,’ John said, now extremely worried.

‘How long has she been like this?’ the soldier asked, keeping his voice carefully neutral.

‘Like…like what? We were attacked by a beast out in the woods! She’s in a state of shock.’

The soldier approached Maria and placed a gloved hand gently on her chin. He tilted her face from side to side, as though searching for something. ‘Cut that out,’ John rasped, growing angry, though he had no strength left to do anything but glare at the man.

The soldier’s examination was cut short as several men and women in military uniform and respiratory masks scurried out of the darkness. Before he knew it, John and Maria were escorted through the rain-soaked garrison to one of several huge residential buildings that must have provided housing for hundreds of military personnel.

The couple were led inside of one of the buildings. Within, every single inch of available space was taken up by sick men, women, and children. They stood or crouched or sat back-to-back, a town's worth of people squeezed in like sardines. Every single one of them wore a blue surgical mask. Above the army of masks, eyes stared at the new arrivals with varying degrees of panic or incomprehension.

With rising dismay, John saw that many of those eyes possessed the same reddish tinge as Maria's. Some were a much darker shade of red. As John watched, a man whose eyes bulged out his skull like they were about to burst suddenly yelled.

His screams were inhuman, like a demon attempting to crawl out of his skin. He lashed out, striking the people around him with his fists. Soldiers swarmed the madman, dragging him away and bundling him out of the building and into the night.

'What's going on?' John said, hardly able to believe what he was seeing. A soldier placed a hand on his shoulder, and he shook it off. The only hands permitted to touch him were those belonging to Maria. The only woman who had ever touched him.

Liar.

The word roared through his foggy mind like an emergency vehicle down a dark road in the middle of the night.

'I fear we had no choice but to quarantine the populace,' said a familiar, cut-glass voice. Lieutenant

Colonel McCormack stepped out of a small room just off the main hall. From within, John could hear the grating beep of a smoke alarm. 'I'm pleased to see you found your wife, Mr Sharrock.'

'What's wrong with her?' John demanded. 'What's happening to these people? What are your soldiers going to do with that man?'

Behind his alien-looking mask, the officer heaved a regretful sigh. 'The virus has spread. It is only a matter of time before those exposed succumb to the sickness. Once the point of no return is reached, the general has ordered the infected be…destroyed.'

'*Destroyed?*' John whispered. 'What the fuck? What kind of monster murders sick people?'

John heard someone move in the small office. Through the doorway, a shadow moved across the wall, cast by whomever waited within. It looked…wrong, somehow. McCormack nodded towards the room. 'Some may call him a monster, but I assure you, the general does what is necessary.'

'But, Maria—' John began. He stopped in surprise as a familiar face appeared from the room. It was Doctor Sutra from the GP surgery. Following behind the distinguished Asian gentleman was yet another face John knew. It was Anu, his daughter, who worked at the sandwich shop on Warminster High Street.

'Hi, John,' she said, offering a small wave. 'We discovered the source of the virus. You remember you told me that Alfie went crazy after you fed him? Our cat, Tango, went mad as well. It turns out the meat used in the Hermes' Gourmet range of pet food carried some sort of disease. The cattle were illegally fed animal remains to cut down on manufacturing costs. The meat-and-bone feed had some kind of faulty protein that infected the cows, and then the entire food chain. Crazy, huh?'

John stared at Anu. She was still in her work uniform. 'That doesn't seem right,' he said sluggishly. 'The timeline doesn't match up. The virus began in Longleat. How does a hive of bees get sick from pet food anyway? I thought it was airborne. None…none of what you're saying makes any sense.'

'Ah, so the writer is a scientist now!' exclaimed Doctor Sutra. He gave John a smile and a wink. 'Why don't you leave the diagnosis to the wise guys? It looks like you've had quite the adventure.' The doctor inspected John's wounds, stared through his gold-rimmed spectacles at the bones poking through his arm. At the ragged hole in his thigh, from which blood still flowed freely. At the deep red gouges in his shredded chest. 'You're a bit under the weather,' the doctor announced. 'Some pills should do the trick.'

Pills?

'What are you talking about?' John rasped. 'What's this nonsense about pills? What the hell is happening?' He rubbed at his face, trying to banish whatever spell had settled over the room, whatever insanity seemed to be infecting the minds of all those around him.

'Easy, John,' said another voice he recognised. It was Adam. His husband Justin was beside him. Both were perfectly well, as healthy the day John had last spotted them in their shop, serving customers with smiles on their faces. 'Why don't you rest now, John?' Adam said kindly. 'Afterwards, you can try some of our brownies. I have a new recipe. You'll love it.'

John was struck by a wave of fatigue so great he almost collapsed. His eyes were heavy. His body was on the point of collapse. It felt like he was Atlas, holding the weight of the world upon his shoulders. It would be so easy to sleep now. To give up and rest. He sagged, his head drooping. Out of the corner of his eye, he glimpsed Maria.

She was staring at nothing, her eyes weeping scarlet tears.

'I…will…not…*stop*,' he growled, punching himself in the head so hard his knuckles cracked. Outside, a sudden peal of thunder rolled across town.

Lieutenant Colonel McCormack tutted. 'He's quite clearly delirious,' he announced. 'Men, if you would be so good as to restrain Mr Sharrock.'

John looked around desperately. There was something he was missing. Some key to unlocking whatever was happening here. Through the rain-streaked windows, he saw Cley Hill illuminated by a streak of lightning. Above, the red star burned in the sky like the Eye of Sauron…

'The other night,' he said, feeling for the truth, willing it to come to him. 'A helicopter landed outside Warminster. At least, I thought it was a helicopter. Flying objects have been spotted in the sky above town for decades. It even has a name, the Warminster Thing. The attacks started soon after. A fucking *red star* appeared in the sky.' John pieced it all together, the sequence of events falling into place at last. 'All of this is your doing, isn't it? You brought the virus to earth. Is this how you plan to conquer us? You want to drive us all crazy, save you the work of killing us yourselves? That red star, whatever it is…it's your mothership. Your way back to wherever it is you came from. You know, McCormack, something's just occurred to me. You and your 'soldiers.' I've never even seen your faces. Why don't you take off that mask and show me what you really are?'

A stunned silence met his words. *I've finally figured it out,* he thought, elated.

Laughter like the tinkling of tiny bells broke the silence. From the darkness at the back of the crowded hall, a dark angel in black and purple strode forth.

'Even now,' said Kim, walking towards him. Somehow seeming to walk *through* the townsfolk, as though she were a thing that existed only partially within this reality. 'Even now you won't see what's right in front of you. Just how long can you keep this up, John?'

'Your diagnosis is incorrect,' said Doctor Sutra, as though he hadn't heard Kim. 'This is the virus at work. Everything stems from the sickness. The *Hostile* virus, we are calling it.'

From the small office, the acrid smell of smoke and burning rubber reached John's nostrils. The smoke detector was going crazy, the harsh beep it emitted louder than an HGV driving in reverse.

Kim smiled her enigmatic grin, and her grey eyes were like portals into the underworld. 'Hostile,' she said, tasting the word as though it were honey caught between her teeth. 'From the Latin *hostillis*, meaning "enemy." Not to be confused with *hospes*, which means "host" or "guest," and from which the word "hospital" comes.'

Another figure emerged from the office. A man. He was slim and muscular, of average height, wearing jeans and a T-shirt. Somehow, the cap on his head cast a shadow that obscured his face.

Lieutenant Colonel McCormack stiffened and threw a salute. The other soldiers followed suit. The man with the cap returned the salute mockingly. A white crescent formed in the shadow of his face. It took John a moment to realise he was smiling.

Maria suddenly cried out and brought her hands up to her face. The shadowy figure beckoned, and before John could stop her, Maria ran to him. Together, they disappeared outside.

'Maria!' John shouted. He went to chase after them, but McCormack caught him by the shoulder with a firm but supple hand. He had thin fingers. Like those of a surgeon.

Kim continued as though nothing untoward had just occurred. 'Here's an interesting fact for you, John. Both *hostillis* and *hospes* derive from the Proto-Indo-European word *g*^{h}*óstis*…which means, roughly, "stranger."'

STRANGER.

Suddenly, John knew the source of the sickness.

2003

The phone rang. John took a deep breath, afraid someone might answer. This was it. This was the moment.

'Hola?' *said a female voice.*

'Hola,' *said John. He tried to remember the phrase Maria had taught him.*

'¿quisiera hablar con Maria, por favor?' *His voice was halting, and he knew he'd mangled the words. He waited for Maria's mum to laugh at him or put the phone down. But there was no laughter. Only a moment of silence. And then:*

'Si, un momento.'

The line went quiet as the sound of receding footsteps echoed down the receiver.

He waited. Anticipation and dread built inside him. What if he said no? What if the letter hadn't worked? What if—

He heard noise on the other end of the phone. The receiver clicked.

'He said YES!' screamed Maria down the phone at him. Her voice burst with joy.

Elation flooded through him. 'What...what convinced him?' he stammered.

'He really liked what you said in the letter. He likes that you work hard and love your family, and that you don't do drugs or anything like that. I can't believe it, I'm going to England!'

He couldn't believe it, either. His life had been turned upside down in the space of a year. First, the accident which had almost killed him. Then, he had fallen in love with the most incredible girl. He had visited her in Spain and experienced things he had never expected to feel. They immediately discussed how she could visit him in England, but her parents were deeply worried. She was only eighteen.

And so, he had written a letter to her father. A letter in English, for he knew very little Spanish. A friend of Maria had very kindly offered to translate for him. Maria had given the letter to her father. She had promised not to read it first. John had never poured his heart out to anyone before, and the things he had written in that letter, he wished to keep between himself and Maria's father.

'I can't believe it,' Maria said again. She was crying now; he could hear the tears in her voice. 'Do you think it will be cold in England?'

'Definitely!' John said, laughing. 'Remember to pack a coat!'

They talked excitedly for the next hour. Maria wanted to know where she could buy the chocolate biscuits her mum loved, the ones he had brought with him the first time he visited. She wanted to know if they could visit Buckingham Palace and the National Art Gallery.

He told her he would love to take her. He hadn't seen them before, either. The thought of going to London by himself and facing the huge crowds was too much. With Maria at his side, though, he knew he could do anything.

'What do you want to do?' she asked him. 'The day I arrive, I mean. We can do anything you want!'

He thought about this for a moment. 'I want to watch Return of the King *with you,' he said. 'It's still playing at the cinema.'*

'But you've seen it!' Maria laughed.

'I know,' he said, somewhat bashfully. 'But you haven't. It's my favourite film. Did I ever tell you how I used to hide in the library and read The Silmarillion *when I was growing up? Middle Earth is my safe place.'*

'That's why I got you the present!' Maria said. 'From Lord of the Rings. *Are you wearing it now?'*

He looked at the golden replica of the One Ring around his finger. 'Yes,' he said. 'I hope that doesn't make me a Dark Lord.'

'Maybe it makes you Frodo,' Maria said teasingly. 'Mr Frodo,' she said, her Spanish voice imitating Samwise Gamgee's west country burr.

'Hey!' he said, laughing. 'Are you making fun of me or Sam?'

'Sam,' Maria said mischievously.

'Fine,' he said. 'If you see anything in my eye at the end of the film, it's not a teardrop, just so you know.'

'What do you mean?' Maria asked. 'Is the ending sad?'

'It's not so much sad,' John replied, 'it's just that everything...changes. I'm not very good at change. I'm not good at letting go.'

'Change can be good!' Maria exclaimed. 'Look at us!' Her voice grew more serious. 'My dad trusts you,' she said. 'He said that in the letter you promised to look after me. You know he's very protective. You'll look after me, won't you?'

'Yes,' he said immediately. 'I promise.'

33

John grabbed McCormack's arm and twisted it, pinning it behind the officer. For a soldier, McCormack was surprisingly weak. With his other hand, John pulled the pistol from the holster at McCormack's belt and placed the barrel against the man's head.

'Drop your guns!' John snarled, as the soldiers in the hall reached for their weapons. 'Stand down or I'll shoot.'

'Do it,' McCormack ordered his soldiers. His voice sounded thin, defeated. Weapons struck the floor like bodies before a firing squad.

John shuffled backwards, the lieutenant colonel held before him like a shield. He barged open the main barracks door, dragging the officer backwards, hardly feeling the cold sting of the rain against his brow. The red star overhead pierced through the storm clouds like a laser, bathing the garrison in a crimson radiance. Like he was stepping into Hell.

John looked around wildly. His eyes stung. Even out in the evening squall, the acrid stench of something burning was overpowering.

'Where is he?' John barked. 'Where is that'—*Man? Thing?*—'Monster,' he spat.

‘The general?’ said McCormack quietly. ‘Where he always is. Wherever the darkness is greatest.’

The lieutenant colonel pointed at a shadowy corner of the garrison. The lampposts failed to pierce the blackness that festered there. John dragged McCormack with him down streets slick with rainwater.

As he staggered towards the darkness, soldiers began filing out of the barracks. They were followed by Doctor Sutra, his daughter Anu, and then Adam and Justin, and finally Kim, her grey eyes curious, face bright with anticipation, as though she were about to receive the long-awaited answer to a question.

None of the soldiers made any effort to stop John. They simply followed in his wake, their bodies moving in sync, as though they were automatons controlled by some unseen puppet master.

Neither did McCormack attempt to free himself from John’s grasp. Not even when John’s arm wavered from exhaustion, and the pistol dipped from the officer’s head. It was as though the lieutenant colonel had accepted his role in some larger design.

John’s breath rattled in his lungs. Even with McCormack offering no resistance, every step was a monumental struggle. Everything hurt so much. John hadn’t so much as cried out in pain when he’d been mown down by the motorbike which had fractured his leg in two places. But this agony was all-consuming, as though his entire body had been smashed beyond repair, his skeleton shattered, bones held together now only by sheer force of will.

As John neared the heart of the darkness, he saw the bodies. Dead men, women, and even children sprawled on the ground, their throats torn out by…*something*. The blue cloth surgical masks they wore hadn't shielded them from the virus. Nor had they offered any protection from the pitiless monster who had brought the sickness to this place.

There came a soft *click*, the ignition of a cheap lighter generating a spark. An orange flame sprung into existence. In the lurid glow of its fire, the stranger was finally revealed.

He stood before what appeared to be a huge pile of detritus. John squinted, trying to make sense of what he saw. It was a mountain of home furniture and appliances, old bed frames and armchairs and wooden cabinets, broken television sets and vacuum cleaners and microwaves. A lawnmower. A garden trimmer that John vaguely recognised.

As he stared, he realised the entire heap was made up of things he and Maria had owned over the years. A married life's worth of possessions, items they had scraped and saved for with little help from anyone. Books had been arranged around the edge of the pile. Despite the pounding rain, their pages were somehow as dry as kindling.

A pyre, John realised, horrified.

Sitting near the top of the pyre, her mouth locked in an expression of horror, eyes weeping blood, was Maria.

The stranger shifted as John approached. He brought the lighter closer to his face, revealing dark facial stubble and a wide smile beneath the shadows of his hat. 'You're here,' he said, in a voice that was strangely familiar. He sounded amused. 'I didn't think you would make it this far.'

'I don't quit,' John replied. His voice shook with anger. 'What are you planning to do with that lighter?'

'You already know the answer to that. I didn't start this fire, John. You did.'

'Let her go.'

'You know I can't do that.'

'I'll kill you.'

The stranger's smile widened. The flame seemed to dance with amusement. 'There's my tiger! Doesn't it feel good, John? The hatred. The rage. *The hunger.*'

'Fuck you.'

There was movement beside John. An enigma in black and purple walked past him and went to stand beside the stranger.

'Kim?' John said, stunned. 'What are you doing? Get away from him! He's dangerous.'

'It's Lilith now,' Kim said coldly. 'You made sure of that.' Beside her, the stranger's smile glowed like a crescent moon. 'This is where I'm supposed to be. I already told you. I prefer the monsters.'

'You don't need to follow men like him. You're too intelligent for that.'

Kim shook her head angrily. 'And you're a guilt-ridden fool, John.'

The stranger's sudden laughter seemed to reach inside of him to the child he once was. Confused. Afraid. Not enough. A thing belonging to the shadows, where none could see how at the very core of him, he was undeserving of acceptance.

Maria moved her mouth as though she was trying to speak, but no sound emerged.

John took a step towards the stranger, McCormack clutched before him. 'What are you?' he demanded, voice shaking with fury. The unresisting officer flinched, as though he, too, dreaded the answer.

'What am I?' the stranger said in his insidious, oddly familiar voice. He raised the lighter slowly towards his face, eating away at the shadow, teasing out the truth as a priest teases out a confession. 'I am the breaking of the chains that bind us. I am the death of fear and self-doubt. I am the weapons the broken find in their darkest places. I am the obsession that can win a heart or rewrite a destiny. I am acceptance of the way the world is and not how the world ought to be.'

The shadow finally melted away. John stared at the stranger's face. It was a visage he had known his entire life.

Without thinking, he released his grip on McCormack. Brought his hands up to his face. Felt his beard, a week's worth of growth. Felt the old, faded black and red cap on his head. It was sopping wet from the rain.

He stared at his hands in horror. The truth was inescapable.

The stranger was him.

As though waking from a dream, McCormack suddenly made a grab for the weapon in John's hand. The stranger, *the other him*, waved a hooked finger. The lieutenant colonel collapsed to his knees, his hands clenched around his throat, gasping wetly. Blood poured through his fingers.

Other John laughed again. 'You see? You understand our power now? The chains are gone, John. You tore them off. You let the beast within roam free. It killed the voice that told you that you couldn't. It destroyed the doubt that threatened to break you. It gave you the strength to *succeed.*'

John squeezed his eyes shut. The memories were coming back to him in a flood. 'I know what you are now,' he rasped. 'You're my psychosis. The trauma that was placed there when I was a child. The trauma I was too young to process, so I turned it into something that could protect me. A darkness, a demon that takes control when I am threatened or afraid. The books, Maria's health, my mum's cancer, my own mental health issues…things I should have gotten help for years ago. I lost myself. I became someone else. I became *you.*'

'Wrong,' Other John laughed. 'I've always been here. You just opened the door too far. This time, I stepped all the way through.'

'I don't want you!' John screamed.

'You need me!' Other John snarled back at him. 'You think you'd have achieved anything without me? A snivelling weakling hiding away from the world? A coward afraid of change, too terrified to poke his head above the walls of his own pitiful, self-imposed prison? Would *he* have jumped on a plane with a broken leg to meet a girl? Would *he* have killed the wolves of fear and self-loathing about to devour his career? *You* sat around with your dick in your hands, feeling sorry for yourself. *I* wrote a book in two months, saved us from financial ruin!' Other John nodded at Maria. She was comatose now, streaks of red running down her cheeks. 'Back when you were writing your first book, she didn't believe in you. You remember, don't you?'

'She was afraid,' John shot back. 'She was worried about our future. She moved to England to be with me. Of course she believed.'

'Always an excuse for everyone else.' Other John sneered. 'What about your father's family? They told you they would look out for you, only to disappear from your life. What about your teachers? They told you that you would never amount to anything. Your friends? Dead or in prison. While you and I, we only get stronger. Get your head out of your ass, Johnny-boy. The world is a jungle. You dominate or you die. Nothing matters, the weak use you or lose you, and the strongest, the smartest, they accept the way things are, and they fucking *thrive*. Here. Let me show you.'

Other John brought two fingers to his mouth and made a silent whistling gesture. Behind John, the soldiers who had followed him into the darkness formed up, rank and file. Other John threw a salute and, like puppets, the soldiers returned the gesture. Other John grinned. He crooked a finger, slashed it through the air. Two of the soldiers collapsed, crimson spraying from their throats.

'Enough!' John shouted. 'You're sick.'

'Sick? I am *clarity*. These sheep, these NPCs, call them whatever you will—you truly wish to be like them? Look at me! Unstoppable. Relentless. I'm a fucking *tiger*.'

'You've destroyed everything,' John whispered. 'I want you gone.'

Other John's eyes narrowed. 'Like I said, you need me. Even now, I'm the only thing keeping you alive.'

The only thing keeping me alive?

'Release Maria,' John said. 'Let her go.'

'You're not listening, Johnny-boy. Letting her go is the one thing I can't do.'

'I won't tell you again. Let her go.'

Other John knelt, brought the lighter close to the pile of books stacked on the makeshift pyre. The flame winked out, plunging him into shadow. 'Or what?' he asked mockingly, a voice in the darkness now. A disembodied predator's grin wide enough to devour the world.

'I already told you. I'll kill you.'

The lighter ignition clicked, and the flame burst back into life. Other John brought the flame within inches of the books. 'You think you're strong enough to kill me?' he growled. '*I am your strength*, you fucking coward. I've already won.'

Other John curled his finger. Slashed it through the air like an executioner's axe delivering the killing blow.

John felt his flesh tear apart. Heard the hideous rip as his own throat unravelled, an explosion of pain and shock and hot, gushing blood. He staggered back, one hand desperately trying to plug the ragged hole in his neck, the other still clutching the pistol. Dully, he looked up. Through rapidly dimming eyes, he saw an angel. He saw Maria.

'Love is what made me strong,' he growled wetly. 'Not you. Go to Hell.'

The stranger was still smiling when John straightened, raised the gun, and shot him through the head.

34

The silence that followed the gunshot was like the calm after a storm. John blinked, trying to make sense of the world. He reached tentatively for his neck, fearful his fingers would touch torn flesh, accidentally probe a gaping wound from which his lifeblood poured like the waters of Iguazu Falls from their honeymoon in South America.

Nothing. His throat was perfectly unharmed, as unblemished as a newborn babe. He looked at his shredded arm, at his wounded leg. They were whole again, the flesh intact. His clothes, too, were somehow repaired, his T-shirt and jeans as fresh as if they'd just been washed and hung out to dry in the summer sun.

John looked at the heavens. It was morning. The skies were clear, the brilliant blue above the perfect canvas for a child's whimsy. On the ground before him, the stranger's body twitched once and lay still. The hole in his head revealed nothing but blackness within, a gateway to some place madness dwelled. Smoke rose from the body. Inky tendrils reached up towards the heavens, only to be dispersed by a soft wind, like the breath of an angel, or a guardian spirit.

'Maria,' John cried. He leapt over the disintegrating form of the stranger—a pitiful, unloved thing, he saw now—and climbed the mountain of furniture and appliances, household items and trinkets, small things from their shared life together that contained the memory of a deep and lasting happiness.

Maria stirred. John saw that her eyes were no longer red with grief and sickness. They were bright, loving, the colour of warm coffee. The eyes that had greeted him every morning for years.

Maria shook her head, as though awakening from a trance. She saw him watching her. '*John?*' she said. It was like she was seeing him for the first time. She raised her hands, the wedding band around her finger glimmering with the brilliance of young love, untarnished by the relentless passage of time. She cupped his face and stared at him in wonder. 'You came back.'

Below them, the sound of a child's laughter drifted up from the streets. It was a young girl, John saw. She carried a red balloon that said, '**Happy Birthday!**' in big letters. Behind her, a man that must have been her father took hold of her hand and produced an ice cream from somewhere, much to his daughter's delight. He saw John watching him and nodded in greeting.

It was his estate agent, John realised. The fellow who had sold him and Maria their first house.

But he was in the Bat Cave, John thought, confused. *They both were. I saw them. Didn't I?*

Other faces appeared in the crowd of people now gathering in the square opposite. He saw Adam and Justin, their faces unnaturally vivid, grinning up at him. His accountant, Denise, who waved what looked like an invoice at him. The woman from the post office, Carrie, wearing the constipated expression of a disgruntled customer desperately searching around for someone to complain to. Maria's friend Elsie was there with little Lizzie, pointing at Maria and smiling happily. A small, familiar shape bounded up alongside them and gave a short, sharp bark. It was Alfie. The little shih zu was looking up in John's direction. His head kept darting this way and that in confusion, as though he sensed but was unable to fully see his owner.

Something about the scene felt wrong, somehow—but when John tried to order his thoughts, they kept exploding into multicoloured particles. Like confetti in the rain.

'John,' Maria said. Her voice wrenched his attention back to her. 'Are you okay?'

'Yes,' he replied, meeting her eyes. He took a deep breath. 'Maria,' he began, 'I'm sorry. I'm so sorry. I let you down.'

'We let each other down,' she replied. Her smile was sad, and tears glistened in her eyes.

'You never let me down,' John protested. 'We were happy. Weren't we?'

'Things weren't perfect,' Maria replied. 'Not all the time. But we had each other. We were a team and, for years, that was enough.'

'I lost myself,' John said. 'I became someone else. I lost sight of what was important.'

'Your books were important to you. And you finished them, just like you said you would.'

'They made us unhappy. I made you unhappy.'

'You did. But I made myself unhappy, too. I'm not perfect, John.'

'You were perfect—' he began, but she raised a finger and placed it gently against his lips. 'Remember what I told you? You always see the best in people. It's one of the things I loved most about you.'

Tears rolled down Maria's cheeks. Not sick tears, not the red tears of the virus the stranger had unleashed upon his world. These were tears of grief. Clear and raw.

'Maria? John said, beginning to panic. 'What's wrong? What aren't you telling me?'

The sound of heavy boots crunching on the mountain of memories beneath them heralded the arrival of a loose end.

Kimberley Grimes looked at the dark outline of what had been the stranger, and then at John. 'I'm no one's loose end,' she said angrily, her grey eyes narrowed. 'And you are *not* the hero of this story, John.'

He stared at her in confusion. Had she just read his thoughts? Maria sobbed suddenly. '*Why didn't you ask for help?*' she sobbed.

John stared around wildly. He had the sudden feeling of weightlessness, like he might drift up and fly away at any moment. The sky seemed to lighten, the colour draining away. Cerulean blue faded to a blank white. White noise, growing louder, buzzing in his brain like flies around a corpse.

'What's happening? he gasped. Below, the crowd now filled the entire street. He saw more faces he recognised. Mike, from the gym. *How? He died! I saw him die!* Nikki Glass. *She died, too. How...how do I know that?* Rosie from The George Inn. Her father, Bill. Bob the boatman from Longleat. *Bob? How do I know Bob?* The two Welshmen seemed to merge into each other, as though they were one and the same. Or perhaps just ghosts, mere figments of his imagination.

Lieutenant Colonel McCormack suddenly jumped up from where he'd been lying at the bottom of the memory mountain. The two dead soldiers rose with him, undying revenants summoned back to life through some unholy magic. John glanced at Kim, but she simply rolled her eyes.

'*We're losing him*,' said McCormack. His voice seemed to come from somewhere very far away. From beyond the military garrison. From beyond the shroud of white that had replaced the sky. From somewhere that filled John with a sudden, mind-numbing terror. '*Rosie*,' McCormack instructed, '*Fetch his family. Quickly.*'

'What is he talking about?' John stammered. Above him, the white canvas cracked. Dark lines spread across it, like a spiderweb woven by an arachnid big enough to eat the sun.

McCormack reached up and slowly removed his mask. His soldiers followed suit. The townsfolk removed their blue surgical face masks.

John stared in horror. None of them had a face. Only a messy blur where their faces should be.

'No writer can fill in every blank,' said Kim. 'Not even you, John. You built this world from memory and fiction to hide from the truth. You created a story in which you could be the hero, escape the guilt of what you've done. It is time for the story to end.'

Adam approached, a kindly smile on his face. 'You stayed, just like I told you to. But now you have to go, John.'

There was a fluttering sound nearby. Tom appeared beside John. A host of death's-head hawkmoths circled his brow like a crown of thorns. 'It's time, laddie,' said the old undertaker. He reached out a weathered hand.

'No,' John moaned. He backed away, desperate to escape the grasping hands suddenly stretching for him. He bumped into his other half. Felt her warm hand on his arm. A hand he had known for most of his adult life, the ring around her finger the confirmation of a promise made long ago.

'John, *we need to leave*,' came Maria's urgent voice in his ear. 'We have to go back to the house. We have to go *now*.'

'Okay,' he managed, surrendering to her.

Together, they fled.

35

They were in the downstairs hallway of their home. How had they gotten back here?

The lights were on. The bulbs were blindingly bright, and he could hardly see. Maria was beside him, her hand clutching his arm. His anchor. His strength.

'Upstairs,' she said desperately. 'The nursery. You need to see.'

'Where's Alfie?' John said, his voice shaking. Nothing made any sense.

He stumbled up the stairs. The staircase blurred. Every step felt like an unknown threat, a car veering out of the night. He wobbled like he was drunk, swaying wildly. Had Maria not been there to support him, he would have tumbled back down the stairs.

They had just reached the upstairs landing when his phone buzzed in his jean pocket.

'Don't answer it!' Maria said in alarm.

But it was too late. He stared at the luminous screen. At the first of several messages between him and Maria.

I'm writing to let you know I've decided to stay at Elsie's for the time being. I don't have anywhere else to go. Ever since you got back from the island, you've become a different person entirely.

Fine. Go stay with Elsie. I'm busy editing my book, and I could use some space. I shouldn't have thrown the plate. I'll buy another one.

You always need space, John. And it's not about the plate. I hope us going to visit my family helps you feel better. Speak soon. Love you.

'John, don't read anymore. Please—'

I've made a decision. I'm not going to Spain with you. I still need to work on my book. Say hi to your family for me.

You're not coming? I don't understand. We've just spent two months apart. I'll come home from Elsie's if it upsets you so much. You always loved visiting my family. My parents will wonder where you are. They love you, John.

John stumbled and the phone almost tumbled out of his hands. Maria's father was going to be celebrating his fiftieth birthday while they were visiting. How had he forgotten that? Maria had spoken excitedly about it for months.

She supported him now, holding him up, but her grip was loosening.

'I'm begging you, John,' she pleaded, 'let it go. Don't read anymore. Look, see what I've done with the nursery—'

John. Just so you know, I popped around the house today while you were visiting your mum. I know about the girl you've been talking to, Kim. I found the hairband in the shower.

I didn't want you to see that. I've told her we can't see each other again.

I needed to experience something different before we committed to becoming parents, Maria. Something other than what I've known my entire life. You agreed. I never lied to you.

I didn't want to agree, John. I just wanted you to be happy. I trusted you. I don't know what's happening. What are we doing? I want my old life back, John. I want you *back.*

'*John.* Stop. STOP.'

Like a moth drawn to a flame, like a lemming drawn to a cliff edge, he brought the phone up to his face and continued to read, his eyes blurring.

Maria, the hospital called. They've found another donor for us. I've decided it's not a good time to think about having children. We're not in the right place. I told them to take us off the list for now.

I can't believe you did that. Why, John? Why, why, WHY? You know I wanted more than anything to be a mum. I can't believe this, I can't believe it. You broke my heart, John. Of all the things you've done. I can't believe it.

I'm sorry.

Guilt hit John like a brick wall. He turned to Maria, determined to apologise again, to attempt to explain himself.

His wife was gone. Vanished, like she never had been there at all. He was alone. All alone once more. He stumbled towards the bedroom door, gripping the handle with a shaking hand and pushing it open. Somehow, the light in the nursery was already on. The window was open again. He couldn't tell if it was night or day. An angry wall of fog had crept right to the edge of the glass, blotting out everything except the sound of a car alarm beeping somewhere in the grey beyond.

The phone buzzed again.

Hey, I'm writing to let you know I finally finished the book. There's a note for you in the Acknowledgments. I hope you read it someday.

I don't care about your bloody book! Can't you see what it's done to us? I spend all day crying. You've destroyed my love for you, John. You destroyed everything. I haven't been happy for months. I loved you so much, John. This is the hardest thing I've ever had to do.

I have to tell you this. I don't want to be with you anymore.

He felt something on his cheeks. He was crying. He never cried.

A nightmare freed itself from the pit where happiness went to die. He recognised it not as a nightmare but a memory, an incident that had happened sometime after he got back from the island. An incident that had echoed a similar occurrence he experienced as a child, a few years after his father's death.

He had been lying in bed late at night when he was overwhelmed by the sense that something, some presence, was in the house with him. He was in the spare room, he and Maria having begun sleeping apart. He sat bolt upright, listening for any sign of an intruder. But the sensation didn't come from anywhere outside.

It was within him. A tingle in his limbs, a sense of building pressure, as though something was trying to force its way into his body. Some alien malevolence of sinister intent.

A stranger.

He had prayed. First to a God he hardly believed in, and then to his father, and then to anyone who might be listening. He saw the sickness with clear eyes then, and he prayed for salvation, some divine intervention to stop it before it was too late.

The phone lit up. The screen's glare offered no mercy.

Destroyed everything? Because I had to go away to work so that we could still have a roof over our heads? I gave you everything, you ungrateful bitch. Now you want to leave me? You won't be happy. You know I'm always proven right in the end.

You're nothing without me. I won't let you go. Ever.

He heard the flutter of tiny wings. Flying insects poured into the room through the open window, the jabbering skulls on their bodies singing a dirge for the soon to be departed.

Death's-head hawkmoths.

The fog followed behind, flowing slowly through the window with tender care. Soon, it would engulf everything. Swallow the nursery, and John with it. There was no escape this time. His strength was gone.

Maria's words echoed from somewhere.

See what I've done with the nursery.

Finally, John Sharrock looked up at the walls.

A colourful zoo stared back at him. A safari park of friendly cartoon animals waiting to greet the nursery's first tiny resident whenever they might arrive. Maria had painted them all with the same enthusiasm she brought to everything.

There was a trio of cheeky monkeys holding oversized bananas; a blue elephant with big, innocent eyes. There was a sly-looking snake. A spider wearing comical red boots. Half a dozen ants dressed as little soldiers, the small squad helping several cheerful bees bring nectar back to their hive. A brilliant blue lake, in the middle of which a pair of hippos sunbathed happily.

Pride of place on the wall, larger than all the other animals and painted in finer detail, was a big striped tiger. It was supposed to look fearsome. As John stared at it, he saw that it also appeared a little confused. Maria had said it reminded her of him. She had gazed at him adoringly as she said it.

He reeled away from the wall. The fog was inches from him now. The death's-head hawkmoths surrounded him, their fluttering circuits through the air bringing them closer and closer with each pass, corralling him. His phone buzzed.

It was the final two messages from Maria.

I wish I never met you. I hate you.

And then, an hour later, a photo.

Their wedding album open on a table.

A bottle of wine.

An empty glass.

A bottle of pills, half its contents scattered across the table. The other half—

I'm sorry I'm sorry I could never hate you, John You were my world I can't live like this anymore us hurting each other. I'm sorry

I will always Love you

Maria

John remembered everything. Phoning Maria in a blind panic, demanding to know exactly what she had taken. Calling 999 and screaming at them to send an ambulance. The guilt. The utter self-hatred that ignited in his veins like gasoline. The roar of something deep within him awakening from its slumber, something stronger and more ferocious than even the sickness that had poisoned his thoughts.

The ambulance quickly arrived and took Maria to hospital. The paramedics confirmed she would probably be okay, perhaps some vomiting, likely a headache for a day or two.

John had downed an entire bottle of Bacardi, his promised reward for finally completing his novel. He waited until almost 3:50am, when the streets were empty. He opened a pack of Hermes' Gourmet Dog Food and filled Alfie's bowl. Then, he went to his car, opened the door of the red convertible that was his pride and joy. He popped open the glove compartment. Pushed the thing for which he had sacrificed everything inside, until it fit.

Two thoughts burned like fire in his tanked-up brain. Two truths he knew were immutable, as much a part of him as his heart or soul. Two truths that could never be reconciled, for some things couldn't exist in the same moment in time. One had to triumph over the other.

I will never let her go.

I need to protect her.

It was time to kill a monster.

He put the key in the ignition and started the engine.

The car swerved as bright lights danced around his face like fireflies. He tried to concentrate on the road ahead, but it seemed to twist and writhe. He caught himself drifting towards the kerb and tried to veer away, but it was as though the steering wheel was locked in place.

Nothing made any sense. A car passed him on the right, and he vaguely registered the sound of a horn beeping. He glanced back, taking his eyes off the road for a split second.

Everything turned red.

The death's-skull hawkmoths crawled all over him now, their tiny wings covering his body like a shroud. The beep outside became one long mechanical *bleeeeeeeeeeeeep.* It was the sound of a car alarm. The sound of a microwave finishing. The sound of a smoke detector warning of potential danger.

It was the mournful cry of a life support machine finally signalling the end.

It was then John finally accepted the truth.

He collapsed to his knees, a terror unlike anything he had ever known putting the lie to his childish belief that there was nothing he wasn't strong enough to cope with. Despite his panic, the fog reached for him with comforting arms, and he thought he saw faces within; one familiar to him, a face he hadn't seen since he was a very young boy, cheerfully pushing a new Transformers toy along the carpet one Christmas morning. It comforted him, but still he was afraid. He didn't know how to give up. He didn't know how to let go.

From somewhere came a voice. The voice of an angel. It spoke his name.

One last time, John Sharrock remembered.

2006

It was a sunny Sunday afternoon in spring. 'Primavera,' in the Spanish language: a season of joy and growth. The lemon trees in the yard were bursting with their yellow fruit. The budgie in its delicate cage sang happily. Maria's grandmother, her abuela, *took a sip of her wine and smacked her lips in satisfaction.*

The smell of the meat on the parrilla *made John's mouth water. Maria's father always cooked the meat to perfection. Her family were seated around the table outside. There was her father, her sister, her sister's boyfriend, her aunt, her grandmother, and, of course, her mother, who was in and out of the house preparing the vegetables.*

John had offered to help, but as always, her family had assured him that he wasn't to do anything except take a seat at the table. Still, he felt awkward watching her father slowly grill the carne, *undeserving of such kindness. John would have to ask Maria's dad to teach him so that he could cook it for them when they were married and living in their own place together.*

'The food will be ready in a minute,' Maria said, smiling at him. 'My dad asked if you want white wine or red.'

'Whichever he prefers,' John said helplessly. 'Honestly, I'm okay with just a beer. You don't have to go to all this trouble.'

'It's not any trouble,' Maria assured him with a smile. 'You're a guest.'

'Are you sure I can't help with anything?'

'Well…you could help me lay the table.'

John leapt up and brought out some glasses and plates, as well as two bottles of cola from the fridge in the kitchen.

Maria's aunt said something to her and looked at John.

'I didn't catch that,' he said, a little self-consciously. 'What did she say?'

'She asked if your leg is okay,' Maria said. 'She said you're limping a bit.'

John glanced down. His leg had been bothering him the last couple of days. 'I think I just need to strengthen it,' he said. 'It's been a few years since the accident. Do you remember when they let me into the zoo for free?'

Maria laughed. 'I remember! It was our second or third date, the first time you visited here. They thought you were disabled.'

'I guess that's one benefit of being hit by a motorbike,' he said wryly. 'I'll join the gym when we're back in England. I always wanted to be strong.'

'You're already strong,' Maria said. 'I knew it the first time we talked.'

Her father signalled that food was ready, and they sat down to eat. 'My dad asks if it's okay,' Maria said. Her dad watched John expectantly.

'It's delicious,' John said around mouthfuls. He thought for a moment, trying to remember the word. 'Riquisimo,*' he said. He gave a thumbs-up for good measure.*

To his relief, Maria's father smiled and nodded in satisfaction.

John finished his plate of food. Maria's father went back to the parrilla to finish grilling the next serving of beef. Maria's sister said something to her in Spanish. John knew she spoke reasonable English, but she was always hesitant to speak it in front of John.

'Sorry, I didn't understand,' John said. He really needed to study harder. He couldn't expect Maria to act as his translator forever.

'My sister asked about your job,' Maria said. 'I mean, what you do for work.'

'I work in insurance,' John said. 'Or at least I did until recently. I had to leave my job to come here and prepare for our wedding. In a few years, I'd love to be a writer.'

'Escritor?*' Maria's sister said. 'You write books?' she added unexpectedly.*

'One day,' John replied.

'¿Qué tipo?' *She thought for a moment, turned to Maria.*

'What kind?' Maria helpfully translated.

'Fantasy. You know, like Lord of the Rings*? Maybe afterwards I'll write a horror.'*

Maria translated this for her family. Her grandmother grinned and said something in Spanish.

'She says you could write about us,' Maria translated, smiling. 'In your horror book.'

John thought about this. 'I don't think I could,' he said. 'I can't write about something that doesn't make sense.'

Maria translated this. 'What do you mean?' she said, translating her aunt's next question.

John felt suddenly embarrassed. 'There's no horror here. Nothing but love. This…' he said, gesturing at everyone around the table, 'is the world as it should be. Todo el mundo.*'*

Maria attempted to explain this to her family, who seemed to understand and appeared happy with his answer. John drained his wine.

'Remember, my aunts and uncles and cousins are coming around later,' said Maria, as her father went to refill his glass.

'Maria!' said her sister disapprovingly.

*John grinned. '*Solo un poco,*' he said to Maria's father, emboldened by his recent practice and the wine to risk a little more Spanish. 'Just a tiny glass,' he said to Maria. She smiled at him, and he knew he'd said the right thing.*

He and Maria cleared the table after they were finished eating. Everyone retired to their rooms for an afternoon siesta.

A few hours later, the guests arrived. Maria's extended family was large, and she had many young cousins who raced around the house and yard like fireflies. They stared at him curiously, this stranger who seemed to communicate only in smiles and monosyllables.

One of them, the youngest girl, had fetched the toy bear he had brought for Maria the first time he visited from England. She pushed its chest, listened in confusion as it played the pre-recorded message John had chosen at the build-a-bear shop.

'I love you.'

She gave John a puzzled look. '¿Qué significa?' *she asked him.*

He knew enough Spanish to understand what the child meant.

'I love you,' he said, pointing at his heart. 'Te amo.'

The girl grinned and stared at the bear in delight. Then, she ran off, the toy clutched tightly in her arms.

The sun went down, and darkness fell. Maria's family were all outside now. There was food and drink and much laughter. One of her uncles brought the portable CD player outside and played a Latin American song in Spanish with a loud drum beat that Maria called 'cumbia.' Her family danced to the music.

They all possessed much more rhythm than John, and he watched them in quiet appreciation, nursing his beer and trying not to appear awkward, smiling and shaking his head whenever someone tried to beckon him to join in.

Soon, they formed a circle around Maria's aunt. The family chanted her name in time with the music, cheering as she danced furiously. She merged back into the circle, and suddenly Maria's sister's boyfriend took the floor, moving with an exuberance John couldn't ever imagine himself capable of matching.

Then, it was the turn of Maria's mum, and then her dad, the two of them dancing together for a time, moving with the easy intimacy of decades of familiarity, before Maria herself was finally called to the floor.

Her name was chanted the loudest of all, for she moved like something else. She flowed like water, danced like fire in the celestial heavens above.

Suddenly, John heard his own name being chanted. He froze, his bottle of beer halfway to his mouth. Maria's family were all looking to him, big smiles on their faces.

Maria didn't leave the floor. Instead, she beckoned him to join her.

'I can't,' he said, staring around in panic, an embarrassed smile fixed to his face. 'My leg...' He knew that was a feeble excuse, shook his head as though to wipe it away. 'I never learned how to dance,' he said instead.

'It's easy,' Maria said. 'Our wedding is in six months, John. I know you can do this.'

'I don't know how,' John protested again, but with less conviction. His name was echoing around the yard now. Maria's family cheered for him. Encouraging him. Calling for him to join in. He felt his barriers, the walls he kept raised to the world, begin to topple.

Maria reached out to him. 'Let me help you,' she said softly.

He hesitated. She smiled at him. And as quickly as that, his fear melted away.

He took hold of her hand.

John let go.

36

Rosie Grace released a deep breath and scrubbed her hands clean beneath the running water. She'd only been an Operating Department Practitioner at Salisbury Hospital for six months, and the most recent patient had been her most harrowing experience yet.

The emergency services had been called out to a critical situation just outside Warminster. A heavily inebriated man in his 30s had collided head-on with a tree in the early hours of the morning while driving at 100 mph down the A350. The police and ambulance had arrived to find his red sports car crushed like a tin can.

No one else had been involved, thankfully, and the duty officers had cut away the wreckage of the convertible expecting to find a body—another tragic victim of careless drunk driving.

Somehow, impossibly, the driver was still alive.

A helicopter had been radioed in to airlift the accident victim to Salisbury Hospital. Rosie had just started her shift when the man, or what was left of him, was wheeled into theatre amidst a flurry of doctors and nurses. His injuries were among the worst anyone on duty had seen: multiple compound fractures, severe internal organ damage, a serious spinal injury, major burns across seventy percent of his body from a fuel tank explosion that had required the fire and rescue service, numerous deep lacerations from smashed glass. The list was extensive.

He also bore a terrible head wound that the doctors said would most likely suggest a catastrophic brain injury. Yet, while he lay stricken on the trolley, being wheeled through reception, Rosie could have sworn she glimpsed him *staring* at her with eyes red from multiple subconjunctival haemorrhages. She even saw him twitch, as though some part of him still fought to rise, to get back up on limbs shattered beyond repair. The only part of his body not broken was his left leg, which ironically still bore a scar from an old injury.

The surgeons and ODPs, led by Doctor McCormack, had done the best they could in the circumstances. It was obvious there was no saving him. The man's mother had arrived shortly after his admission to hospital. She had wept over her dying son, wailing like a thing possessed. In a tragic irony, her husband, the man's father, had also perished thirty years ago in a road traffic accident.

No one had been able to contact the man's wife. Apparently, they had recently separated. Somehow, he had survived for several hours after the accident, and later in the morning, the victim's mother had received a call from the spouse. She was in Bath hospital, having herself been admitted to hospital the previous evening. She discharged herself as soon as she was able, but the victim had just suffered a massive brain haemorrhage and wasn't expected to live beyond the hour.

Against all probability, he clung to life. The machines he was hooked up to even detected a flurry of unusual activity in his brain.

When his wife was only minutes away, he had suffered a devastating cardiac arrest. It ought to have killed him then and there, and the doctors were baffled when the ECG machine again resumed its weak, mechanical beep.

His wife reached his bedside just as the red lights on the vital sign monitors began flashing urgently and his heart finally gave out. Dr. McCormack pronounced his death as he passed peacefully, his wife's hand in his.

Rosie wasn't religious—she preferred to put her faith in medicine than prayer—but even she had to wonder at times like these if someone up there wasn't in the business of handing out small mercies.

'Tough shift, huh?' said Brandon, her fellow duty ODP. He looked tired. He waited until she had finished washing her hands, then took his turn at the sink. 'You working tomorrow?'

Rosie shook her head. 'I have the weekend off. I'm back on Monday.'

'Me, too,' said Brandon. 'I mean, I'm on holiday all next week.' He seemed to hesitate.

She knew he liked her—one of the other girls had told Rosie he kept asking if she were single. She was indeed single, sometimes painfully so, but dating was the furthest thing from her mind right now. She had too many work commitments. Besides, she wanted to travel soon. There was a whole world out there to explore. She was a realist; long-distance relationships never worked.

'I was wondering if you wanted to grab a drink tomorrow?' he blurted out. He turned a shade of red.

'Really?' said Rosie. 'That's very nice of you. I think I might be busy, but I'll let you know.'

'Cool, awesome,' said Brandon. He gave her a smile, but she could see the disappointment disguised in his eyes. 'Um,' he said. 'One of the responders dropped something off at reception. The Welsh fellow? Cardiff fan. I think his name was Bob, or Bill.'

'Welsh fellow?' Rosie said. 'You mean Bert.'

'That's the one. They recovered it from the victim's vehicle. Bert asked if you could make sure it gets forwarded on to his wife.'

'Shouldn't Rachel take care of that? It's her job.'

Brandon gave a helpless shrug. 'I think he trusts you more.'

'I guess so,' she said. She grabbed her things from her locker and made her way to reception. Rachel was taking a call. Her aunt gave her a wave and beckoned for her to let herself in to the office through the side door.

Rosie loved her aunt dearly, but even she had to admit that she had a habit of misplacing important things. It wasn't the worst flaw in the world, she told herself. Her aunt had a big heart.

She noticed the package Bert had left immediately. It was on a tray just next to Rachel's computer, right beside a stack of empty cans of Pepsi and Tango and other soft drinks. Her aunt ought to have been cutting down on the sugary beverages, but she had begun her shift at the same time as Rosie and was probably running on fumes, as were many of the overworked staff. The extra £350 million per week for the NHS couldn't come soon enough.

Rosie picked up the parcel, felt its considerable weight in her hands. For a moment, she stared at it in confusion.

It was a pile of A4 paper, she saw. It was hundreds of sheets thick. Somehow, it had survived the crash and subsequent fire, and the pages were only lightly singed. Black text was printed in the centre of the topmost page, but it had been crossed out in red pen and was unreadable.

Rosie flicked through the document and realised it must be a manuscript of some sort. Every single line on every single page had been struck out in red pen. She shook her head in bewilderment. Was this what the victim had been doing prior to his accident? It must have taken him hours.

She was about to put the manuscript back on the tray when a sheet fell from somewhere near the middle. This sheet looked different to the others. The paper was blank and shiny, and as Rosie turned it over, she saw that it was a photograph. Unlike the hundreds of pages of text that had surrounded it, the photo was unmarred.

She stared at it.

It was a photo of the accident victim and his wife. They stood on a boat together somewhere on a lake. Something about the lake looked familiar, and it took Rosie a moment to realise the photo had been taken at Longleat Safari and Adventure Park.

On the afternoon the photo had been taken, the sun was a bright coin overhead, casting a warm glow over the pair They looked lovingly into each other's eyes and grinned. The deceased had his arm wrapped protectively around his wife.

Behind them was an island.

Alone on the island, gazing out over the lake and the happy couple like a silent guardian, was a huge silverback gorilla.

Rosie was suddenly overcome by a deep sense of sadness.

'Bye, Rachel! Bye, Rosie! I'll see you when I'm back from holiday.'

Brandon's boyish voice called out over the reception counter as he made his cheerful way towards the exit.

'Bye, lovely! Have a great time,' Rosie's aunt called back, briefly interrupting her call to give him a friendly wave.

Rosie looked up from the photo. She saw Brandon watching her. He gave her a smile and turned away.

She made a decision.

'Hey…Brandon?' she said hesitantly.

He turned back around, his brow furrowed in confusion, big eyes gazing questioning at her.

'I've just checked, and it turns out I'm free after all. Did…did you still want to do something tomorrow? I was thinking maybe…Pizza Hut and bowling?'

Brandon's eyes lit up. His face folded into a big grin. In that moment, he looked just like the man in the photo. 'Really? I'd love to! I, um, shall…shall we meet at 6pm?'

'That sounds perfect.'

He bid farewell to Rosie and her aunt, positively skipping out of the door.

Rosie placed the photo carefully on top of the stack of paper. She waited until her aunt was off the phone and gave her strict instructions to ensure it was posted via special delivery that afternoon. Five minutes later, she followed Brandon out of the door.

It had been a rough shift. Still, the sun was shining and the birds were singing. There was still some daylight left. One had to cherish one's blessings.

Tomorrow was another day.

RESOURCES

If you have lost a loved one to suicide, or know someone who has, you can find a listing of local suicide loss support groups at the Survivors of Bereavement by Suicide website, or uksobs.com. You can contact them on 0300 111 5065.

If you are suffering or want guidance on how to help someone who is, and live in the United Kingdom, you may find the following resources of use:

The Samaritans: Call 116 123, 24 hours a day, 365 days a year.

Campaign Against Living Miserably (CALM): Call 0800 58 58 58.

Suicide Prevention UK: Call 0800 587 0800.

Mental Health Foundation: www.mentalhealth.org.uk

Mind: mind.org.uk. Also provides a list of other organisations that provide support for anyone affected by suicide or suicidal thoughts.

ACKNOWLEDGMENTS

Many thanks to my beta readers: Nim, Ian, CJ, Chris Corke, and Gcd. Thank you to Phil Williams for his wonderful cover design, and to Tim Marquitz for his excellent work editing this book. Special thanks to Laura Dodd and Mark Lawrence for their sage advice, encouragement and support. Finally, a big shout-out to British horror legend James Herbert, whose 1974 debut *The Rats* helped inspire my own halting first steps into the world of horror.

To everyone who helped inspire any of the characters or situations described in this work of fiction, I wish you only love, peace, and prosperity. Thank you to all the emergency workers who continue to put their own physical and mental well-being at risk to protect the lives of their fellow citizens.

The Warminster Thing is a real phenomenon that was first noted in 1965 and to this day continues to engender rich discussion for UFO enthusiasts. I don't believe I ever encountered any extraterrestrial life during my time living in town—though there was one occasion when what turned out to be a helicopter landed what felt like 20 feet back from my back garden, and I briefly wondered if I was about to find myself in a *War of the Worlds* scenario. Perhaps that's an idea for another book…

The Old Fire Station is an actual restaurant-café located just behind the Athenaeum, Warminster's local theatre. The original owner and founder, Mike Magee, a former police officer, was sadly killed in August 2021 in a road traffic accident, two months before he was due to be married. The restaurant is currently #1 in Warminster on Tripadvisor, with a hard to beat average rating of 5.0 out of 5.0.

The George Inn in Longbridge Deverell is also very real. It offers good food, a fantastic garden, and a lovely atmosphere in which to relax and enjoy a quiet beer, or your drink of choice. I am reliably informed that no perverts stalk its guest rooms.

Longleat House continues to operate Longleat Safari and Adventure Park, delighting over one million visitors each year. In 2024, it celebrated its 75th anniversary as a tourist attraction. The park supports vital conservation projects around the world and works hard to protect endangered species through vital conservation programmes.

Nico the gorilla sadly passed away in January 2018, aged 56. He was at the time the third oldest gorilla in Europe. In his many years at the park, Nico delighted countless children and adults and inspired the imagination of at least one decidedly peculiar author. Nico's mate, Samba, passed away in 2007.

Printed in Dunstable, United Kingdom

64322529R00188